Zero Hour

———•◆•———

"All that is needed to understand World War I in its philosophical and historical meaning is to examine barbed wire—a single strand will do—and to meditate on who made it, what it is for, why it is like it is." —JAMES DICKEY

Zero Hour

Georg Grabenhorst

NEW INTRODUCTION BY ROBERT COWLEY
New Afterword by Casey Clabough

THE UNIVERSITY OF SOUTH CAROLINA PRESS

New material © 2006 University of South Carolina

German edition published as *Fahnenjunker Volkenborn* by Koehler and Umelang, G.M.B.H., Leipzig, 1928
English cloth edition published by Little, Brown and Company, 1929
English paperback edition published by the University of South Carolina Press in Columbia, South Carolina

Manufactured in the United States of America

15 14 13 12 11 10 09 08 07 06   10 9 8 7 6 5 4 3 2 1

Library of Congress Cataloging-in-Publication Data

Grabenhorst, Georg, 1899–
    [Fahnenjunker Volkenborn. English]
  Zero hour / Georg Grabenhorst ; new introduction by Robert Cowley ; new afterword by Casey Clabough.
      p. cm.
    ISBN-13: 978-1-57003-662-0 (pbk : alk. paper)
    ISBN-10: 1-57003-662-4 (pbk : alk. paper)
    1. World War, 1914–1918—Fiction. I. Title.

PT2613.R15F313 2006
833'.912—dc22

                                                          2006024983

This book was printed on EcoBook Natural, a recycled paper with 50 percent postconsumer waste content.

To Graf Maximilian Wiser
with thanks

Contents

Series Editor's Preface

The Joseph M. Bruccoli Great War Series republishes fiction and personal narratives—the demarcation is not always clear—from the belligerent nations of World War I. Formal military history is excluded.

"The war to end all wars" generated a vast literature—much of it antiheroic and antiwar. The best books of the war convey a sense of betrayal, loss, and disillusionment. Many of them now qualify as forgotten books, although they were admired in their time. The intention of this series is to rescue once-influential books that have been long out of print.

The volumes are drawn from the Joseph M. Bruccoli Great War Collection in the Thomas Cooper Library, University of South Carolina.* This collection is named for a private in the AEF who was severely wounded on the Western Front. Joseph M. Bruccoli's medal has seven battle bars, and he claimed two more battles. He was not embittered by his war.

M.J.B

* The Joseph M. Bruccoli Great War Collection at the University of South Carolina: An Illustrated Catalogue, compiled by Elizabeth Sudduth (Columbia: University of South Carolina Press, 2005). See also *The Joseph M. Bruccoli Great War Collection in the University of Virginia Library,* compiled by Edmund Berkeley Jr. (Columbia: MJB, 1999).

Introduction

ROBERT COWLEY

In book publishing, the years 1929 and 1930 marked the crest of what came to be known as the war boom. Erich Maria Remarque's *All Quiet on the Western Front* and Ernest Hemingway's *A Farewell to Arms* were huge commercial successes, the former especially, selling hundreds of thousands of copies in the United States alone, and millions in the rest of the world. *Journey's End*, R. C. Sheriff's play about a group of doomed British officers, became the equivalent of a best seller on the West End and Broadway. They paved the way for other novels and memoirs about the First World War (as it was already beginning to be called). Publishers know a main chance when they see one. In quick succession, Robert Graves's *Good-bye to All That*, Edmund Blunden's *Undertones of War*, and Siegfried Sassoon's *Memoirs of an Infantry Officer* appeared in England and were picked up across the ocean. The outpourings of these former citizen subalterns were matched by similar ones in Germany: Ernst Jünger's *Storm of Steel* and *Copse 125: A Chronicle from the Trench Warfare of 1918*, along with Ludwig Renn's *War*, were notable books translated into English. (The French were curiously silent. For them, the war with its huge casualties remained a memory best unremembered.)

A decade after the armistice, people at last seemed ready, even eager, to confront the first great trauma of our times. As Robert Penn Warren wrote in a later introduction to *A Farewell to Arms*, "Those who had grown up in the war, or in the shadow of the war, could look back nostalgically, as it were, to the lost moment of innocence of motive and purity of emotion."* Men (and even a few women, such as Vera Brittain) now felt ready to commit their pasts to paper, and

*Robert Penn Warren, introduction to Ernest Hemingway, *A Farewell to Arms* (New York: Scribner, 1949), viii.

publishers did not hesitate to snap up their manuscripts. The time for denying the war was over.

It had not always been so. Edwin Campion Vaughan, whose diary of 1917, *Some Desperate Glory* (1981), is now recognized as one of the notable documents of the war, had tried to get it published in the early 1920s. He found no takers and the manuscript languished in a cupboard for nearly half a century, long after his death. In 1927, Max Plowman published his memoir, *A Subaltern on the Somme*, under the pseudonym Mark VII. Critics did not even bother to savage the book; they ignored it completely. "Ne'er a one of them has touched it with a barge pole," the author wrote to a friend.* Not until *All Quiet on the Western Front* appeared did readers—and reviewers—begin to appreciate, and buy, *A Subaltern on the Somme*.

Had it not been for this surge of interest in the war, one book that might never have seen the translated light was Georg Grabenhorst's *Zero Hour*. The novel had been published in Leipzig in 1928, and it was one of the numerous Great War titles picked up in Great Britain and the United States the following year. Little, Brown of Boston became the American publisher, and one imagines that its editors hoped to capitalize that fall on the popularity of *All Quiet*, which the house had brought out in June. Perhaps the dour impact of the stock market crash made a difference, but sales of *Zero Hour* apparently went nowhere. Perhaps, too, it was because the novel did not strike the then-fashionable pacifist tone that had captured the imaginations of the readers of *All Quiet*. *Zero Hour* can be regarded as much as a memoir as a novel. *All Quiet*, whose author had never seen a front-line trench, was less a memoir than a work of pure imagination, embellished by myth, exaggeration, and a healthy dollop of what the critic Samuel Hynes has called "battlefield gothic." No matter that the novel lacks any sense of time or place. It has provided generations of readers with a comforting frisson of war as they fancy it really is.

The author of *Zero Hour*, Georg Grabenhorst, was twenty-nine when his novel was published in Germany. Little is known about

*Malcolm Brown, introduction to Mark VII (Max Plowman), *A Subaltern on the Somme* (reprint, London: Imperial War Museum and Battery Press, 1996), third page, unpaginated.

him—though biographical details about his war career can be picked up by inference from the pages of his novel. He came from a good family and was well educated and reasonably gifted in the arts. He felt at home in Berlin society and appreciated the luxury of a good hotel when on leave. Like so many British and French junior officers, his commission belonged to him almost by birthright. He served with merit but no special distinction in the 3rd Naval Division, German marines, and was invalided home at the end of the war. On the evidence of his novel, he was a victim of shell shock.

The German title of the novel is *Fahnenjunker Volkenborn,* after its protagonist, Hans Volkenborn. A *Fahnenjunker* was a probationary officer, a private with privileges who would in due course advance first to *Fähnrich,* ensign, and then to lieutenant—if he survived that long. The English publisher slapped on the title *Zero Hour,* which may be more dramatic, but it is not wholly accurate. The novel describes only one real attack, a minor but important one that occurred on the Belgian coast in the summer of 1917, as well as some trench raids a year later. Most of the war action, it should be noted, found Grabenhorst/Volkenborn and his comrades on the defensive. The zero hours, then, are largely those of the enemy, most memorably the ones experienced on the mucky flats below Passchendaele.

Grabenhorst's war service and the novel that came out of it seem to have been high points of a long and industrious, if not notably illustrious, career. One can only guess that through the novel he attempted to write his way out of a serious bout of post-traumatic stress disorder. After the publication of *Zero Hour,* Grabenhorst lived another sixty-nine years; he died in 1997, at ninety-eight. He flirted with National Socialism, but not ardently enough to disqualify him from serving after World War II as executive officer of the Regional History Society for Lower Saxony or as a functionary for that West German state's Ministry of Cultural Affairs. He also worked as an editor and wrote novels, poems, essays, and travel accounts. *Zero Hour,* however, was his one book translated into English.

"Storm" is the title of Grabenhorst's opening chapter, although the event he describes, and took part in, actually happened on a cloudless evening in July 1917. It was one of the most successful spoiling

attacks of the war on the Western Front, and in that sense the title
"Storm" is appropriate. Since the beginning of the war, the Allies
—first the French and then the British—had held a narrow bridgehead on the Belgian coast north of the Yser River. In the summer of
1917, the British made plans to invade that coast—at the same time
pushing north from the Yser bridgehead. The object was to create a
new flank and to join up with Field Marshal Sir Douglas Haig's
Ypres offensive, scheduled to jump off on 31 July. Their intention
was nothing if not audacious: to beach three 550-foot-long steel
pontoons pushed by huge, heavily armed shallow-draft monitors,
landing nine tanks and an entire division of 13,000 men.

The Germans guessed that a landing of some sort was about to
take place and resolved to forestall it by wiping out the bridgehead.
This they accomplished on the evening of 10 July in the attack in
which Grabenhorst/Volkenborn participated. The operation began
at dawn with concentrated shelling, a softening up that lasted all
day. Three hundred thousand high explosive and gas shells smothered a mile of sandy front. Then, at 8 P.M., the marines of the 3rd
Naval Division surged forward in three waves. It took twenty minutes to reach the river and a couple of hours more to mop up. The
code name of the operation was Beach Picnic, and for the attackers
it was. The British lost three thousand men, the equivalent of three
battalions, the majority of them rubbed out by the bombardment;
less than seventy made it back across the Yser. The invasion never
did take place.

Grabenhorst's account squares with the memories of British and
Australian survivors, as well as the matter-of-fact narrative of the
British official history. His vivid impression of the battle on the
dunes is special in another respect: It is the single German eyewit-
ness account of the event that seems to have come down to us.
Memoirs of infantry attacks in that war are, surprisingly, not that
plentiful, perhaps because too few survived to write them. Grabenhorst did, and his is a good one. Take his description of the use of
flamethrowers, one of the storm troopers' weapons of choice:

Two English dugouts stubbornly hold firm. No way of getting at
them.

They keep a lashing hail of machine-gun bullets! . . . Two of
the attackers are already lying dead, when the flamethrowers
come on the scene. . . . Twice, three times, the flaming, scorching tongues lick through the galleries of the trench; it belches
pitch-black fumes. The machine guns are abruptly silent. From
behind the one nearest to Volkenborn, staggers a charred something. It makes a queer forward movement and collapses. Burnt
alive! (*Zero Hour*, 24–27)

This may be the most extreme bit of battlefield gothic in the novel,
and I find it comparable to the description by the American novelist
Hervey Allen of being on the receiving end of a *flammenwerfer* in
Toward the Flame, one of the best personal accounts of the war.

Several days later Volkenborn marches back to Bruges, that
canal-ringed relic of Hanseatic times that was far enough behind the
lines to be still unblemished by war. He spends three months there
in machine-gun training. "Belgian women walked beside the troops
and from time to time exchanged open or secret greetings with the
men; one might imagine that it was a regiment returning to its own
garrison town. 'My girl has known for a week that we were to arrive
to-day,' said the man marching behind Volkenborn" (*ZH*, 133). Frat-
ernization with the locals (and to a lesser extent, with French
women) was the rule rather than the exception. The men are
"roughly quartered" in a monastery, "all sleeping in one great cheerless room with a stone floor" (*ZH*, 29). But Volkenborn, as an officer candidate—he has been promoted to lance corporal after his
efficient performance in the Battle of the Dunes—is billeted in a private room in a priest's house. Class counts, and it is a prominent, if
understated, theme of the novel. Class and command go hand in
hand. As the author comments, the men are more impressed by officers decked out in tailored blue breeches, silk caps, and dog-skin
gloves than by the ones of slender means who wear badly fitting uniforms cut from the same cloth as theirs.

But even in this urban idyll, the war is always a presence,
whether it is the rockets that shoot up after dark "like glowworms"
or the distant drumfire coming from the direction of Ypres. Or it
may be the constant traffic, the "endless lines of pioneer [military

engineer] lorries and ammunition columns" that "rattle and pound along" all through the day and night. These are the "workers of war" (the phrase was coined by one of them, Ernst Jünger), the proletariat of a new industrial revolution. War in its modern incarnation required a vast workforce recruited to man the assembly lines of mass destruction. As Grabenhorst notes, "War is a whole-time job, like running a lift, or stoking in the gas works. The same thing has to be done over and over again. It's all a matter of habit, and a soldier soon becomes used to it. He may have killed someone in doing his duty, but it is all in a day's march, so what is the good of thinking about it? Our turn tomorrow—who knows? After all it is—war!" (ZH, 45).

This perception undoubtedly enhances the Bruges chapter but is hardly its most prominent feature. There is too much else of an emotional nature going on. What is the reader to make of the relationship of young Volkenborn and the pale, handsome, and fatally cynical company adjutant, Lieutenant von Kless? In the fall of 1929, an anonymous reviewer in the *Times Literary Supplement* declared, with what may seem unnecessary priggishness, that the novel "hints at sexual perversion." It is undeniable that the Bruges section does have its homoerotic moments. "The adjutant is a fine chap," Volkenborn writes to his parents. "If I were a girl, I should fall in love with him right away." (ZH, 33) To an extent he does—but for the Fahnenjunker and the lieutenant, there will be other romantic distractions.

The first time the two men actually talk they discuss books. Volkenborn admits that he carries with him a copy of Josef von Eichendorff's *Taugenichts*—or, as it is known in English, *From the Life of a Good-for-Nothing*—a diverting but depthless nineteenth-century saga about the wanderings of a young man on the make. It must have made for perfect trench reading. (He feels that perhaps he should have mentioned Faust, the other book he carried but rarely cracked.) The lieutenant is interested in Volkenborn for another reason: He has observed him drawing in his spare time and asks to see his sketchbook. So a friendship begins. They meet most afternoons. They talk. Von Kless plays the piano—well. "To Hans Volkenborn there seemed something strange about those afternoons with the lieutenant, but perhaps the only strange thing about them was that he made no mention of them to his fellow soldiers." Staying

silent "was not always quite an easy matter, and occasionally it entailed lying. But this troubled him no more than do the evasions that
lovers so often practice as a safeguard against the prying world" (ZH,
48, 49).

More to be hidden, perhaps, is von Kless's disenchantment with
the war, which could land him in trouble, as it did Sassoon and
Plowman in England. "The assassination at Sarajevo was a crime,"
he remarks, "but isn't the expiation too great? Do you still know
what we are fighting for? I don't" (ZH, 50). Volkenborn is flustered
to find himself in the presence of a man who has little past and,
apparently, less future. "Hans believed in everything, the lieutenant
in nothing. . . . He had reached the stage where there was neither
light nor dark, only half lights" (ZH, 77, 78). In trying to grasp the
reasons for the lieutenant's disillusionment, Volkenborn will find
himself on the same slippery slope.

Perhaps to ease the minds of censorious readers such as the
anonymous critic of the *Times Literary Supplement*, Grabenhorst at
this point inserts not just a triangle but, well, a quadrangle. Volkenborn finds that he has a rival for von Kless's attentions—indeed,
affections. It is the daughter of the house where von Kless is billeted, the beautiful Fleming, whose father is an officer in the Belgian Army, an unreachable twenty miles away. At first she is just a
mysterious presence that Volkenborn senses behind a curtain in the
music room as the lieutenant plays the piano. Then he actually sees
her as he is sculling on the canal that runs by the house. She is looking from an open window of the music room, and Volkenborn hears
familiar piano chords. They will in fact meet once in the music room
when, wordlessly, she offers Volkenborn her hand. In the meantime,
the Fahnenjunker has begun a passionate correspondence with a girl
back home. But, as he remarks, his liking for the lieutenant "was in
no way affected by his love affair" (ZH, 73). Maybe it is just a stage
that Volkenborn is passing through, although one thing is certain: If
the novel appeared today, it would be much steamier, a martial
"Sunday Bloody Sunday," no doubt.

The lieutenant—curiously, we never learn his first name—will be
killed. Death is clearly his destiny, and he is resigned to it. Von Kless,

delivering a message on horseback, spots Volkenborn marching to the front at Ypres and pulls up long enough to remind him to pick up his sketchbook, left behind in his Bruges room. He gallops off. Volkenborn is "struck by the fact that the lieutenant has never before said good-by" (ZH, 92). It remains only for him to make a confirmatory sighting of the expected outcome some days later, almost as a narrative afterthought, a chance passing of canvas-covered figures waiting for burial. Volkenborn and a fellow Junker are lugging boxes of machine-gun ammunition back to the front when his companion remarks, in his upper-class manner, "I say, there's Lieutenant von Kless." Volkenborn stands for a moment, looking at his dead mentor's face and remarking only, "We must be getting back" (ZH, 104, 105).

That night, the lieutenant visits Volkenborn in a dream: "He can see the face of his dead friend before him. It seems to confront him from the floor of the shell hole, lying on a muddy service cap. It looks quite peaceful, but as though cut in marble, like Michelangelo's Madonna. Withal it is the face of a stranger. . . . There is something almost menacing in the expression." Then von Kless is joined by the shade of the Flemish woman, wordless as always, extending her hands—which suddenly take him by the throat." As a psychiatrist might say, "What does the dream suggest to you?" (ZH, 105–6). An unease with past emotions, perhaps. But Volkenborn, coming awake in a shell hole, has greater threats to deal with than phantom choking hands.

As a record of individual experience, the Ypres chapter is not just memorable but also historically important. Grabenhorst's description of life (and death) in the mud reminds us that the British did not have a monopoly on suffering at Passchendaele. The same rain fell on the Germans, and the mud was just as deep for them, just as intractable. Drowning in water-filled shell holes was a common fate. The Germans, too, needed four (and sometimes more) stretcher-bearers to carry a wounded man back to a forward aid post:

> The stretcher seemed as heavy as lead. . . . On they pushed, mud spouting up into their faces and pieces of shell whizzing around them. They came to a ditch, and the bearers wanted

to go round it, but Volkenborn made them go through the water. The bank bristled with barbed wire and the water was breast high, but they got through somehow, helping themselves by means of the wire, and tearing their hands badly. . . . One of the bearers stumbled and was nearly carried away by the stream. A moment later another bearer slipped into a shell hole and they had to put the stretcher down in order to pull him out. (*ZH*, 126)

Those words might just as well have been written by an Englishman —as could Grabenhorst's memories of a watery ruination that was universal. His account of going up to the line can stand with the best that has been written about the doleful 1917 campaign.

Were there differences? Of course. The British, forever on the attack, had farther in the mudscape to travel; they had to slog through three and a half miles of cratered fields to reach Poelkapelle, where the actions Grabenhorst describes took place and where the 3rd Naval Division fought from mid-October to early November. The Germans could escape the worst after a mile or so, the limit of the most concentrated shelling. But the Germans experienced one special kind of suffering: near starvation.

At one point Volkenborn happens on a horse that has just been hit and fallen. Though the animal is still alive, two men are already carving thick pieces of flesh from it. Volkenborn puts three quick bullets "into the poor beast's brain. 'They ought to be in your skulls, you brutes!' he shouted" (*ZH*, 117). The next day he passes the same spot and finds "nothing there but a bare skeleton, from which all the flesh had been hacked away, leaving the ribs staring at him like the rafters of a burned-out house" (*ZH*, 118.) Volkenborn himself admits to living on nothing but bread, probably made from potato flour. "As a result of insufficient food, the whole division was suffering more or less from dysentery, and at the Dressing Station there were pails of lime—and opium pills with which to meet this epidemic" (*ZH*, 118).

Poelcappelle, a village of little consequence on the plain below Passchendaele and Westroosebeeke, was the scene of some of the most inconclusive fighting of the inconclusive campaign the British called the Third Ypres. An attack on 12 October landed the British in the middle of the village, where they stuck fast: They never, in fact, fully drove the Germans out. That seems to be the day Volkenborn arrives at the front and, manning a machine gun, helps to beat back three waves of enemy attackers, easy targets plodding in slow motion through the mud. What the author describes so well is a kind of combat, new to the Western Front struggle, in which fixed trench lines had ceased to exist: It was the open warfare generals had long dreamed about, but without movement or maneuver. One German regimental historian speaks of "invisible garrisons": "Our lines were such that they were unrecognizable to the enemy's ground or air observers. There was no lack of accommodation, wet and filthy though it was; for every crater made by the heavy shells was a potential shelter for a machine-gun nest or a few men, with a tent or strip of corrugated iron as their only head-cover and a few planks as their only chairs and beds."* But by this stage of the battle, everyone, German and British alike, was invisible, or tried their best to become so. Only the dead were conspicuous.

If Grabenhorst's fictional imaginings following the Ypres chapter stall in a stretch of anticlimax, can the author be blamed? History itself has trumped him. Volkenborn stops briefly in Bruges, where, retrieving his sketchbook, he has a final sorrowful meeting, as always wordless, with von Kless's beautiful Fleming; then he continues on to Germany. He will enjoy eight months of reprieve in an officer's training course. He returns with an Iron Cross and with the expectations of peace before long. No one doubts that Germany will be victorious. Volkenborn will sneak home for Christmas, and for a first embrace in a snowy wood with his hometown sweetheart. He lets himself be seduced (presumably) by a voraciously neurotic war widow, a desperate hausfrau, one might say, who soon after conveniently dies of a heart ailment. He repels the homosexual advance by a fellow probationer: "there were still things in this world that were beyond Hans Volkenborn" (ZH, 179). So much,

---

*Quoted in Capt. G. C. Wynne, *If Germany Attacks* (1940; reprint, Westport, Conn.: Greenwood Press, 1976), 312.

presumably, for homoeroticism. Besides an occasional chilly and lightless railroad car or the odd comment about food queues and the scarcity of tobacco, little is said about the privations that the ordinary German had to endure. As always, it helped to be upper class.

The most noteworthy section of the novel follows—one that, without the author meaning to do so, stands apart from almost all other personal accounts of the Great War.

In the months that Volkenborn has been away from the Front, everything has changed, and not for the better. By the time he arrives in northern France in the spring of 1918, the promise of a favorable peace is fast disappearing. Field Marshall Erich Ludendorff's successive offensives may have gobbled up unimaginable amounts of Allied real estate, but at great cost in irreplaceable lives. They had not succeeded either in driving the British and French apart or in reaching Paris, leaving the German army with vastly longer lines and fewer men to hold them. Volkenborn finds that many of his friends are gone. "The death of so many of his comrades seemed almost to reproach him for his absence." The new recruits he commands aren't the same enthusiastic young men he had fought with a year earlier. He leads them into a man-made desert empty of life except for the occasional sight of other marchers. In a description suggestive of the increasingly dispirited mood of the war, the novel evokes the Somme wastelands, a landscape swept over and devastated by battle:

> They spent two days on the march, the sun blistering their
> faces. . . . The guns seemed to have left nothing standing.
> . . . There were very few trees, and consequently no shade,
> which made the heat very hard to bear. They seldom came
> across water of any kind; the whole district seemed one mass
> of brown, dried-up fields, with a feeble crop of grass here and
> there. The only objects that relieved the monotony of the land-
> scape were the many white crosses that they kept passing.
> . . . The young soldiers passed by the graves of their comrades
> and, many of them, without knowing it, were drawing closer to
> their own. (ZH, 191)

Volkenborn's destination is the wood of Aveluy, a square mile of former hunting preserve on heights overlooking the Ancre River, and beyond, the 1916 battlefields of the Somme. The German advance had stopped at Aveluy Wood at the beginning of April. Now the British are trying to get it back, and raids, usually at night, are constant. The river valley at Volkenborn's back is flooded, crossed only by pontoon bridges that are constantly being destroyed by shellfire: he describes the position as "a regular mousetrap" (ZH, 200). The fighting is at close quarters and has the quality of 1915, though with none of its malevolent energy. There are no continuous trench lines now. Both sides are running out of men—which is why the coming of the Americans that summer would make all the difference. Everyone is exhausted. These obscure and isolated struggles amid shattered trees might be forgotten today were it not for books such as *Zero Hour* and Ernst Jünger's *Copse 125,* which records similar encounters in another blasted wood only a few miles distant and in the same period.

Copse 125 is notable because the author never admits to doubts about himself—which perhaps might account for his famous courage—or about the rightness of his cause. Though he comes to recognize that the German bid for victory has failed, he feels that even so the war has been worthwhile, that out of its ashes will emerge a new kind of man, self-confidant and resilient. "Our hour will come; and then at last we shall see that the loss of this war brought us to our full height. Hard timber is of slow growth."* Jünger was, of course, teetering precariously close to the superman edge of National Socialism—from which, in the end, he would draw back.

Grabenhorst, however, in the person of his novel's protagonist, is increasingly assailed by doubt and disillusion. One evening he looks across the valley and spies a shrine dedicated to the Virgin Mother. For what is almost a last moment, he feels that his faith is still like the shrine, which he compares to "a candle that all the guns of the enemy could not extinguish" (ZH, 218, 252). A month and many

---

*Ernst Jünger, *Copse 125: A Chornicle from the Trench Warfare of 1915,* trans. Basil Creighton (New York, Howard Fertig, 1988), 184.

troubles later, he passes by the shrine. It is lying in ruins. Soon after, as he is about to lead a raiding party, fear overcomes him for the first time. He has had a premonition of death. The zero hour, a small one, is the catalyst. "A dreadful paralysis seized on his whole body. . . . Then, shame and honor both spoke to him, and with desperate haste he mounted the parapet, and with two quick leaps found himself in the wood, which closed over him like a wave" (*ZH*, 235). The man following a step behind Volkenborn is the one who will be killed.

A mortar shell (which the translator incorrectly calls a "mine") buries Volkenborn alive; companions dig him out in the nick of time. It is then that he first experiences the strangeness that will envelop and all but destroy him: "As he stared into the darkness, smoking, tiny white spots danced before his eyes, and then he saw the violet ball" (*ZH*, 240). The ball, that symbol of his unhinging and its almost mystical crystallization, will disappear—this time. But it leaves a numbing aftertaste: "Everything seemed still and empty and dead within him" (*ZH*, 240). Worse, his eyes begin to deteriorate and he experiences night blindness. The violet ball returns, "a beautiful yet terrifying round sphere of color with radiating circles" (*ZH*, 249). And then another shell explodes next to his head. The company commander meets the half-blind and dazed officer staggering along the trench and reprimands him, all but accusing him of cowardice. A regimental surgeon, who detects nothing physically wrong with Volkenborn's eyes, intimates the same thing. But his eyes get worse, and he is eventually sent back from the line and invalided home, feeling that he has somehow dishonored himself. Even when the war ends, the torment of shell shock—an appropriate term in that artillery-driven war—and the accompanying emotional numbness will not disappear. In Volkenborn's case, the currently fashionable "battle fatigue" was not wholly accurate.

Zero Hour has an importance that no one could have suspected when it was published. It was still too close to the event in 1929. The novel is one of the few, perhaps the only, accounts of what it was like to suffer from shell shock. True, in *Sherston's Progress* Sassoon describes his experiences at Craiglockhart, the Scottish hospital for shell-shocked officers, and his brilliant therapist, W. H. R.

Rivers. But Sassoon was mostly free of shell-shock symptoms. He had dared to protest the war openly: The medical board that examined him decided that he had to be crazy and packed him off to Craiglockhart. Wilfred Owen, a fellow patient, was killed before he could write a memoir, though he did leave letters and one memorable poem, "Mental Cases." (Owen had experienced a brush with shellfire death much like Grabenhorst/Volkenborn's.) In his novel *The Secret Battle*, A. P. Herbert did write about an officer—"one of the bravest men I ever knew," says the narrator—who suffered from shell shock and was shot for deserting. That happened with distressing frequency in the British army. And Hervey Allen was a sufferer, although his superb memoir, *Toward the Flame*, ends with the incident that sent him over the edge. But no novel, memoir, or poem comes closer to evoking the actual experience than *Zero Hour*. For that reason—and there are certainly others—this novel that was forgotten almost from the moment it was published in the United Kingdom and the United States deserves to be rescued from the hecatomb of the overlooked and the discarded accounts of World War I.

Zero Hour

CHAPTER ONE

STORM

I

The coast of Flanders shimmered in July sunshine. A perfect summer day! Not one of those
rare fine days that dawns unexpectedly, filling us
with a feverish anxiety to enjoy it while we may, but
one of many sunny days that we allow to pass with
a careless acceptance of their golden splendor.

His midday dinner over, young Volkenborn
strolled from Nieuwmünster to the seashore, a distance of something under two miles. At Wenduyne
he stopped to buy a bathing costume, and with a
pleasure that was almost childish carefully selected
one of a silky, black material with a white border.
On reaching the sand dunes, he threw himself
down to rest. His company was to be there at half-
past five for a bathing parade. Whole hours lay between now and then: a peaceful interlude of soli-
tude, sunshine, and sky. Nothing to do but lie at
full stretch and dream. . . .

He inhaled the smell of seaweed and dried shells
on a breeze which, thin and light, caressed his relaxed body and softly stirred the sea grass and gorse
bushes. As he lay listening to the faint rippling of

the sun-kissed waves, it seemed as though he could feel the pouring sunshine and taste it on his tongue like warm rain: it seemed to irrigate his body, to penetrate to his inner being.

Peeping from time to time through half-closed eyes, he saw nothing but glittering sunshine: sky and clouds seemed to be absorbed in its splendor, and to have vanished into nothingness.

Dreamily, he seemed to become a part of the warm sand dunes. He was scarcely conscious of any difference between himself and the sun-soaked sands. He could hear his blood pulsating in his veins, and the sound of the waves curling into foam on the shore — equally remote and equally near.

When he woke, it was half-past five, but the company had not arrived. He looked around for any sign of his comrades, and then slipped into the sea. How pleasant the feeling as the water gradually grows deeper, deeper and cooler! It is as though the earth were gradually leaving one like a mother parting from her child who is going out into the world, and turning again and again for a last wave of the hand.

To swim, free and strong, far out into the sea! To feel the cool crested waves breaking! To dive deep down! To rise again to the sunshine! To drink in the salty tang of the air and sea! Volkenborn struck out boldly until with a start, he became conscious of the war — there behind him! Quite distinctly he heard it: the dull sound of guns thudding. It seemed to penetrate him. . . . The company! Why hadn't they come? In sudden fear, he swam back to the shore.

Dressing, and buttoning his tunic as he ran, Volkenborn left Wenduyne behind him. He could see far ahead down the main road, which had but a slight bend in it. Not a sign of the company. The bugles! "Fall in!" . . . Absent from parade? That it should happen to me! Me! The Fahnenjunker![1] *Won't* they be down on me! Just my rotten luck! But I must keep cool, breathe deep — there's only a little over a mile still to run. Hardly that! I shall just manage it. What's that? Ah. There's the company. Falling in! Marching orders, or the recall? In front of the orderly room! No good getting flustered, but I've got myself into a hell of a mess, all the same!

Hand-grenades were being handed out. It was a raiding party. Volkenborn slipped quickly in among the rest without being noticed by the lieutenant. Section-leader Corporal Friedrich Schiller merely gave him a chummy wink and a nod. Everything was going to be O. K. after all. Karl Wulff had already received his grenades for him, and had by mistake taken two extra. All correct! Pistols, luminous ammunition, and emergency rations were served out.

"Cells for any one who starts nibbling at his ra-

---

[1] *Fahnenjunker.* In the German pre-war army every officer had to complete a period of service as a private soldier before qualifying for a commission. During this probationary period he enjoyed certain privileges over his fellow privates and was known as a

tion beforehand, I tell you; just let me catch you at it," warned Sergeant Major Peterson, the "Spur." Young Volkenborn was always greatly impressed by the S. M.'s ferocious manner, and held him in high esteem.

"Identification discs to be hung round the neck on the bare chest!"

The non-coms. in charge of the raiding party inspected their men.

"To hell with these bloody old tickets for Heaven! What's the good of 'em to the likes of us when we're sprawling with our toes turned up? Not a bit of good. Mucking us about!"

"Pietschmann! Shut your ugly mouth, you grouser!"

The captain scowls at the raiding party, where Fritze Pietschmann is standing on the flank. Volkenborn finds it difficult not to laugh right out.

"The letters will be given out afterwards. Address and regimental number to be destroyed!"

"That's enough of that," growls Pietschmann again, swinging his biscuit bag. "Sounds just as if we was going to let ourselves get killed. Well, we aren't! See?"

Again Volkenborn has to bite his lip. This almost uncontrollable desire to laugh is dangerous — with the captain looking. Pietschmann — a hefty brute — is a source of endless amusement to him. What

---

Fahnenjunker. The Fahnenjunker in due course became a Fähnrich with the right of wearing the officers' sword knot, and then a lieutenant.

shoulders! What arms! The way he rolls his eyes, showing the whites! What a big fellow! But Volkenborn is proud of every one of his raiding party.

After an evening march of two hours they get aboard the train. The station lay westward, so they marched with the golden rays of the setting sun in their eyes. The sunset seemed to form a golden gate at the end of the road before them.

Volkenborn was reminded of a book that he had read as a schoolboy. It was very sad, and was called "The Golden Gate." He could not remember much about it. There was a girl — he thought her name was Marie — and she died, and it was all in some way connected with the Golden Gate. Yes, it was Albert Schulze who had given the book to his brother Kurt. Albert had written something on the front page; something good, and honest, and true. Written it in his nice, careful, upright hand. Albert Schulze of Walsrode. How well he remembered his sturdy handclasp, the fair stubble on his chin, his correct stand-up collar, and his nice, honest face, that always looked as if it had been just washed! He could not help thinking about him. . . . Albert had already passed through the Golden Gate. Killed three or four months before. Over there, where they were going to attack. Poor old Albert Schulze! The thought of his fate obsessed Volkenborn.

"Seem a bit down in the mouth! Got a touch of cold feet? This won't be much of a scrap, my lad.

Not worse than pig-sticking. You just keep close behind me!"

Volkenborn started, flushed with confusion — and then burst out laughing. Pig-sticking! Pietschmann *was* funny.

"No, I'm not funking. I was only thinking of — "

"Thinking of your little bit. I know. What's her name? Mine was called Erna; a nice sort of name too, but she couldn't wait for me to get my leave. So I just told her to go to blazes. I can always find a girl to cuddle. Queer birds — girls, eh?"

Volkenborn was going to reply lightly, but instead he fell to thinking again, and forgot all about Pietschmann.

Night fell quickly. It was so dark in the small, low trucks of the field-railway that they could hardly distinguish one another. As a pipe or cigar was lighted, faces would show up suddenly, looking white and grim in the darkness. Volkenborn found that, if he stared at them steadily as long as the match burned, they grew human and animated. In his heart there grew up a brotherly feeling towards these stout fellows. The darkness that hid them no longer seemed a barrier between them, and something in the sinister atmosphere of war seemed to be linking them more closely together; a bond of common destiny. As the strong faces stood out for a moment in the gloom, they seemed to be nodding at him, as though they would say: Don't be afraid, you won't be alone; we shall be there, you can depend on us.

One began to sing; just to himself, as men will sometimes hum a tune over unconsciously, without thinking what they are doing. It was Pollmann, the time-expired man who had signed on for a period of long service before the war. In the company they nicknamed him the "Sprinter," a name that he lived up to, in spite of his short legs. A second joined in, then another; the simple, plaintive melody unconsciously affected their thoughts, all enveloped them in a flood of sentiment, gave expression to their sorrows and anxieties, relieving the loneliness that they felt in the eerie darkness. Soon, nearly all were singing. Even those who, like Pongs, the sceptic, at first only smoked in silence with a mocking smile on their faces, in the end joined in the chorus. They were all drawn into the wave of sentiment, which grew and grew. It was a sad song, and it was sung sadly by tired men. But it heartened them for the dread work lying before them. Fear and anxiety, suppressed longings and vain hopes, haunting remembrances and eager desires — all the obsessions of the hour found their expression in this song.

At midnight the train halted at a spot only half a mile away from what the English guns had left of Middlekerke. The companies began their march. The night was cool and starry. Ammunition columns were passing at the gallop. Automobiles. Dispatch riders dashing recklessly onwards. Motor cyclists. Field batteries lumbering along. Oaths.

Words of command. Orderlies. Field kitchens. Heavy guns. Lorries loaded with mines, duck boards, barbed wire. The road shook under the weight and rush of the traffic of war; hurtling vehicles, as they passed, fanned the air into a steady current of wind. Moonlight hovered brokenly over the frenzied movement of the night, flooding the shell-scarred streets and ruined alleys, glinting on shattered windows, and palely illuminating the dark masonry of the remnant of a shattered church tower. In the uproar and turmoil horses were rearing and plunging, their drivers holding them in by main force.

II

Volkenborn's company has taken over their sector of the front line. They are out reconnoitering, and Volkenborn is lying beside Karl Wulff. The company which they had relieved had not much to tell them. They had been in a hurry to get off, and, as an excuse for their haste and at the same time as an encouragement, had reported quite optimistically. The barbed-wire barricade had been pretty badly knocked about. They had been kept busy the night before patching it up, they said. "The pioneers are to repair it to-day, so you'll have company."

It is pitch dark. The trench lies some fifty yards to the rear. From time to time the picket sends up a star shell. With a *whiz!* up go the rockets and bore their way through the darkness, bursting into a blinding flash of light, spraying the gloom with a train of fiery rain, and falling, leaving blacker blackness behind them.

Volkenborn is quite calm. As the rockets roar upwards he keeps his eyes fixed on the ground in front, but there is never a movement until they fall. Then menacing shadows seem to rise from the ground, move backward, crawl along, bending low, and throw themselves down. When the rocket dies, all hold their breath and creep nearer together threateningly. Machine guns begin to bark, there is the whine of passing bullets.

Karl Wulff whispers something. Volkenborn cannot catch what he says, but instinctively stretches out his hand for the grenades lying in front of him. Wulff looks sharply behind him to the right and puts his hand on Volkenborn's arm. Nothing to be seen, and scarcely a sound. But both realize that some one is near them.

In a low voice Wulff calls, "Who goes there?" No answer. Volkenborn drags himself up to his knees, grenades in hand, ready for throwing. He too cries, "Who goes there?", but this time louder. The answer comes quickly in a hoarse whisper: "Shut up, you damned fool, it's me — Fritze Pietschmann."

Slowly he crawls up to them. "Just wanted to have a squint, to see how you're getting on here. Wish it wasn't so damned dark. Just going to lob a bomb at me, wasn't you, Junker? It's cool as does it!"

A quarter of an hour passes. Pietschmann is lying beside Volkenborn. When the rockets flare, nothing is to be seen. As soon as they fall, those menacing shapes loom in the darkness. Suddenly a machine gun begins to hammer out on the right. *Rat-tat-tat!* More rockets go up. Nothing doing. Does it mean that our sappers are coming over the top? Sooner or later they are bound to come. The machine gun continues to splutter nervously at short intervals. "Something up!" All quiet again for a few seconds. Pitch dark.

Volkenborn fixes his eyes on the barbed wire, and waits for the next star shell. A whole battalion might be lying in front, he thinks. Couldn't see it. One hears nothing, or one hears too much. "I'm getting nervy. Must keep cool. Pietschmann's an ass. Must be our sappers. Why the hell are they so late?"

On the right, somewhere in the direction of the machine gun, a grenade explodes. Very lights flare. Wild firing. Volkenborn can see nothing, but suddenly he becomes conscious of a movement. In front of him, slightly to the left, he can distinctly hear some one. Something cracks. There is a muffled sound of hurried motion. A queer noise, as though a straw mat were being dragged along the ground. He leans across to Pietschmann, who at the same moment springs to his feet. Another rocket goes flaring and roaring up into the sky. Pietschmann stands motionless. Not thirty paces from him forms are crouching beside the wire entanglement. Perhaps twenty men, perhaps twice as many.

Friend or foe? Are they the sappers or — Tommies? "Who the hell are you?" shouts Pietschmann.
Bullets go singing past his head. "I knew something
was up! And now you're going to get a packet!"
Three grenades fly across the space. Then the
scouts fall hurriedly back. Karl Wulff tumbles into a
shell hole. Volkenborn goes to help him out, and
himself sinks in up to his knees. The Tommies are
firing at him, but the bullets are high; all pass over
his head. Then the big guns get busy with a sudden
roar.

They have reached the breastwork. A bomb
bursts right in front of them down in the trench.
Clods of earth go tumbling down. The acrid fumes
of the explosive catch their breath. Volkenborn
does not know where he is jumping to, but jumps
all the same; his knees crash against something
hard, he loses his balance and pitches forward on
freshly broken-up earth, his right wrist buckles under him. Good thing he's fallen soft, he thinks. As
he grabs for a hold on something in the dark, blood
streams over his hand. With a shudder he realizes
that he is clawing at a lacerated corpse.

The next morning opened dull, but cleared up
towards noon. There was the roar of approaching
airplanes. To the south of Lombartzyde, a combat
in the air was raging. With what dash the Germans
zoomed down, and how cleverly that Tommy
swooped clear! Then, suddenly, the English plane
burst into flames, fell into a spin, and crashed. For

a long time a tall column of smoke rose into
the clear air, and then died down. To Volkenborn,
who was watching, the end seemed very horrible.

Once again the airmen were circling warily in
great, graceful curves, their planes catching the sun
with every turn. Now it was like a scene in fairyland. The war seemed far away. No firing! No
sound but the far-off drone of the propellers high
in the air! Fleecy clouds floated in the heavens,
drifting gently along. Volkenborn imagined himself
sailing along with them. Imagined them carrying
his unspoken messages to those he loved at home.
For a long time he stood near the dugout, watching their silent flight.

The mail came up with the evening rations. From
his brother Lothar there was a parcel of grapes,
tomatoes, some pastry, and a small bottle of cognac.
Enclosed was a scrappy note:

"Hello, young 'un. Greetings from Kurt, who
has just 'phoned through. Keep your courage up!
Yours L."

All three brothers belonged to the same corps.
Lothar was adjutant of an artillery regiment, to
which Kurt was attached as orderly officer. To Hans
Volkenborn it seemed a sort of family affair, and
he always thought of it as "our corps," just as he
spoke of "my company." It gave him a sense of
security, a feeling of being at home among friends.

And there was a card from Elma:

"Thanks for yours. How nice for you brothers to

have been together! Love and good wishes to you all!" He looked at the picture on the card. The Kaiser in full uniform wearing many decorations. He tried to make out all the different orders. I should only have put on one, he thought; it would have been better form. Then he ripped the card across. The half with the address and the orders he tore into little bits, and let them blow away out of his hand. The other half, with the message and the Kaiser's head, he put into his pocketbook with Lothar's note.

The commissariat men brought rumors of an attack that was to be made at eight o'clock on the following evening. They had it from "an absolutely reliable source." Fritze Pietschmann and the others sat talking it over in the dugout while Volkenborn was sharing his tomatoes and grapes, and shaking the remains of the pastry into Pietschmann's outstretched hand. To Wulff had fallen the task of getting the cork out of the cognac bottle. Whilst they sat yarning, eating, and drinking, Volkenborn's thoughts wandered to the card in his breast pocket, and he kept repeating to himself the few simple words that it contained — trying them over in his mind with varying intonations. Later on, after Lance Corporal Schiller had extinguished their little Hindenburg lamp, Hans Volkenborn's hand strayed to his breast pocket, to the little book in which lay the torn-off half of the field post card. Soothed by its presence, he passed from pleasant thoughts into dreamland.

The batteries had been blazing away unceasingly since half-past nine in the morning. The sky was as blue as in a child's picture book, and the clouds as clear-cut and perfectly shaped as if they had been stuck on by hand. Airmen were up. In formation like migrating birds, darting here and there, reconnoitering, looking for the enemy. From time to time there would come a momentary lull, only to be followed by a still louder droning of propellers, as the planes came sweeping lower through the invisible walls of the sky, seeming to shake the very earth with the roar of their flight. The guns made the noise of an earthquake with the thud of falling buildings, and the shrieks of women. Ceaseless, without pause, came the sweep of these roaring, droning planes. The sky seemed to be vibrating with the explosion of shells, to be gaping as though cut into strips by millions of red-hot shears. The earth beneath seemed to quiver, helpless, like a tortured martyr in the hands of merciless inquisitors.

Hans Volkenborn, crouched behind earthworks thrown up at the edge of a shell crater, was breaking off lumps of dry soil from the edges and letting them fall into a pool of dirty, yellow water. They fell almost without a sound; just a splash, and they disappeared. Bending over, he could see his own gray image reflected in the muddy water. He began taking shots at it with the clods, amused to see how his face became distorted by the splashes. Then he stopped. A filthy rat crept over the edge and stood looking at him, its ugly head stretched out, listening.

Little eyes like boot buttons, a pink snout with quivering smellers, shining flanks moving in and out with
the action of its quickly pulsating breath, a long
dark-gray ringed tail. Hans reached for his pistol,
but in a flash the rat had scuttled over the edge of
the shell hole. He pushed his pistol back into the
holster. Tired of pelting his face in the water, he
gave it one last look, jumped up, and made his
way quickly into the trench.

Pietschmann, returning from a visit to a neighboring sector, found him sitting in front of what
they called the "arbor", legs crossed, open pocketbook beside him, looking at photos.

"My parents, Pietschmann."

Pietschmann held the pictures out between two
fingers. Hans Volkenborn, hardly hearing what he
said about them, put the photographs back.

Time passed drearily. Towards five in the afternoon the official order to attack was given out.
Everybody already knew what it was to be. From
six-thirty to seven o'clock Volkenborn was on duty,
observing the hits through the periscope slit in the
company commander's observation post.

Fountains of dust and débris were being blown
into the air. Hardly a clump of earth near him
but was hammered and crushed into powder every
second or so by the impact of shell splinters. It was
like a panorama or a cinema — or a nightmare. He
tried to convince himself that the humming and
groaning and thundering was all his imagination.
That it was not really audible. That it was merely

some hideous din that he had heard before, now reëchoing through his protesting brain. A buzzing in the ears, as the men called it. It would pass. He leaned his temple against the damp concrete wall. No, it was no longer a panorama, no longer like being in a cinema. The sounds were not a mere echo in his own brain. They were not beating merely in his ears, not thumping in his temples only. No! The earth beneath his feet was shaking. There was the same trembling of the wall against which he was leaning as in his own head. The air that he was breathing, this thick, sticky mixture of condite, sweat, tobacco smoke, rotting straw and urine, was poisoning him, sucking into his lungs. His head ached vilely. It was as though he were being scalped, as though his head were being steadily knocked against some padded object. An irritation, a sort of tickling, made itself felt in his ears, ran like a clammy trickle through the back of his head, and down his neck and spine. He could even feel this prickly, tingling irritation in his bowels and thighs. Three days of this and I should go mad, he thought, and looked at his watch. Presently Wulff relieved him.

Volkenborn and Pietschmann had their meal together. He had no appetite for it, but Pietschmann had insisted that it would buck him up. Then he again examined his hand grenades, tested his automatic, and put the three reserve cartridge clips in the right-hand pocket of his tunic. His gas mask was close up to his chest, where it would be easier to get

at if he got caught in the wire. The first field dressing packet was handy in its proper place.

Black, white and red bands were served out to
the storming party, and they bound them on each
other's backs. The idea was that officers directing
the artillery fire might know how far the attack had
advanced. For a moment Volkenborn found himself
standing alone near the breastwork. Nervously he
shifted his handkerchief from one pocket to the
other, readjusted his white arm brassard, buckled
his belt a hole tighter, and then let it out again. He
would have liked to take out his pocketbook with
the photos, and read once more what was written
on the torn field postcard, although he already
knew it by heart, but he refrained from doing so.
Then he looked at his watch, and held it while the
second hand ticked out two, three minutes. With a
quick movement he snapped it off the chain, opened
the case with his knife, closed it again, put it back
on the chain, and then into his pocket.

Close behind the trench, poppies bloomed. He
was about to pick one, but becoming aware of the
sentry, who with his back turned was looking out
through his peephole, he gave up the idea. A lance
corporal passed at this moment and barked out an
order. Then they assembled at the company leader's
post. The lieutenant made them a speech. While
they stood waiting at the outlet from the trench,
Volkenborn tried to recall what the officer had said,
but could not.

Pietschmann was smoking a cigarette. It seemed

to Volkenborn as though all the hidden sweetness of the life that lay behind them, a life that would perhaps have no morrow, was concentrated in this thin stream of up-curling smoke. Schiller was holding his watch in his hand, and Volkenborn stared at it. . . . It was one of those solid silver watches that can be bought for thirty marks, such as his father still carried. You wind them up with a key. There would be engravings on the inner case. On some there was a full moon with a smiling face, or a Venus with fantastic leaf ornamentation. Some even had a compass. Schiller carried his in an out-side metal case, a very superior one of nickel. He'll have it on him to the end, thought Volkenborn, and then his boy will inherit a thirty-mark watch, almost a new one. To the end! Then Volkenborn looked at his own watch. It wanted just five minutes to eight. Zero!

Like peas falling through a burst bag, they tumble out of the trench, wondering how long it will be before they find themselves up against the wire entanglement. Surprising that no machine guns get busy on them. All quiet; nothing moving. The good German artillery throws a screen slowly in front of them — the creeping barrage. The wire entanglement is shot to pieces. The earth has been pounded until nothing has been left standing. Like a box of toys upset by a naughty child. Those three dead bodies are no part of this evening's work. They are a horrid memento of the night before. Originally there had been a greater distance between them, but

two or three shells had blown them up and dumped
them down close together, although in the hurry of
this reassembling a few of their limbs had been left
behind. There they lie, like broken marionettes after
the performance is over. Despite something of vio-
lence in their attitude, they look almost comic and
grotesque . . . which is as it should be.

Five minutes pass slowly. Pietschmann is almost
through the wire. Schiller is standing, looking right
and left, and then at his thirty-mark watch. He is
very excited. If all goes well, he is to get his stripe.
No wonder he's so eager, thinks Volkenborn.

Eight o'clock! Like horses under the lash they
start forward, Pietschmann, with his long legs,
leading. Just in front of the trench he gets caught in
the barbed wire. By the time he has wrenched his
way out with bleeding hands, Schiller has passed
him. Leading by ten paces, he plunges into the
trench, headfirst like a diver, but with a curiously
clumsy and undecided movement. Volkenborn jumps
almost on top of him. Schiller has not moved from
where he landed. Volkenborn shakes him, turns him
over. Then rushes on, his only conscious thought the
beautiful thirty-mark watch! Nothing doing for
Schiller in the corporal line!

The first line has been pretty well blown to
pieces by the guns. They have to jump and climb.
Fire begins to spit from the second line, — first one,
then a second, then a third machine gun. So the
Tommies are still alive! They advance in savage
rushes. If only the artillery would look where they

are shooting! "Damnation! Their job's to drop a curtain in front of us, and now we're running into our own fire! The fools will end up by letting us have it in the backside."

Star shells go up. Pallid and strange they look in the strong evening light. Pietschmann and Volkenborn stalk the nearest machine gun warily. At length they get inside bombing range. After the third grenade it is silent. "You did that fine, Junker." The third squad is just behind them. Now for it! At last the artillery comes to their aid. "All clear to the left!" Hands are stretched out as though in welcome. Tired, worn, dust-coated faces. A sergeant leans, heavily against a tub, as though drunk. He is spitting blood, trying to die on his feet. Shots come from behind a breastwork! Karl Wulff yells out in agony, *Ow!* — like a hurt child. He has only barked his shin bone. Fritze, who is pressing forward, shouts to him in passing, "Don't make such a hell of a fuss, fathead."

At the mouth of a communicating trench there is a pistol duel. Volkenborn finds himself opposite an English officer. In answer to Volkenborn's *"Surrender!"* the Englishman aims his big pistol at him. Volkenborn jumps back. For a few seconds there is wild shooting. Then Volkenborn feels something hard hit him on the temple. He puts his hand up; there is no blood, but his head aches like fury. As he fires again, blindly, the Englishman has sunk to his knees, mortally wounded. With his left hand he clings to a post of the timber-lined trench. His head, as though in dreamy expectation, is inclined to one side. But he aims at Volkenborn again. Thrice his revolver misses fire. The third shot from a falling arm merely hits the earth and the English officer slithers sideways against the wall of the trench. Volkenborn rushes past him.

While he runs he inserts a new clip into his automatic. Machine guns on the left hammer out. They seem to have brought the attack to a standstill. Pietschmann and Baluschek, a sturdy little East Prussian, come up. They had been with another party, which had been making good headway. The only check at the moment is on the extreme left. "We'll deal with them, while you get round and take 'em in rear."

The company has occupied the enemy's captured second line. A group of men from the third squad join in the attack. The English artillery, though badly knocked about by the German guns, is still blazing away furiously in the direction of the lost ground. A group of prisoners is simply blown to pieces. In front of the third position machine guns are giving trouble. They are firing from behind a solid mass of broken masonry. In vain has Volkenborn showered grenades on them.

Pietschmann raises his rifle and fires five carefully aimed rounds. A heavy machine gun is brought up, but its crew of two are killed outright before it can open fire. The same fate befalls a light machine gun that is rushed ahead of the company. The English guns will have to be taken with a rush. Volkenborn

calls to Pietschmann. At the same moment Baluschek, who is on the extreme left, has stopped firing,
and has slowly wriggled his way towards the heap
of brick work. He now makes a rush forward, cool
and confident as a detective raiding a thieves'
kitchen. Either the machine gunners do not see him,
or they cannot fire at such an acute angle. He stops
just short of his objective, and leaning forward, like
a boy at some playground game, hurls his grenades
in quick succession, and then drops instantly to
earth. As though by arrangement, Pietschmann and
Volkenborn swerve round to the right and are behind the barrier while the crash of the exploding
grenades is still in their ears and the fumes and dirt
in their eyes.

"Hands up!" The answer is the muzzle of a car-
bine, but Pietschmann is too quick for the Englishman, and shoots him down at ten paces. "Swine!"
he roars, and catches his next opponent, who ducks,
right across the skull with the butt of his automatic.
The man doubles up like an empty sack. The company presses on. "Keep a move on, Junker, we're
just getting into the swing of it." Hands go up. Prisoners are surrendering sullenly. With a gesture
Pietschmann indicates the way the English are to go.
"Any cigarettes on you, Fritz?" One of them actually stops. They shake hands. Forward!

"We'll be jumping Calais before we know where
we are, and that'll put the lid on the war."

Two English dugouts stubbornly hold firm. No
way of getting at them. They keep up a lashing hail

of machine-gun bullets! Hand grenades are called
for. It develops into a desperate siege. Baluschek,
venturing too much, drops. Pietschmann and Volkenborn drag him back, and then Pietschmann is hit.
Two of the attackers are already lying dead, when
the flame-throwers come on the scene. On the left
wing, where the attack had been held up, they quickly
blaze a way for a further advance. Twice, three
times, the flaming, scorching tongues lick through the
galleries of the trench; it belches pitch-black fumes.
The machine guns are abruptly silent. From behind
the one nearest to Volkenborn, staggers a charred
something. It makes a queer forward movement and
collapses. Burnt alive!

Volkenborn shudders. Horror grips him. Burnt!
Burnt alive! Hell . . . ! He follows Pietschmann,
who is looking for some one to bandage his wound.

Twenty yards beyond flows the Yser — a strip of
dirty gray water, with swampy banks — and every
moment falling shells pitch splashing into it. The
mud rises in spurts. On the other side, behind a
thick veil of smoke, dust, and falling mist, lies what
the guns have left of Nieuport. We have reached
the Yser. Why don't we cross? The din of battle
fades and slowly the night falls, casting its cool
shadow over the horrors that lie hidden in trench
and shell craters. A gentle breeze, salt with the
brine of the sea, carrying with it the murmur of
quiet waves lapping a distant shore, brings peace
after the fury of the day.

Two hours' work temporarily restores the de-fences of the captured position. Pietschmann is firing an English machine gun. Volkenborn has bandaged his arm. Pietschmann, who has proved unusually docile during the operation, remarks, "Straight, Junker, when you first blew into the company, I thought here's another nut — like the rest of 'em. But I was all wrong, because you aren't."

"Thanks."

Shortly after midnight the storm troops are relieved. Pietschmann takes charge of his group. On the way to the rear, they pass an artillery observation post, and Volkenborn rushes in and makes for the telephone. The man on duty looks doubtful, but gives way.

"Give me Weichsel — Weichsel! The adjutant, please! Hello! That you, Lothar? Good morning. All went off splendidly! What? Yes, I'm O.K. All quiet now. Thanks. Say hello to Kurt for me! See you soon! Good-by!"

In Middlekirk there's a fresh bombardment. Shrapnel! A spent bullet hits Volkenborn's steel helmet, hardly making a mark. A pity! A deep dint would have been something to remember the day by.

Cars, retreating columns, and batteries are clattering past. Pietschmann and Volkenborn ask for the field hospital. Baluschek is still there. He lies motionless, evidently in great agony, but smiles faintly as they are going. His eyes follow them. Volkenborn turns back with three cigarettes that he has bought from a hospital orderly. He holds them before Baluschek's eyes, and then crams them into the breast pocket of his tunic. Then he runs to catch up his section. He again has a pain in his temple, and can feel a swelling there. It was probably only a bit of stone, but if it had been a bullet . . . There would have been an end of me. I should have been lying in the cold-meat cart like poor Schiller. To-morrow they would have shoved me into the ground. Or I might have hung on to life for a bit, just like Baluschek. I should have been sent to hospital at Arnstadt. Ursel would have nursed me. They would all have come to see me and the colonel would have sent me the Iron Cross. One fine morning it would have been there, lying on the counterpane, or on the night table, covered with roses from the garden. And Mother and Father, both very proud of me. And then when I could begin to walk again —

Dreaming as he marched, he came to a place about a kilometer from Middlekirke, where the regiment entrained. For a while Volkenborn and Pietschmann chatted together. Without noticing it, they had both dropped into the familiar "thou." Soon they grew weary and made themselves comfortable for a nap. Pietschmann smoked a cigarette that he had begged from Volkenborn, who was already half asleep. He was just conscious of the glow of the cigarette when Pietschmann took a pull at it. Lulled by the steady rumble of the train, he slipped off into dreamland, and was once again in the hospital at Arnstadt. So clean and inviting. Everything snow white! Everybody so kind and considerate! Ursel sweetly smiling. Then suddenly Pietschmann is there.

No, it isn't Pietschmann, after all. It's Albert
Schulze. And Mother has made a pudding, a dump-
ling with strawberries. Father is lighting one of
the big cigars he keeps for special occasions. Elma
blows the match out for him. What cheek! She takes
father's cigar from his mouth and pulls at it until
it glows again and then — God! The flame-thrower!
That hellish blaze licking up the gallery of the
trench! A half-calcined body lurches out. Burnt
alive! Burnt alive!

Volkenborn opens his eyes. Pietschmann is just
knocking the end of his cigarette out. "Now for a
snooze, Junker! Shut your peepers and off you go."
Volkenborn again falls into the sleep of exhaustion
and again has queer, distorted dreams.

III

Three months later the regiment was again "at
rest" in Bruges. A hard batch of trench fighting lay
behind them. Volkenborn had been appointed a
lance corporal (on Goethe's birthday) and Pietschmann had secured the shanks of the collar buttons
denoting his new rank with broken match sticks. It
was quite a while later that Volkenborn wrote the
news home, pretending to treat it as an item of no
importance. In secret he was tremendously proud.
It made him more sure of himself in his dealings with
his comrades. He felt now that he really did belong
to *the* company, and that he was a proper "old
soldier."

He had some scruples of conscience in taking possession of the officer's billet assigned to him in a priest's house. This compunction was not on account of his sour, reverend host, in whose establishment there was such a coming and going of clergy that it was difficult to distinguish the good man himself from his colleagues. Neither had he any scruples with regard to the slovenly housekeeper, who had removed the *prie-Dieu* from his room after he had hung his dirty tunic and the rest of his equipment over it, rifle belt, steel helmet, gas mask, and all. No; his conscience only pricked him with regard to his less fortunate comrades, Pietschmann and Wulff, who, healed of his wound, had rejoined the company some days before.

They were roughly quartered in a monastery, all sleeping in one great cheerless room with a stone floor. Of course it was very pleasant to be allotted a private billet as a *Junker* — with marble staircase, white walls, red stair carpets, a great white bed, green blinds, a little brass lamp on the bedside table, sacred pictures, fireplace with the mirror over it, and a table in the window with a faded red cover. Every day he revelled anew in these luxuries and was thankful to be allowed to enjoy them. But the thought that his comrades were not so comfortably housed, that they slept on straw sacks instead of in a comfortable bed — that worried him. It seemed a sort of betrayal not to be sharing their rough quarters, not to be sleeping on straw and washing at the cold pump in the monastery yard every morning.

One day when Pietschmann visited him, Volkenborn cautiously approached the subject. But Pietschmann could not understand his scruples. "That's how it ought to be — you're quite different to the likes of us. In six months you'll be an officer and you won't want to pass the time of day with Fritze Pietschmann any more. Army's like that, you see."

A few days before Volkenborn had received a packet of cigarettes from Elma, and a card in it on which she had written, "Anneliese Lengerke is here, we have been talking about you." And Anneliese Lengerke had added a couple of lines.

There was nothing much in the two lines of faint, rather unformed writing. But something in the sound of the name and the picture that it brought before his eyes touched some secret spring in his nature, and a longing, that he had succeeded till now in sternly suppressing, suddenly seized upon him.

He was only six years old when he had first met Anneliese Lengerke: it was at a private school kept by that dreaded disciplinarian, Rector Welke. His mother told him that he used to walk across the church square arm in arm with his little friend, a well-behaved, serious little boy, keenly conscious of his dignity. Then for a long time they saw nothing of each other, and only came together again at a charitable show, just a week before he joined up. As befitted grown-up persons they addressed one another with the formal *"Sie,"* and drank a bottle of champagne with Ursel and Elma Scholander, who

were to dance a minuet and were suffering from a
bad attack of stage fright. It had all been very fes-
tive and he had remembered what lovely, great blue
eyes she had. On the staircase leading to the cloak-
room he had said good-by to her and pressed her
hand — rather hurriedly because her mother was
standing near! But the novelty of a soldier's life had
banished all thought of her. It also made him forget
all about his unrequited love for Gert Sowansky —
who wrote such delightful letters and fell in love
with his brother Kurt, when he came home on leave.
Hans Volkenborn had been very proud of the indifference that he, as a soldier, felt for both of these
girls. Even after the attack and after receiving
Elma's post card and dreaming about it, and imagining himself lying in the hospital in Arnstadt and
being nursed by Ursel, he had written a long paragraph in his diary about his indifference, and how
the stern duties of a real soldier's life excluded all
such things as love.

Despite this proudly expressed conviction, he now
found himself frequently thinking of Anneliese. Especially when he was smoking a quiet cigarette would
he think about her, about what she and Elma might
have said about him, and whether she ever thought
about that evening at the show. Did she still remember the Rector's school, and how they walked arm
in arm together across the square? One day, he
bought some elegant, tinted writing paper and composed a very long letter, read it through twice, and
tore it up. He wrote a second hurriedly, which he

posted without reading through; posted it as hurriedly and felt as if the fate of an army corps de-
pended on it.

Volkenborn was not reserved, and spoke often
with his comrade Werner of the Seventh Company
about his home, his parents, his brothers, the two
"Scholander girls": Ursel of the dreamy sea-blue
eyes, and dark motherly Elma with her beautiful
hands and trim ankles. He and Werner used to add
little postscripts to each other's cards, but of his
letter on the elegant, tinted note paper, and of
Anneliese Lengerke, he never spoke.

One day the Fahnenjunkers of the regiment were
paraded before the acting colonel. This officer, whose
chief characteristics were a close-clipped thick, fierce-
looking moustache, and a short riding crop, in no
way disappointed their unpleasant anticipations of
the interview. It began with an explosive lecture and
resulted in their being handed over to the adjutant
of the Second Battalion for daily instruction from
three to four.

This afternoon drill under Lieutenant von Kless
was not exactly in the nature of a punishment. Nevertheless the Junkers regarded it as a bore, especially
as the lieutenant selected the neighborhood of the
Lac d'Amour, where a fine promenade seemed to
him to provide a suitable spot for their exercises.
Volkenborn's chief grievance was that this duty made
him late for the evening swim with Pietschmann and
his other comrades of the company. But Lieutenant
von Kless proved a pleasant fellow. In fact, so

greatly taken was he with this officer that he wrote
to his parents, "The Adjutant is a fine chap."
Volkenborn wrote in one of his letters, "If I were
a girl, I should fall in love with him right away."

CHAPTER TWO

THE LIEUTENANT

I

Von Kless was an exceedingly smart soldier and might have been voted the most popular officer in the regiment; but he was too self-contained and reserved to become a pronounced favorite. Not that he was "stand-offish" in his intercourse with subordinates; they liked him, but the mess complained that he was too impersonal, kept too much to himself, and never let himself go, even in the hours of greatest gayety and good-fellowship. A few thought him proud and cold. Not one of them was intimate with him.

At the conclusion of their third meeting, Lieutenant von Kless invited the eight Junkers to a café. Volkenborn was delighted, and made a special toilet for the occasion: his best uniform, a new service cap, and gloves. He also paid a special visit to the barber's.

He sat next to the lieutenant; not as the result of any special effort, but just by chance — or because the others hung back. At first he was rather shy and awkward, and was more silent than usual;

having secured the place of honor, he began to feel ill at ease.

"Pleased you're appointed to the Machine Gun Company, Volkenborn?" said Lieutenant von Kless, as they were leaving the café, and the two were walking side by side.

"Very pleased, Herr Lieutenant."

"Have you been inside Notre Dame?"

"Yes, Herr Lieutenant, I have."

"Did you see Michelangelo's Madonna?"

"No, Herr Lieutenant."

"My dear Volkenborn, when we are off parade let's leave out the Herr Lieutenant." He smiled kindly. "And how do you amuse yourself in your spare time?"

"I'm very keen on swimming. I go bathing every day."

"Are you fond of reading?"

"Oh, very!"

"What do you read mostly?"

Volkenborn was silent for a moment, as though he were reflecting, but he was not really in doubt as to his answer.

"I'm very fond of Eichendorff, Herr Lieutenant. I carry a copy of 'Taugenichts' about with me."

The lieutenant looked at him keenly — a quick sidelong glance. Volkenborn flushed. Perhaps it was not exactly a book for a soldier. Dreams of that kind have nothing in common with war. He wanted to say something; wanted to say that he had been fond of Eichendorff when he was a schoolboy, that he also had a field edition of "Faust," but that he had neither leisure, patience, nor tenacity to study it, that he always fell back on Eichendorff. But he said none of this, only walked in silence beside his officer, uncertain of the impression he was making. It was a relief to him when the eldest Fähnrich gave him a sign that it was time to separate from the lieutenant. Von Kless shook hands with each of them.

"Till to-morrow afternoon! You are living quite near me, Volkenborn; you may as well come part of the way with me."

I wish he'd say something, thought Volkenborn, as he walked beside the silent lieutenant. I expect it's because of Eichendorff. Why on earth did I say that? After all, what's it to do with other people? I can hardly think that he's the sort to be displeased about a thing like that . . .

"Didn't I see you sketching at the bridge yesterday, Volkenborn?" So he had seen that too, thought Volkenborn. Now for it. A Fahnenjunker is not expected to do things of that sort.

"Yes, Herr Lieutenant."

"I expect you've made some sketches in the church too, in Notre Dame?"

"Yes, Herr Lieutenant."

"Perhaps you'll show me your sketchbook one of these days? And please cut out the Herr Lieutenant, when we're alone together. It's unnecessary under any circumstances." Volkenborn felt perplexed. All sorts of ideas ran through his head.

He's just feeling your pulse. Be careful! Although he's friendly and familiar with you, you mustn't be familiar with him. He's an officer and you're only a Junker. Don't forget that. Rules of the service are rules of the service.

But he managed somehow to check the "Herr Lieutenant," though with difficulty.

"I should very much like to show you the sketch-book, but there's nothing much to see in it. It's not worth looking through."

"That remains to be seen, Volkenborn. You must come and see me. I've a delightful room, looking on to the canal. I can give you a good cigarette and a glass of bad wine. Come to-morrow after drill, will you?"

"Yes. I shall be delighted to come, Herr Lieutenant."

II

Three days after his first visit to Lieutenant von Kless, Volkenborn got a day's leave, to visit his brother Kurt. The morning was still young when he reached the Brigade Staff Quarters. It was a Sunday; Kurt had returned at eight o'clock from duty, had slept a little and was just shaving when Heinrich Kosemund, his batman who was also from Piskallen, brought him in his top boots, and announced "The Fahnenjunker."

"What? Who? Man alive, Kosemund, do you mean my brother?"

Kosemund grinned affirmatively and kept tight hold of the tops.

"Slacks, Kosemund, and my brown shoes. We'll make ourselves comfortable. — How splendid to see you, Hans! Of course you'll lunch with us. I'll send word to the general that you're here. How glad I am to see you! You can stop till the evening? Splendid! We'll have a bathe, and then lie down in the grass and yarn — make a regular holiday of it. I sha'n't be long. Take a pew till I'm ready. Yes, over there at the writing table! Seen this photo of Ursel? Now tell me all the news! How jolly to have you here, Hanseken!"

In due course Hans Volkenborn was presented to the general — a little, clean-shaven gentleman, with perpetually raised eyebrows, a bald head that rose to a peak at the back, and eyes of an uncertain hue. At midday they all had a plate of soup together, and it was arranged that they were to meet again in the evening.

The officers of the staff were quartered in a two-storied house on the bank of the canal. Near it was the "Gefechtsstand," which consisted of a vast concrete work, roofed in, with doors and windows painted on it. In the rear of the yard, which contained stabling and garages was a meadow surrounded with bushes, poplars, and elms, which ran down to the canal. Three parts of it were mown, but near the water the grass had been left long for the greater convenience of bathers.

Three horses were grazing in the meadow. One of

them was Kurt's chestnut; a beast with a coat like a pattern on a plush rug, — as Hans, who knew nothing about horses, described it. Fond of all animals, he at once took a fancy to the heavily built Frisian, a gentle creature, but with a look of roguish mischief in its eye.

They lay down where the long grass began, their pink bathing wraps showing up picturesquely against the green background. Stretched out on their stomachs, they chewed grass stalks, gazed from time to time up at the sky, that was of so pale a blue that the fleeting clouds were hardly distinguishable against it, bathed their shoulders in the September sunshine, and permitted ladybirds to crawl unheeded over them.

"Can you still tickle your nose with your big toe, Kurt? Do you remember how we used to practise that in the old days on the Baltic? It's almost like Brunshaupter here, isn't it? No sign of the war! No guns! Can you hear anything?"

They both hold their breath and listened. High over Lombartzyde circled airplanes. There is a light, buzzing sound, almost like gnats. Little puffs of smoke, that look like clouds, suddenly form round the planes. An anti-aircraft battery starts firing. There is nothing in the least alarming in the sound, which is not an aggressive one. Rockets rise. When the shells burst high in air, there follows a slight harmless crack, like the breaking of gingerbread. *Crack! Crack!* How lovely the clouds look, sailing along in a circle, like celestial maids of honor!

"It's just like being at a rifle meeting. We lie here and enjoy watching it all, and perhaps presently one of the chaps up there will bump up against one of those harmless looking puffs and crash, and then there will be nothing left of him but a lump of squashed pulp — as Fritze Pietschmann would say."

For a while they lay in silence. Then Kurt asked for the home news. In October, father and mother would be celebrating their silver wedding. Kurt had already applied for leave. Hans hoped to get at least a few days from his captain.

"The adjutant thinks it will be all right — Lieutenant von Kless, he's a fine chap. I visited him the other day. He is quartered on a barrister. A tip-top house! He has the free run of the music room. The barrister, who is a captain in the Belgian army, is fighting against us. Rotten luck for the wife to have to put the enemy up, the very man who perhaps some day will put a pill into her husband. We had some music. He plays beautifully, and I like him awfully. When I first met him I had no idea that he was so simple and unpretentious. He is said to be our keenest officer. They say he was a marvel on the Somme. But when you're alone with him, he's quite another man. In the evening —"

Kurt had been vainly trying to coax his chestnut up to him. The beast was now approaching cautiously, his head stretched out, snorting slightly; nibbling from time to time at tufts of grass and stopping periodically, head down, to steal a look at Kurt.

"Come on! What are you so scared about, Hans, you silly beast? We haven't got many clothes on, which makes us the more like one another. This chap here is called Hans too, as you are! Allow me to introduce him."

Step by step Hans, the chestnut, with a coat like the pattern of a plush rug, draws nearer. He seems to have no purpose, hardly to be aware of their presence. In reality he is consumed with curiosity; he tries to conceal it under the guise of an uninterested stupidity and does it well. He lays his ears back, points them again, looks around him, lashes flies away with his tail, wasting much unnecessary vigor, until finally he is standing within eighteen inches of Hans Volkenborn's foot. He sniffs, then stretches his neck out as far as he can without losing his balance. He can't quite make it all out. Again he draws his head back and lays his ears flat, points them again, looks, and leans forward.

"Sheer curiosity," whispers Kurt. "Keep quite still!"

The beast ventures still nearer, advancing one foot and sniffing at the grass in an attempt to conceal its real intention. Gradually it advances its muzzle until it touches Hans Volkenborn's foot. The contact tickles frightfully, and the man has a difficulty in keeping still. Then its cool, trembling, cautious lips nibble tentatively at his toes. Exercising all his self-control, Hans withdraws his foot slowly. The chestnut snuffles foolishly with its lips, as though to make sure that the toe is no longer there; then lifts its head, puts its ears back, points them again, stares, and trots away with its tail in the air.

Hans jumped up. "Now for the water! My whole body is itching with the tickle of that velvet muzzle. This is great! We must ring Lothar up afterwards. What a pity he couldn't come. Yesterday his man brought me a whole packet of soldiers' comforts. Next time I sha'n't accept them."

For half an hour they swam side by side, lying on their backs and splashing with their feet, swimming under water or racing one another to some selected spot, such as the twentieth poplar.

As they swam they exchanged remarks with each other: about their parents, about Jenno, their dog, about being appointed to the Machine Gun Company, about Lieutenant von Kless, Michelangelo's Madonna in Notre Dame, about Ursel and Elma and the presents of cigarettes they sent.

"Anneliese Lengerke added a line to the card. Do you remember her?"

"The little girl you used to walk with arm in arm across the church square?"

"What! You remember that? Did Mother tell you about it? We must both write to Father and Mother afterwards. How glad they'll be to hear that we are together. Shall we turn back now? Is your mess dinner a very formal affair? A mere worm of a common soldier from the trenches can hardly be expected to know how to behave in such august company! Do you sit long over your meal? Thank goodness! Then we shall still have some time to ourselves afterwards."

The dinner had passed off quite pleasantly — up to a point. The artillery section commander, who shared their quarters, was celebrating his birthday — an agreeable man, with hair graying at the temples, and bright, dark eyes that Volkenborn took a pleasure in looking at. In honor of the occasion wine was drunk, and the *Armen Ritter* that they had for a sweet was such a success that it recalled memories of childhood. Kurt sat blinking across the table, and the other orderly officer kept filling his glass up. Hans Volkenborn decided that it was quite jolly in the brigade mess.

The general, too, seemed in high good humor. He made a long speech in honor of the gunner's birthday, and took wine in turn with his adjutants, his orderly officers, and finally with the Junker. As he did so, his eyes drew still nearer together, and he made a movement as though his collar had suddenly grown too tight. Volkenborn felt that the general was looking at him as though he were the bugler posted in front of the regiment, to give the time for the manual exercises. He sat bolt upright, as prescribed, held his glass level with where the buckle would have been, had he worn his belt, and waited for the general to make up his mind to drink, which seemed to take a long time. Apparently he was waiting for something; perhaps in his mind's eye he really did see the regiment lined up proudly before him. Whatever the cause, his face took on a sternly

regimental look, until Volkenborn felt himself gradually becoming petrified. At last the general withdrew his eyes and took what appeared to be a resigned sip from his glass.

Hardly had the brothers reached Kurt's room,
when an orderly brought word that the general
wanted to see him. He came back white with anger.

"To-morrow I shall apply to be sent back to the
regiment! I'm tired of being treated like a silly
schoolboy! It's time he learned that I'm not here to
play the clown in his circus! I'm fed up with it all."

Little by little, it all came out. The general had
reprimanded Kurt because Hans had not stood up
when he had taken wine with him. He expected his
officers to have the education of gentlemen.

"My goodness, yes! I was half asleep. We don't
do that sort of thing in our regiment. Our lieutenant colonel hates all that jumping up and down at
table. Damn it! What am I to do? Report the matter
to my colonel?"

"Your colonel? Bunk of that kind? Why, he'd
die of laughter — or turn you out. But it's not the
first time that I've been thinking of applying to be
sent back to the regiment. I have had it in my mind
for a long while. I'm thoroughly sick of it all. Fed
up, I tell you. We're soldiers and not performing
monkeys."

For quite a long time they talked it over. Kurt
was very bitter about it all. Meanwhile Kosemund,
his batman, was going about the room on his toes, as
though he would say, "Oh, I know all about it; the

old 'un again! All he can do is to lay out flower beds and bully his lieutenants. How glad I am that I'm nothing but a plain soldier servant!"

Ursel's photograph stood on the table between them, and, catching sight of it, Kurt began to calm down. "If it were not for one's people at home, one wouldn't stand it for a day longer!"

It was nearly midnight when Hans rose to go. Kurt went a part of the way with him. They walked arm in arm until they came to the bridge at Leffinghe, where they stood still for a moment and looked back. The sky was alive with summer lightning, flashing here and there; pale as the phosphorescence with which the seashore sometimes illuminates the night. Rockets, like glowworms, shot up from time to time, and showed sharp and clear against the blackness of the sky. There was the sound of far-off guns. It was all vague, like murmurs one hears in dreams, or whispers that drone in your ears as you fall off to sleep, sometimes growing louder, and then dying away like a sigh. Suddenly a gun answered quite near them. There was a train of red sparks; a rumbling like the sound of bowls on a skittle alley, a noise like the wind passing through broken pipes. The heavy batteries were opening a general bombardment on strategic approaches, crossroads, pioneer parks: all the appointed targets. Many rounds per gun in such a length of time. Not until the supply of shells was exhausted would the firing cease. Then there would be a chance for the gunners to get a short sleep. War is a whole-time job, like running a lift, or stoking in the gas works. The same thing has to be done over and over again. It is all a matter of habit, and a soldier soon becomes used to it. He may have killed somebody in doing his duty, but it is all in a day's march, so what is the good of thinking about it? Our turn to-morrow — who knows? After all it is — War!

Pioneer detachments march hurriedly and quietly by, shouldering their entrenching tools and smoking as they go. Men on leave come and go, parcels bulging under their packs, their bread rations on top. Cyclists, batmen, are returning from Bruges and Ostend. Field kitchens and field kitchen lorries give off invisible fumes, the aroma of sweetened coffee, dried vegetables and cheese; endless lines of pioneer lorries and ammunition columns rattle and pound along; all through the night the roads are alive with traffic.

The brothers part from each other at the church, giving each other both hands. In daylight they would be ashamed to do so. But it is dark. White, with blue-black shadows between its columns, the church tower rises serene above the turmoil of the night. Countless stars quiver like tensioned nerves; the ruddy harvest moon suggests wounds and blood. They give each other both hands. Their eyes are in shadow, of which they are both glad.

III

Since Hans Volkenborn had been transferred to the Machine Gun Company, there has been for him no more afternoon instruction under Lieutenant von Kless. Volkenborn missed this afternoon hour very much. Occupied as he was with his new duties, there seemed something lacking: something that he hardly admitted to himself, something so personal as to be almost inadmissible in a soldier.

The instructor of the Machine Gun Section, Lieutenant Gallatz, was a smart officer and an excellent fellow. He wore the most fascinating blue breeches, tan leggings, and a blue silk service cap — altogether a most irresistible combination. He knew his work well, too. Patience, however, was not his greatest virtue, and on occasions he could be rough, rough to the verge of brutality, to his men. But his whole demeanor, his tan leggings, his blue breeches, his silk cap, his dogskin gloves, his eternal cigarette, his witticisms, and his ruthless decision — all this impressed the men; it was what they admired. These were the qualities that they looked for in an officer, the characteristics that they respected. Often Volkenborn found it difficult to understand the private soldier's point of view. On one occasion, when the men were cleaning their rifles, he overheard a conversation which provided him with much matter for thought. They were discussing a young officer of the Reserve, who could not afford breeches of blue cloth, silk cap or dogskin gloves, but saved up his pay and sent it home; who never stood the men a cask of beer, never swore at them, or addressed them with the familiar but contemptuous *"Du."*

"If he can't damned well afford to do the thing

proper like, what the hell does he bother with it
for? Calls himself an officer! A miserable, gutless
swine of a skinflint, that's what he is. Would like
to be a swell, and ain't got it in him to do the thing
in style."

With astonishment, Volkenborn listened to this
tirade. How cruel the men were in their judgments!
Cruel and foolish, like children! But he had to confess to himself that he, too, preferred Lieutenant
Gallatz of the dogskin gloves and the smart, brutal
tongue to the officer of whom they were speaking,
who wore a badly fitting uniform made of the same
cloth as the men's and wore ammunition boots, but
was decent and polite, just like an ordinary human
being. There were moments when Volkenborn could
not even understand himself.

What he greatly regretted was the "labor of
love," as Werner had named the afternoon instruction with Lieutenant von Kless near the Lac
d'Amour, but he found compensation in a standing
invitation to spend his free afternoons with the
Lieutenant.

"Come as often as you like, Volkenborn. I shall
always be glad to see you."

To Hans Volkenborn there seemed something
strange about these afternoons with the lieutenant,
but perhaps the only strange thing about them was
that he made no mention of them to his fellow soldiers. These visits and his letter on the nice blue
paper were the only things which he kept absolutely
to himself. This was not the result of any definite

decision, come to as the result of careful consideration, but simply because he felt it impossible to talk
about these visits, and so remained silent. It was
not always quite an easy matter, and occasionally
it entailed lying. But this troubled him no more than
do the evasions that lovers so often practise as a
safeguard against the prying world. It seemed even
as though these subterfuges strengthened his determination to throw a veil of mystery over this
friendship. If he had been able to realize clearly his
own secretiveness, he would have been ashamed, but
he acted entirely on impulse, and without any conscious reflection. What was there to confess?

One day the lieutenant asked him, "Are you fond
of soldiering, Volkenborn?"

The question astonished him; flushed and tongue-
tied, he could find no answer but a smile. What reply
could he make to such a question? Not knowing, he
smiled; just as he had smiled when, as a schoolboy,
he had been called up to the blackboard to solve a
problem that had been set him. His schoolfellows
had tried to help him in whispers, but he had paid
no attention to them, perhaps from pride, perhaps
from honesty. He had simply turned the chalk round
and round in his fingers, and smiled at the mas-
ter with his merry, honest eyes, as though he would
say, "How can you exepect me to solve such prob-
lems?"

"I mean to say, do you take any pleasure in the
soldier's calling? Does the war appeal to you?"

"Yes — of course," replied Volkenborn quickly,

almost defiant in his embarrassment, painfully conscious of having turned so red.

The lieutenant remained silent, standing in a careless and seemingly despondent attitude at the window. How old he was looking! Never before had it occurred to Volkenborn to consider what his age might be. Suddenly he saw that here was a study for his pencil, and he turned over in his mind the thought whether he might venture to suggest making a sketch — in profile, just as the lieutenant was standing there.

"Don't you think the war terrible, Volkenborn? Unspeakably terrible?"

Volkenborn let his cigarette go out. He was standing to the left of the window, behind a tall red leather chair, and he kept prodding the upholstery with the forefinger of his left hand. When he prodded hard enough, a crater formed round his finger, and the red leather seemed to take on a deeper hue. What made him think just then of the night attack, of his fall as he jumped into the trench, of the quivering body that he had made a grab at, to save himself — what could have recalled all this to his mind at that moment?

"Three years of war, Volkenborn! Three years of ceaseless bloodshed! The assassination at Sarajevo was a crime, but isn't the expiation too great? Do you still know what we are fighting for? I don't. I seem to have known once, but to have long since forgotten. A bad business, Volkenborn! A bad business!"

Beneath the chair lay a small, hand-knitted rug, with a fantastic pattern of flowers, black and gold on a deep blue background. Its edge had curled up a little, and the gold threads underneath caught the sun. Volkenborn kept smoothing the corner down with his foot, but it obstinately curled up again as soon as he stopped. As he flattened the corner down he was listening to the lieutenant, feeling moved by what he was saying, especially by something in his voice, which suddenly seemed to be far-off and strange. He felt afraid. Of what? Of the lieutenant or of the war? What were we fighting for? Surely for our homes, parents, brothers, womenfolk, children! How could one forget that? What did the lieutenant mean? Were not the Fatherland, freedom, right, honor, all at stake? Were we not battling for the very soul of Germany — for God even?

Volkenborn felt distressed and uneasy; so much so that he could not muster up courage to lift his eyes from the glittering gold thread that was peeping out from beneath the turned-back corner of the rug. He wanted to say that the struggle was for God, King, and Country. Were not these words or words like them engraved on the eagles of their helmets? Had not their fathers fought and died for the same cause?

But the words would not come and he remained silent, staring at the pattern of the rug. Perhaps he had not grasped what the lieutenant meant. Perhaps it was but a passing moment of depression. The lieutenant was still looking out of the window, apparently watching a boat that was disappearing under the little bridge, being swallowed up by the black archway. It was growing dusk. The sound of a concertina in the distance broke the stillness, and gradually faded away. Volkenborn became conscious of the sound of his own breathing, and did not even venture to glance at his companion, so afraid was he of startling him, and bringing him back too sharply from the daydream that held him in its spell.

How quiet and peaceful the town looked as the afterglow fell on windows, gables and roofs, making them stand out clearly against the darkening background of the evening! Below, on streets, canals, doorways and steps leading down to the water, lay the twilight, softening their contours as with a veil. Slowly the shadows stretched upward until the red glow faded from the roofs. Still higher stretched the shadows until they finally touched the great tower, on which the dying sun had lingered lovingly to the last.

As dusk enveloped the town Volkenborn sighed — sighed as when something pleasant or beautiful has drawn to a close. With a smile the lieutenant turned to him.

"You'll stay to supper, Volkenborn, won't you? We'll have a little music. The lady of the house doesn't mind our using her piano. Do stay. I'm always so glad to have you here. I'll send my man over to the mess, to say you're not coming. That will make it all right."

The music room, downstairs on the first floor, had three large windows looking on to the canal. The walls were cream-colored, and without pictures or ornamentation, their severity broken only by jutting bronze candelabra. The floor was entirely covered by a plain carpet of bluish-gray and to the right of the third window stood a grand piano. Of the two doors, one was covered with a heavy curtain. Against the walls were comfortable low divans of some black wood, piled with blue cushions. The room seemed almost chilly at first, but when the lieutenant threw the casement windows open, the air from without flooded it with summer warmth.

Volkenborn sat down beside the larger of the two doors, and then moved to another seat against the wall on the left, from which position he could see the lieutenant in profile. As he sat watching him, the distance between them seemed to grow greater.

The lieutenant began to play, improvising. To Volkenborn it was like coming unexpectedly on to the sea, and finding it surge up all round him. He seemed to be carried away on a wave transported to some distant spot. To be drifting peacefully, passing gently and without effort over vast depths, seeking for something mysterious and beautiful that lay hidden beneath, something strange and secret, like fairy music. He was being borne onwards, gently, softly, and then suddenly the waves grew high and foam-tipped and crashed together over gaping depths; rising, falling, exulting. The secret troubles of youth with their stormy longings and desires;

days full of sunshine and high courage, of laughter and song, of life: all these came to him on waves of sound. Then the waves grew angry, broke upon ragged, menacing rocks; it seemed as though green breakers surged all around and swept masterfully over the jagged, rugged points, and then died down into foaming surf.

With folded arms Volkenborn sat listening, motionless. Inwardly, he was conscious of a tingling in his limbs as though an electric current were passing through him, of something carrying a tension to all his nerves that was almost unbearable. A tingling, prickling feeling, as though bubbles from sparkling wine were seeking to force their way through his veins.

The music held him in thrall to such an extent that he was lost to all consciousness of himself, of his companion at the piano, of everything. He was only aware of floods of sound that swept over and submerged him like a vast incoming tide, waves and surf burying all beneath them.

Now with tightly clasped hands, intent on nothing but the music, he felt himself called sharply back to earth. There was no actual movement of the curtain behind him. No current of air played on his hand. No sound of a door being opened reached his ears, nor did even the sound of a breath betray a presence; but he felt — an uncanny certainty that sent a shudder through him and almost stopped his breathing — that some one was standing behind him, that the curtain concealed a listener. He opened his eyes, and for a moment hardly knew where he was. Yes! There were the bronze candelabra and the grand piano, and there sat the lieutenant. Was he still playing? No, there was no sound from the instrument, though his hands rested on the keyboard. To Volkenborn, everything in the room looked, for the moment, unreal. The lieutenant had turned his head away, looking out of the window and sat without movement, giving no sign of life. How dark his hair looked! It had never looked so nearly black before.

An atmosphere of mystery seemed to pervade the room. Volkenborn was seized with the desire to move, to speak, but invisible forces held him motionless and silent. Presently the lieutenant rose from the piano, and stood, one hand resting lightly on the case, looking in Volkenborn's direction. Then he took a step forward, looking intently at something, something invisible behind Volkenborn, and as he looked he smiled. Volkenborn, freed from the strange obsession that had been numbing his faculties, rose to his feet, and heard his own voice saying quite naturally but in an inquiring tone:

"Lieutenant?"

The lieutenant passed his hand over his forehead, as though he would banish some troubling thought, and, as he did so, the strange smile faded from his face.

"I beg your pardon, Volkenborn, I had forgotten — "

Together they passed through the wider of the two doors, and the lieutenant turning on the threshold, glanced back into the room. The candles were still burning.

"I'll put them out afterwards. Come, Volkenborn. It must be getting late."

As they parted at the outer door, he laid his hand for a moment on Volkenborn's shoulder. Making his way homeward through the empty streets, he still seemed to feel the pressure of the lieutenant's hand, still seemed to sense that unseen presence behind the curtain. Even as he lay in bed, with the cool white sheet folded back from his face, uneasy thoughts of something guessed at, but unseen, pursued him through a restless night of troubled dreams.

IV

Lothar and Kurt came to Bruges, to see their brother Hans. Together they strolled along the quays, visited the Béguinage, sat for a while in silence on the wall outside, stood reverently in the Chapel of the Holy Blood, and, at last, at Kurt's suggestion, mounted to the top of the belfry. So blinding was the sunlight after the darkness of the stairs, that at first they had to hold their hands before their eyes. That dazzling stretch of silver over there was the sea. To the right lay Zeebrügge, and there in front of them was Ostend. Below stretched the roofs of the ancient Hanseatic town. A wonderful place in a country full of old and marvelous things!

For an hour they rowed up and down the canals that encircle the whole town. Dahlias and asters were blooming in the tiny gardens that lay hidden away mysteriously behind gaps between the moldering walls of the houses. The medieval atmosphere of the place lay heavy on them, and only the light splash of their sculls broke the silence, as their boat glided through the stagnant waters of the canal. Under the arches of the bridges the light played tricks with the water, making it look like mother-of-pearl.

Lothar was steering and Kurt sculling, whilst Hans huddled in the bows, embracing his knees with his arms. They were talking of home, parents, girls of their acquaintance; of sailing parties on the Steinhuder Meer, of the new U-boats; exchanging stories about commanders, and batmen and Reichstag deputies who had paid visits to the Front. Then the talk was of the latest official report, and of whether they would all three be able to get leave for their parents' silver wedding.

"This is where Lieutenant von Kless lives!" said Hans, pointing to a red sandstone house on a little terrace just over the bank of the canal. From the terrace an imposing flight of broad steps led down to the water.

"There to the right, on the second floor, where the window is open. That's his room."

"He is not at home," he thought, and felt relieved that it was so. He could not have explained to himself why he was glad, why he had been afraid that the lieutenant might be at home on this day when he would be unable to visit him. He would have laughed at anybody who said that he was afraid for Von Kless on account of the mysterious being behind the curtain on the evening before.

"What a beautiful woman!" cried Lothar.

On the first floor a window was open, one of the three windows of the music room, the one farthest away from the grand piano. It was a casement window and opened inwards. One wing was thrown back, and from the opening peered the pale face of a young and beautiful woman. She seemed to be looking down at something, perhaps a book, on the window sill; or was she looking down at the water? To Volkenborn it seemed as though her eyes saw nothing of what lay before her, that she was dreaming.

"A beautiful woman!" repeated Lothar. Just as the boat had passed the house, the sound of a chord, a scarcely audible chord, came to Hans Volkenborn's ear. Some one was at the piano. The beautiful woman was still standing there as they passed out of sight of the house.

Why should some one not be playing the piano? But the beautiful face at the window, with the strange rapt expression! The look of one who is listening to something very far away, or to something so near that all else is inaudible.

Lothar began to talk about Elma, whom he loved in secret, whilst Hans sat watching the dip of the sculls into the muddy water, listening to the sound of each stroke, to the murmur of the little ripples against the stone embankment, and above it all hearing the sound of that one, long, sustained chord, played with the touch that he knew so well. And again he became obsessed with a strange fear — a dread in some way connected with the curtain behind the divan on which he had sat the night before.

"Let me take the sculls, Kurt; we must turn back."

When they passed the red house on their return, the window on the first floor was closed. Hans Volkenborn's eyes dropped again to his sculls.

"Don't put your back into it so, Hanske; we've lots of time!" said Kurt. But Hans continued to pull as though haste were imperative. They had their coffee in a *patisserie,* iced coffee which they sipped through straws. The two elder brothers arranged to give the youngest a small monthly allowance, so that he might have the wherewithal to pass more of his spare time as they had done to-day.

They wrote field post cards. On Elma's card Hans wrote, in very small letters round the edge, "Am going to smoke the last of your cigarettes this evening. If you knew with what thoughts."

"With what thoughts then, young 'un?" asked Lothar, after deciphering it.

"Oh! that's only my little joke."

On the way back from the station, Volkenborn turned over in his mind whether he should look Werner up as promised. For this purpose he made a slight detour. It was a beautiful evening, and he was very fond of walking right along the canal to the spot where the windmills began and the grain barges lay. For walking and thinking at the same time, there's nothing like the bank of a canal. There's little to distract the attention and usually nobody about. But it is dangerous to dream too deeply. The horizon is far off, where the water runs into the sea, and thoughts, amid such surroundings, have a tendency to stray beyond everyday bounds to the mysteries of life and death.

The vanes of the windmills seemed to assume a sinister aspect as they showed up against the quickly darkening sky. Only a small disc of sun still remained above the western horizon; its blood-red rays come to Volkenborn from under the lowest vane of one of the windmills. So vivid was the impression that it was on fire that he seemed to hear the crackling sound of burning.

On his way back disturbing thoughts went with him. Had he ever seen the sun so red before? The regiment was not likely to stay much longer at rest behind the lines. Where would they be sent to next? When he stood still for a moment and the sound of his footsteps ceased, he could distinctly hear a sound like distant thunder. Ypres! The guns from Ypres! It had been continuous since yesterday. We were on the defensive. Just holding our positions. The rest behind the lines has lasted a long time. Would they get their leave? Lieutenant von Kless had said they would, but he was not infallible. Funny, that he should never speak of leave or of

going home. Was he in his rooms now? This afternoon he had been at the piano playing. "I should
know his playing anywhere. What a beautiful
woman! She must have asked to be allowed to sit
and listen to him. Did he know that yesterday evening?" Volkenborn felt sure that it must have been
that woman. Why did the thought alarm him? Was
she — could it — ? No, he could not think that.

Just before he came to the barracks, which lay
near the canal, behind the road leading to Ghent,
Volkenborn was about to leave the narrow towpath.
As he looked up — it was already very dark — he
saw the silhouettes of two people walking closely side
by side. The falling dew had developed into a slight
mist, but something in the walk and carriage of one
of the figures showed Volkenborn that it was a
woman. A German soldier with a Belgian girl! His
gorge rose at the thought, but much as he disliked
passing them, he refrained from turning off into the
road, and kept on the towpath.

Soon he was close behind the couple; they did not
hear his footsteps, which fell almost noiselessly on
the muddy bank. His eyes fell on the soldier's side-
arm. It was slung right round to the back, and was
smaller and of a better finish than the ordinary
private's side arm. No company tassel hung from it.
The hilt had been polished until it shone again.
Despite this mist, all these details stood out clearly.
Without a doubt he knew that side arm. Those high
broad shoulders, too, could belong to only one
man.

In the closeness of his inspection he nearly ran into them as they suddenly stood still.

"Now then!" came Pietschmann's voice. Volkenborn, started, stepped aside and went on his way, hurrying as fast as he could without actually running.

Intentionally he passed the house where Werner was quartered. What was the good of going in to see him? Then he stopped before his own quarters and was about to raise the knocker, but changed his mind and walked on. There was a small square in front of the house where the lieutenant was billeted, and in the middle of it stood a monument. On it was engraved the name of a poet in bronze letters. Volkenborn tried to decipher the name, but there was not enough light. He looked across at the red house, stood watching it for a long time. The sound of approaching steps disturbed him. It was the sentry from the monastery. Volkenborn went up to him.

"Good evening, Comrade; infernally dark, isn't it?"

But the sentry seemed disinclined for conversation. As Volkenborn turned to go, he remembered his cigarettes. Elma's cigarettes. For a moment he hesitated. There was only one left in his case. Then he handed it to the soldier.

"Smoke it when you've time to enjoy it, for it's a good one. Good night!"

On the march out to field exercises next day, while Werner was chattering beside him, Volkenborn's thoughts kept returning to his dreams of the past night. The Belgian girl, and Elma, and Pietschmann all had played a part in them. Elma had changed into the beautiful Flemish woman; she had come quite close to him and kissed him; kissed him wildly and passionately, and then recoiled from him and cried, "Is it true that you killed him? Where is he? I want to see him!" And the lieutenant stood at the window, pale and old, and, as he turned away, he had laughed. His laughter had sounded horrible in Volkenborn's ears, so full of suffering and bitterness.

"Mind you look me up to-day, Volkenborn," said Werner, nudging him gently with his elbow. "I've just received a monster parcel from home: grub and a lot of jolly good cigarettes. They're from Luise, and I've got a new photo, too."

Volkenborn nodded, and they fixed up an evening hour for his visit.

V

That afternoon Hans went to Lieutenant von Kless' rooms. He had originally intended not to go, but the lieutenant had met him by chance, and asked why he had not shown up the day before, and then carried him off with him. The feeling of awkwardness that Hans felt at first soon wore off, and he asked the lieutenant to sit for his portrait for half an hour. The half hour soon ran into an hour, without Hans noticing the passage of time. The sketch turned out a success; the best thing he had ever done. Hans was so delighted that he forgot all about his worries and forebodings with regard to the lieutenant. Proud though he was of his work, he felt so nervous when he passed it over for inspection that he got up and walked quickly over to the window. It was on the tip of his tongue to say something, to make some modest excuse for the quality of the sketch, but he himself was so pleased with it that he felt ashamed of his own timidity, and left the words unsaid.

For quite a time Von Kless looked at the drawing in silence, until Volkenborn began to feel quite uneasy as to what his verdict would be. Perhaps, after all, it was not as good as he had thought. He would have liked to turn round and have another look at it, but had not the courage. If the lieutenant would only *speak,* if only to say that he did not think much of it!

A hand fell on his shoulder.

"My dear fellow, how cleverly and with what insight you have hit me off! You may well be proud of having such an artistic eye — and such discernment. How glad I am for you! May I keep this?"

The evening at Werner's was a merry one. Never before had Volkenborn been so natural and let himself go so freely. Gerhardi was there too. Gerhardi, who wrote daily letters to Gert, the girl he was engaged to. In fact, it might be said that he passed all his free time in writing to her; hardly an hour passed without his taking a writing pad from his pocket and adding a line or two, just as the thoughts came to him. This was a standing joke with his comrades.

"Poor girl! How we pity her! Does she have to wade through all that tripe? God help her. Fancy having to go through such an ordeal three hundred and sixty-five times a year!"

It was not only that the name of Gerhardi's fiancée happened to be Gert that caused Volkenborn always to connect him in some way with Gert Sowanski. Although he was fair and she dark, there was a remarkable likeness between them. The same broad nose and rather full lips, the same dimple in the chin, the same note in the way they both laughed, their peculiar manner of shaking hands! Every time they met, Volkenborn was reminded of this resemblance. As a soldier Gerhardi was a miserable failure; the slovenly way he wore his uniform and the slouching manner in which he walked were a source of constant irritation to Volkenborn, who was ashamed to be seen out with him. Gerhardi, for his part, made no secret of the fact that "playing at soldiers" did not appeal to him in the least; that he had only joined up so as not to disgrace his family, and that he had no desire to become an officer.

"You've both got a bee in your bonnet," he argued. "As for me, I'm damned if I'm going to wear all this truck a moment longer than I can help it. Hell and blazes! I was born for something better than to wear myself down to skin and bone, and wind up with a bullet in my head. And now leave

me in peace for five minutes, while I finish my letter!"

Speeches of this kind fell frequently from Gar-
hardi's lips, but he had such an irresistible way of
turning all the serious things of life into ridicule that
no one could be angry with him for long.

They drank an immature red wine that Werner
had bought for Burgundy, and ate sweets, figs and
apples, just as they came to hand out of the packet;
puffed away contentedly at the good cigarettes, chat-
tered incessantly, and arranged to go to the theater
together on the following evening. A German company was performing an operetta — "Der Fledermaus." When conversation languished, they wrote
field post cards, each adding some remark. By the
laughably extravagant wording of his postscripts,
Volkenborn beat them all out, and the fun grew fast
and furious.

Gerhardi's quarters were quite near Werner's, so
they both saw Volkenborn home to his house, which
was about a quarter of an hour's walk away. They
began to talk about Lieutenant von Kless, and Volkenborn felt that Gerhardi knew something about
their intimacy, and wanted to know more, but he
adroitly switched conversation off to other subjects.

As he was lighting his bedroom candle afterwards, it occurred to him that he ought to see more
of his comrades, that they were downright good
fellows. Then his thoughts wandered off to his home
and parents, to Lothar and Kurt and to Anneliese
Lengerke.

As he lay in bed with his hands folded across his chest, he wished that there might be a letter for him in the morning from Anneliese. Then it struck him that his wish, in the form in which he had imagined it was impossible. First of all he must wish that Anneliese had written to him three days before. For field letters took at least that time in coming. Then the idea came to him that all that had nothing to do with it, and if one only wished hard enough, nothing was impossible. In this way it became possible to bring about something that should have been done the day before, so that all the different stages — the writing of the letter, the posting of it, the emptying of the box by the country postman, the sending it on from Arnstadt, and the journey to Flanders — all these stages could be brought about by a second of thought. Neither Anneliese nor the postman would ever know how earnestly he had wished them to do these things. It would just be a sort of miracle.

VI

Nearly all the Junkers of the regiment were at the theater the next night and met together in the foyer for a chat. There was Kerksiel of the Third Battalion, with his young, honest gray eyes and lanky limbs. He was one of those long youths who, when they stand still, always sag at the knees, which certainly does not make for a soldierly appearance. In Kerksiel's case both arms and legs seemed to be a source of general and permanent inconvenience. There was too much of them, and his trouble was to know what to do with them. To meet this difficulty, he would at times stand with arms folded across his breast. For a change he would try resting his hands on his hips, and would then vary this attitude by cupping his chin in one of his hands, or folding his hands on his breast in a devotional attitude. These strange contortions afforded his comrades endless amusement.

He was also afflicted with an abnormally large head covered by thin fair hair so pale as to look almost white. A small and much freckled nose, a large mouth and a chin that was not remarkable for firmness, completed a rather unfortunate personal appearance.

"Pity we come across one another so seldom, Volkenborn, isn't it. There's such a lot to talk about."

"Yes, I suppose there is. Well! You must look me up one of these days."

After Werner, Kerksiel was the one he liked best of the Junkers. A decent, sensible modest fellow, deeply attached to his mother, who had lost her husband at the beginning of the war. He had a sister whose photograph he had shown to Volkenborn, who for ever after connected him in his mind with a demure-looking, flaxen-haired little girl in a black velvet dress.

"Ah! I might have known that I should find all the highbrows here! How are you all? Going strong?"

Von Hartwich of the Eleventh Company was a rather insolent youth, and not a pleasant messmate for a lad like Kerksiel. Loud and artificial in his manner, and given to bragging, his favorite topic was his alleged luck with the girls and the telling of smutty stories. On one occasion he had gone so far in this direction that Volkenborn had told him to stop his filthy talk, and had been on the point of striking him. For a time they had avoided one another. Of late Von Hartwich had made attempts to renew their friendship, but Volkenborn ignored him.

Gerhardi, Werner, Kerksiel and Volkenborn took a box together, and little Möbius, late as usual, managed to procure an extra chair and crowded in with them. Anything to get away from Hartwich, who was his special aversion.

Möbius was a little chap whose lack of inches had been made the more conspicuous by his having been posted to the Second Company, among all the tall men. He was a pale, delicate lad, who wore horn spectacles, and whose blue veins stood out on his temples. With his head always on one side like a sparrow, and a thickness in his speech, the result of adenoidal trouble, he was one of the many unlikely ones who cut a poor figure in a uniform. Coming of people who, although gentlefolk, were extremely poor, he had no extra uniform, and sought to make good this deficiency by the addition of a silk scarf and a pair of kid gloves, which he wore on every possible occasion.

Why he had not claimed exemption, and above all

why he had elected to serve as a Junker — the first step towards becoming an officer — was a mystery. The rigors of the service were a great hardship for him, but he set his teeth and struggled hard against his bodily weakness. His father, a colonel, had died a soldier's death, and it was pride and the desire to follow in his father's footsteps that had mainly influenced him. As an only son, a petition would have led to his withdrawal from the Front. His colonel had even written to his mother, to advise her that such an application should be made, but the petition had never been sent in. "There is more at stake than our lives and personal wishes," he had once said to Volkenborn.

The overture had not yet started, and Volkenborn was in no hurry for it to begin. He was glad of the delay, for the later it began, the longer it would last. The curtain once up, how quickly the act would be over! Then, two more falls of the curtain, and it would be all finished: there would be an end to this delightful evening in the box, and he would be back in his quarters again, and amusement would once more be superseded by the irksome duties of a soldier's life.

But to sit here in the box in his best uniform, programme on his knees, his hands resting on the red velvet ledge, chatting, passing remarks, every one looking gay and happy, — all the joys of anticipation were his at this moment, compared with which fulfillment only too often proves a disappointment.

Presently Eichholz arrived with Leisewitz and Benninghoven, the two Fähnrichs. They took their seats beside Hartwich in the opposite box. Eichholz, the "Knight of the Rueful Countenance," or "Don Quixote" as he was dubbed by those who found the alternative too long, though as thin as a lath, had such an appetite that nobody liked to sit next to him at mess. Always good-tempered, but impudent as a town-bred sparrow, like Gerhardi, he was one of those whom it was impossible to dislike. When the Junkers were alone together in the mess he would hammer with his fist on the table until the glasses rocked and rang again, and then yell out to the mess waiter who would come rushing in, "Man alive, don't look frightened! I'll pay double for every glass I break, but I *must* have a good time!"

There was an exchange of the latest stories; Leisewitz was grinning in his blasé way and Benninghoven looking as foolish as possible — a sure sign with him of profound meditation, probably resulting from an effort to see the point of the story Von Hartwich was telling.

It was like the good old days at the Cadet School. They stared into the boxes and pointed out new arrivals to one another. In the old days, the newcomers had been schoolmasters and schoolgirls, now they were officers and regimental comrades, but in reality there was no great difference, for it all resulted in the same tension and excitement that forms one of the delights of an evening at the theater.

"Lieutenant von Kless is here. There! In the next box! If you just turn your head a little, you'll see him."

Volkenborn had seen him long before. When he looked in his direction at the end of the second act, his seat was empty, and it remained so for the rest of the evening.

Volkenborn wondered why he had left so early, and this fact troubled him. After the performance they wanted Volkenborn to accompany them to the mess, where they intended winding up the night, but he managed to slip away and make his way home.

By the time Volkenborn had climbed the airy staircase of the priest's house where he was quartered, the opera, the lieutenant and his comrades were all forgotten.

With a hand shaking with excitement and anticipation, he lighted the lamp on his table, and took from his pocket a letter — a letter that had come with the field post that afternoon. He had already read it — an inconspicuous letter in a pale blue envelope and addressed in a spidery, irregular, unformed hand. Within the folds of the envelope lay three large sheets of the same pale tinted paper, all closely covered with the same spidery writing. To tell the truth, it was rather a higgledy-piggledy sort of letter, and one in which a Rectory School and a church square were rather hopelessly mixed with ducklings and tomato plants, and a charity fête, a glass of champagne and a squeezing of hands, jostled remarks about one Elma, a Klingler concert, violin lessons and complaints of trains that were running anyhow.

Volkenborn had already read this letter twice; in the afternoon his hand had, on several occasions, strayed towards it, although he already knew much of it by heart. Before supper, he had glanced at the beginning again, dipped into the middle, and carefully reread the end, and now he was once more going through it for the fourth or fifth time. His task concluded, he sat down to write an answer, which he evidently had no difficulty in composing. Notes of exclamation and dashes were scattered here and there in profusion, and the ducklings played their part, as did the lamp, the red plush tablecloth, Lieutenant von Kless and his wonderful grand piano, the theater, and "Der Fledermaus," and to wind up, there was a eulogy of the soldier's life. Then came the final paragraph, which seemed more difficult to get into shape, and was finished off with several great thick marks of exclamation. This final sentence haunted his dreams and nearly caused him to tear the letter up again next morning. However, he at last decided to let it go as it was, and sent it off to the post, and sat for quite a time dreaming about it after it was gone.

His liking for Lieutenant von Kless was in no way affected by his love affair. Nearly every afternoon after duty, he spent an hour or two in his company, chatting and playing the piano. Sometimes Hans would sketch while the lieutenant read or wrote letters.

The only difference was that the lieutenant sometimes seemed preoccupied, and was often so absent-minded that he did not hear the answers to his questions, or repeated them again long after Hans had replied. But he was always kind, and frequently so impulsive and brotherly that Hans felt ashamed of his own temperament, which made it difficult for him to be responsive. There were days, however, when the lieutenant was taciturn and almost unapproachable. On such occasions he would not touch the piano, and either remained silent or spoke disconnectedly and continuously, smoking all the time furiously, and even forgetting to offer Hans a cigarette. The boy noticed these queer transitions and thought a great deal about them. He was equally haunted by the face of the woman he had seen at the window, and every time he entered the house he half hoped, half feared to meet her. But he never did, and in time her image faded from his mind, and with it all the talk there had been in the mess about the lieutenant and the way he kept apart from the others, and how strange he had become.

His own new happiness, straightforward and simple in its character, kept his mind from dwelling for long on other matters. It was his first serious love affair, and it fully occupied his waking thoughts. He was not ignorant of the facts of life, but passion had not yet stirred his veins, and he was still unconscious both of its beauties and dangers as an essential element in existence.

VII

The beginning of October was still sunny and bright, but towards the end of the first week there was a change to rain and mist. The evenings grew longer and the depression that comes with the fall of the year brought moods of weariness and melancholy, while for others, younger or less sensitive, the change passed unheeded.

Hans Volkenborn, busily engaged in reading and writing long letters on pale blue paper, was indifferent to both rain and mist. So little was he affected by them that when the men cursed the downpour and mud that made their field service exercises a penance, he felt amused at their irritability, and ventured to chaff them on their ill humor with a careless freedom that he had never shown before. What was the good of worrying? What more was there for him to wish for, when Anneliese Lengerke of the beautiful blue eyes loved him? There it was in three separate words — written down in plain German! And the day after to-morrow, she would say it once again. In three weeks he would be with her, holding her hand, speaking perhaps about the Rectory School, perhaps of something quite different. What cause was there for ill humor, for worrying about anything?

Lieutenant von Kless delighted in having this cheerful, confident youngster about him, but at the same time the gayety of the young man's mood brought painfully home to him the contrast of his own depressed and hopeless outlook on life. Volkenborn's unconscious assurance, his unbroken spirits, his healthy nerves that gave no sign of being affected — all these qualities that the lieutenant himself had once possessed caused him to realize only too plainly to what an extent his own nature had broken down under the strain of war. And the tragedy of it was that there was no escape; no hope for the future! Nothing before him but an abyss.

On the first day of the mobilization he had joined his regiment as a Fähnrich; for valor in the field he was given his commission. Then came three years' service with the regiment. During that period there had been no daring reconnaissance, no desperate attack, in which he had not played a part, and an important and decisive one. Not a man in the ranks but respected and trusted him, but none knew what impelled him to such a reckless disregard of danger. Neither did any one know why he suddenly applied to be attached to the staff of the battalion, why he gradually withdrew from all intercourse with his fellows, although there were gossip-mongers who professed to be able to explain the mystery, when his attitude was being discussed and commented upon.

The few words on this subject that the lieutenant had once let fall had been incomprehensible to Volkenborn. They had shocked him, but although he had long tried to read some clear meaning into them, he had been unable to do so. In reality, there was at that moment closer contact between them than at any other time during their friendship, but the Junker was too young and inexperienced to seize the occasion, and it passed.

Hans believed in everything, the lieutenant in nothing. Hans was full of conviction, gratitude, love, pride, confidence and hope. He had home, parents, brothers; people that he loved, dear ones for whom he prayed and fought. The lieutenant had nobody to pray or fight for; his struggle was with and for himself. In the beginning this had sufficed to carry him through, but in the long run it failed him. The emptiness of his life gripped him. Loneliness raised its gray walls round him. Disgust seized on him, conscience began to work within him until all sanity and common sense fled. The reason for the war, for this awful slaughter that went on day by day and hour by hour; the reason to which nobody any longer gave a thought, the reason that had long since been buried and smothered under masses of empty words and phrases; the reason, the cause for which he was fighting, had escaped him. As he had once said to Volkenborn, he no longer knew what it was. Instead of a cause he saw only mountains of misunderstandings, errors, lies, crimes and guilt.

His was no sudden mental transition. For long he had struggled against it, determined not to allow himself to be conquered by it. The most dreadful thing about this struggle was that it remained unde-

cided always. There were hours when he was again
able to persuade himself of the justice of the cause
for which he was fighting, and to find solace in this
thought; times when he regarded the struggle within
him as a mere crisis of nerves, the result of mental
and bodily exhaustion and weakness, something de-
grading to a soldier who wore his country's uniform.
But this point of view was always an evanescent
one. The happy state of those who can see matters
only from their own point of view, and who are
never in doubt as to where their duty lies, was never
his. He had the gift, or the curse, of seeing things
from both sides, and the result was mental torture
that gave him no rest and made conviction impossible. He had reached that stage where there was
neither light nor dark, only half lights.

Volkenborn wanted to bring the lieutenant some
of the Gravenstein apples that Anneliese had sent
him. Werner and Kerksiel had looked him up and
tried to carry him off for a jolly evening with Eichholz, whose birthday it was. He had been obliged to
promise to come on later. This had delayed him,
so that it was rather late and already beginning to
grow dark when he knocked at the door of the red
house.

The porter let him in as usual with no other greeting than the slight nod that seemed to convey a sort
of resigned protest. To the Junker there was something distasteful about the man, whose felt slippers
and noiseless movements suggested slyness, latent

hostility and danger. Often when sitting with the lieutenant in his room, he had an uneasy feeling of being spied on. Perhaps it was all imagination, the result of the general tension which he invariably felt on entering the house.

The way led up a cool and airy staircase and across the first landing, from which there mounted another flight to the lieutenant's rooms. As Volkenborn passed the folding doors leading into the music room, he thought he could hear a voice that he could not recognize, speaking in a low tone. He resisted an impulse to stand and listen, and passed on up the stairs.

He knocked at the lieutenant's door, went in, laid the apples, which were wrapped up in pink tissue paper, on the table, closed the door softly, and went downstairs again. He had not reached the bottom step when the door of the music room was suddenly opened, and the lieutenant stood before him.

For a moment Volkenborn was speechless. Perhaps it was surprise at this unexpected appearance, perhaps it was that stupid feeling of being caught to which some people are subject when they suddenly come on somebody in a strange house; perhaps it was the definite confirmation of a suspicion that had haunted his mind. Whatever the cause, he was so startled that he could find no words, and simply stood looking at the lieutenant.

"You — Volkenborn!"

The lieutenant seemed startled too, and his voice sounded strangely hoarse and abrupt. A ray of

light came through the half-open door, faintly lighting the dark corridor.

Within the room, at the window where she had
stood when Volkenborn passed in the boat, was the
beautiful woman with pale face, looking down at
the dark water below. Against the darkness of the
window frame, her figure was only faintly defined,
as she stood with folded hands. She turned to glance
at Volkenborn and then gave him her hand in silent greeting. To him, she seemed hardly a creature of flesh and blood. Many a time afterwards
he tried to recall the details of this meeting,
but they remained elusive, vague, like a dream
that fades away on our awakening and cannot be recalled.

A ban of silence seemed to fall on all three as
they stood looking down on the water. The lieutenant was the first to move, to make some remark
that Volkenborn did not hear clearly, but in appar-
ent answer to which the beautiful Fleming lighted
the candles in the silver candelabra. With their lighting, strange and gigantic shadows played in constant motion over walls and ceiling, like a bird that
flies wildly and desperately about in its terror at
finding itself in a room from which there seems no
escape. Then, as in a dream, Volkenborn saw the
lieutenant cross noiselessly to the piano, on which
the silver sconce with the candles in it had now been
placed, the flames flickering in the slight draught as
if they were dancing to the music. Then the breeze
from the window dropped, and the light fell steadily

on two faces — the faces of two who should have been enemies, but —

With this picture of these two still before his eyes, Volkenborn passed down the dark staircase and through the door; worked by a mechanical contrivance from the porter's room, it opened and closed in mysterious silence behind him.

Volkenborn kept his promise and passed the evening with Eichholz and the others. It was not the wine that he drank, as Gerhardi and Kerksiel thought, that made him sit silent and thoughtful, but the recollection of that strange hour in the candlelight, the realization of something that was a new and strange discovery to him.

CHAPTER THREE

I

Bugles!

At eleven of the forenoon the regiment paraded at the railway station. Nobody knew where they were bound for, but everybody guessed, and as the long train steamed away westward, all doubts were set at rest; they were on their way to Ypres!

Volkenborn sat beside Werner in an ordinary passenger compartment of a Belgian carriage. There was rain on the window; at first only a few fine drops that had been carried on the wind. Volkenborn polished the inside of the window with his sleeve, watching the drops as they settled on the glass. They grew bigger, began to run together, until finally a very big one came along and carried all the other drops down with it. Every time the train gave a lurch, on rounding a corner, all the drops ran together on the pane, sank into a pool at the bottom, and left the glass quite clear for some seconds.

Raindrops, thought Volkenborn. That is all we ourselves are, and when the big lurch comes, we too shall all be swept away!

He still had some picture post cards in his pocket-book, two of which he gave to Werner, keeping the remaining four for himself. The first one he addressed to his parents. Then he began to write, very plainly and choosing his words with care, which was quite contrary to his habit. Usually he just scribbled "With love!" across the back of the card. To-day, after some hesitation he wrote. "I send you a kiss." His card to Anneliese, too, he worded with special care. It was an open post card that the country post-man, the servant and everybody could read, but despite that he wrote on it, "We are off to the Front again. My thoughts are with you, and I am very happy. Your Hans." It was the first time that he had signed himself "Your Hans," and he read it aloud several times, to see how it sounded. In reality, he was feeling anything but very happy. What was she doing at that moment? Where was she at the very time that he was sitting in the transport train for Ypres? Was she sleeping? Perhaps she was in the garden, or playing the piano. Was she thinking of him, just as he was thinking of her? Had she any foreboding that he was off to the Front, was on his way to Ypres? Surely she *ought* to feel it! Then he wrote cards to his brothers. Short, soldierlike cards, such as he always wrote, but as he read them over, they seemed to him more full of meaning, more important, perhaps more final. Werner wrote to his parents too, and to Luise. They added a few words to each other's cards, and signed them.

"They are pretty cards," said Werner. On one

there was a field of ripe, golden corn, on another a rose garden in full bloom, with a fanciful cottage and a deep blue sky overhead. A third showed a chestnut tree in blossom, with a white garden seat beneath it. For quite a time they sat looking at the pictures, and then Werner began to talk about Luise and of how he used to play duets with her. Volkenborn listened, and in return told him the old story about the church square in Arnstadt, and about the glass of champagne and the handclasps on the staircase. Then they lapsed into silence, looked out of the window, watched the raindrops as they descended, each down its particular groove, and stared out at the gray, misty, flat country through which they were passing, the bareness of which was only occasionally relieved by a tree, farm or village.

Two or three times the train pulled up, and they put their heads out of the window or got out to stretch their legs. It seemed an endless journey. The low rumbling like distant thunder that they had heard faintly on many an evening in Bruges increased in intensity when the train drew up. It was always in the ears; not even the rattling of the train along the line could entirely deaden it.

A little after four, the train stopped again, and for a long time they sat waiting. At last the order came: "Get out! Take your rifles!"

A close fine drizzle was falling, and the road was thick with mud. The truck with the machine guns could not be drawn up to the platform, and it proved a long and tiresome task to get them out.

II

The regiment is marching along the Flemish road;
marching through the rain and mist. A line of bare
poplars rises at regular intervals on either side of
the way. As they approach each tree, it proves a
duplicate of the one just passed, — dark, dripping
and depressing. After a time they cease to glance
to the side, but each man keeps his eyes doggedly
fixed on the back of the file in front of him, and his
heels, his bayonet, his knapsack, his helmet. Occasionally Volkenborn watches the wheels of the
machine-gun carriage, and then glances at the two
men who are drawing it. Then his eyes wander to
the company commander, with his eternal cigarette
and his rain-soaked dogskin gloves, as every half
hour or so he rides down the ranks. From under
red and inflamed lids, his small piercing eyes run
over the men with a smile that is half friendly, half
derisive. Perhaps this derisive expression exists only
in Volkenborn's imagination, as an excuse for his
own smile; that smile of his that he is never able to
suppress, although he always grows red and self-
conscious when he realizes it. Each time the company commander's look meets his, he feels as if he
were being tested, as if his answering glance were
a promise.

They come out on to the great military road,
where the mud is less solid: it splashes up in their
faces as they march. Here the traffic moves in three

lines. Cars, dispatch bearers, trolleys in the middle; right and left, marching columns: on the right those for the Front, on the left, those returning. The rain begins to fall less heavily, decreases to a fine drizzle, then to a wet mist which seems hard to breathe, irritates the chest, and leaves a sticky, foul taste in the mouth, as though the air were impregnated with tiny particles of fungus.

Automobiles come tearing wildly along! Ahead, in the infantry column, one of the marching men is knocked down, but seems little the worse for it. "Hard luck," says a man beside Volkenborn; "it would have been a fine chance to get out of all this!"

Then a horse shies at a passing car and backs into Volkenborn, who jumps aside. As the animal just grazes him, he can almost feel its maddened pulses beating through its rain-soaked and steaming hide. Poor beast! he thinks.

Werner has a raindrop hanging from the end of his nose; larger and larger it grows, wobbling with every step he takes. Fascinated to see how long it will be before it falls, Volkenborn watches until something else causes his eyes to wander off in another direction.

Along the opposite side of the road come returning infantry. They are marching in small sections, ragged, dirty, hunched up under the weight of their equipment; their faces are gray and haggard and they cast furtive and almost hostile glances at their comrades going to the Front. They have the scared miserable look of those who have endured more

than men can endure and retain their manhood, — a
look that seems to say, "Now you're for it — why
not? We've done our bit."

Ammunition columns try to pass. There are pro-
tests. Insults are hurled from one to another. "Lum-
bei troop; damned taxi-drivers!" The company commander rides up and gives them a look. The columns
pass them.

They are marching towards that dull, grumbling
sound that never ceases for a moment. It is like the
roll of a giant's drum. They can no longer be said
to be marching, but are just being propelled onward,
their legs swaying automatically in step. They are
now so thoroughly wet through that they no longer
notice the rain. They are quite warm, and their uniforms cling as if they had been poured into them.
Everything on them is taut; even the belts fit better.
Their holsters are quite hard. Their whole outfit
seems more closely connected with them than ever.
It forms part of themselves, is their ally against the
foe.

They are now so near that they can distinguish between heavy mortars and railway siege
pieces. On the left the line has been bent back a
little. A thousand metres farther on, their position
is being enfiladed. The dull monotonous drumming
has become sharper, livelier, more distinct, but still
in the distance they can hear that obstinate, unbroken roar, as though a drummer were beating a
roll on a great drum, but on the metal frame instead
of on the parchment. That is the field artillery! Less

noisy but more effective are the heavy shells that are directed at batteries, pioneer forts, depots, cross-roads, and the strategic line of march by howitzers and long-range guns of heavy caliber.

Air and sky seem one sheet of metal along which shells rush like luggage along a moving platform, like boxes bursting open from time to time and discharging their contents in every direction. One grows accustomed to these infernal noises, and learns how to distinguish between them. The only ones to be dreaded are those that bury themselves like a flash of lightning, bore their way in, and then burst with two or three separate explosions. The effect of these is as though one's nerves were being cut through by a great saw. It seems to get at the very marrow of one's bones, to seize one's limbs like a cramp.

The battle draws nearer. Twice, three times, many times, they come to a halt. The leading column may already be under fire. Red Cross stretchers, trolleys pass in an almost unbroken line. "If we were only in one of those," says somebody.

The men avoid looking at one another, sure neither of themselves nor of others, and not knowing exactly how they are expected to look and behave. Werner takes a packet of soaked cigarettes out of his bread bag. They try to light them, but cannot. They pretend to find this extraordinarily comic, and laugh hysterically because their hands are so stiff and the cigarettes droop so limply. Somebody in the first rank makes a remark, perhaps says something really funny. Everybody inquires what he has said.

The joke passes from one to another, is added to, elaborated and laughed at. Their laughter sounds rather hard and forced, but still they laugh. They all realize that they are "for it"; going to "get it in the neck."

Lieutenant Gallantz, no longer wearing his blue silk service cap and tan leggings, is not looking as smart as usual. "He ain't no different to the rest of us when he's up against it," say a tall lance corporal. "Less guts, that's the only difference!"

The company commander rides for a while beside the second section, to which Volkenborn and Werner belong.

"Buck up, Grasshof, old man. In we go and out we come. We shall come out of it all right, never fear."

"May be, Herr Lieutenant, but what'll we be like when we do come out? That's what I want to know?"

"Well, Grasshof, with a chap like you, with a head or without, it does not much matter. Nobody would know the difference."

Grasshof grins from ear to ear. "Heads aren't all what we've got, by long chalks, but both you and me'd look sketchy without 'em, Herr Lieutenant. Besides, if our dial was gone, they wouldn't know you from me, and you an officer an' all."

The lieutenant puts spurs to his horse. "Long may your long tongue wag, Grasshof!"

Grasshof is very proud of his remark and repeats it all over again; repeats it several times, adding,

"The lieutenant knows how to take a joke. He understands us, he does. He's a fine chap! A fine beast!"

Then he grows tired of talking and marches on in silence, as they all do. No one feels loquacious with the battle raging in front.

Motor ambulances continue to pass in an endless stream, tearing along as if fleeing before the enemy. Shrapnel is bursting on every side. Bits of gray sky peep out at intervals through the flare and flame of exploding shells.

Again the advance is held up. The village in front of them has suffered little from the bombardment. Amid all the wreckage around, it seems a marvel it should remain almost intact. The men eye it suspiciously.

The regimental staff halt at the church, at the spot where the great road makes its last slight curve and runs straight onward from the village. Volkenborn recognizes the commander and then sees that Lieutenant von Kless, who has delivered a message, has pulled his horse around, and is galloping past the company. He seems very pale, but perhaps it is only the shadow from his steel helmet that makes him look so.

"That was Lieutenant von Kless! Did you see him?" whispers Werner. Volkenborn nods and turns around more than once to look back as he marches onwards. The lieutenant is no longer in sight.

On the other side of the village they overtake the

First Battalion. It is again raining heavily and Volkenborn keeps his eyes on the heels of the file before him. When the latter splashes right into a puddle, Volkenborn wakes from his daydream. "Swine!" cries Werner. At this moment, as Volkenborn steps to one side, he sees Möbius of the Second Company standing in a column that has halted on the other side of the road.

"Hullo, Möbius! Filthy weather!"

As they march onward, they speak about him. "Poor chap, with his spindle shanks, having to struggle through the swamp." That's all the comment that they make. The march goes forward for five hours. It grows dark. The blaze of bursting shells becomes more clearly visible. The traffic increases. Ammunition columns for the front, kitchens, new batteries, pioneer lorries, and, slipping in between them, orderlies and dispatch bearers on motor cycles.

Once again Volkenborn catches sight of Lieutenant von Kless. That is to say, he recognizes his horse, but he is gone again in an instant. Farther up the line he slows down and appears to be asking something. Volkenborn hears his own name. He is marching on the left flank. The lieutenant waits till he comes up to him, and then gives him his hand.

"Ah! And there's Werner too!" And he shakes hands with Werner.

"Oh, Volkenborn, I've left your sketchbook in my quarters. Don't forget to fetch it. Do you hear? Good-by, I must get forward."

It is almost night and so dark that Volkenborn can hardly see the lieutenant's face. His voice sounds strange and hoarse as on that evening in the corridor. Volkenborn's thoughts return to that incident and to the woman with the pale face. He is struck by the fact that the lieutenant has never before said good-by. Try as hard as he may, he cannot remember to have heard the lieutenant use those exact words before. And then, "Don't forget, do you hear?" What a strange thing to say!

A shell falls among the company, and there are casualties. The Third Section receives a direct hit. Horses bolt. There is nothing to be gained by leaving the road, however. The fields are under water, some of them completely submerged. Forward!

Finally they came to rest in a partially destroyed hut in a deserted wood. Right and left are long sleeping benches. Only the longitudinal walls are left standing; the others are blown away, but the roof still holds.

The rain has increased in volume, and they are all glad to find themselves with a roof over their heads. Lieutenant Sollmann has strips of canvas hung over the open ends of the hutment.

The Third Section — held up by the shell — arrives. There had been two killed and five severely wounded. They learn the names of the dead men.

It suddenly seems to grow cold and the chill of their soaking tunics begins to react on them all at the same time. Like an icy shower it runs over their bodies and down their arms, where the wet cuffs cling clammily to their wrists.

Lieutenant Sollmann has ridden off. Most of the men lie on the benches. How long are they going to remain here? Will they be going right on? To the Battalion Staff Headquarters? Will they go into action that night, or to-morrow early? This infernal cold! Everything soaking wet! What a miserably bloody hole!

Shrapnel flies over the hutment, but fails to disturb them. They feel sheltered and in safety. The mere presence of a roof, this thin roof of half-inch planks with a layer of pulp and tar over them, this roof that is so leaky that every second great drops of wet come falling on their faces, this wretched, almost useless roof exercises a wonderfully comforting influence on the exhausted men. A roof is a roof; it is always an advantage to have something between you and the sky. The fact of not being able to see anything is also a comfort in itself. Not to be able to see the Front, with its perpetual flares and explosions, and star shells. Their present darkness has at least boundaries, even though they be but damp planks.

Volkenborn and Werner lie side by side, talking in whispers about quite indifferent matters. They share their last cigarette, each taking a puff in turn.

The din of the battle reaches them uninterruptedly. The guns seems to be getting still busier. It is a regular drum fire, the customary prelude to an attack. The very earth groans, twitches and gapes;

even the benches on which they are lying shake with the concussion. The air they are breathing seems heavy and exhausted, as they lie shuddering with cold, their very lips trembling.

Volkenborn can hear Werner's teeth chattering, and he himself is nearly in the same plight. They shudder and shiver openly, being past all pretence.

The shells are coming nearer, and it seems as though a giant were shaking the whole hutment with his great hands, panting with rage the while. At any moment the whole crazy building may be blown into the air, but nobody moves, nobody seems to be concerned as to what may happen next. They are too tired, or perhaps none of them are willing to admit to what extent their morale has suffered, how fear seems oozing from their wringing clothes, and terror from the dank walls of their shelter. Terror of what lies before them! A terror that is almost the same thing as hatred. Hatred of their unhappy lot; a lot that is not theirs alone, but that of millions of others who are being sacrificed to fulfill a nation's destiny. To fulfill? Can destruction be fulfillment? Are we born but to slaughter and be slaughtered?

Are there any among these shivering men lying sleepless on their wooden benches — waiting to be ordered into the firing line — who feel sustained by the thought that they are fulfilling a nation's destiny? Are their minds busy with abstract conceptions of high ideals, or are they not rather simply thinking of the rain, and that on the Somme it had been even worse, and of their luck in having escaped that last big shell? Wondering why some are lucky and some are not, finding comfort in the thought that, dead or alive, they will be all out of it, some day. Thinking of home and wife and children, of parents and brothers and sweethearts; thinking of those for whom they are cowering here with chattering teeth on bare boards, of those for whom they will presently be fighting and dying. Thinking of their last spring leave, of a red dress, of a meadow, of a tree, a tree with fresh young leaves that shimmered in the sun!

Some clench their fists in rage; but who notices them? Who has any heart left to trouble about the woes and needs of others?

The same fate broods over all, yet each feels himself alone. Each struggles to maintain his individuality and yet is conscious of the ties of comradeship; for comradeship is, by now, the one splendid and ennobling thing that holds them all together. It is a thing they all accept without asking themselves on what it is based. Is it another word for duty, regiment, country? There are many names for it, for those who have imagination enough to find them.

Volkenborn feels for his pocketbook, the one that his cousin Li had sent him. What a long time ago it seemed! They had been sitting in the garden together after dinner, in a little arbor overgrown with creeper. Quite suddenly she was on his knee — kissing him. At that moment the maid had come with the coffee, and he had welcomed the interruption which put an end to an embarrassing situation. While they sipped their coffee Li had pressed her foot against his under the table. He had turned red and laughed, and his aunt had asked him what he was laughing at, and shook her finger at him. That was all there had been between him and his cousin Li; afterwards she had sent him the pocketbook with a passionate letter, which he had never even answered.

Against his will, he finds his mind dwelling on this foolish business. What he wants to think about is Anneliese's letter that lies inside the pocketbook. About her photograph too! The little oval one, with the tomato plants that were her special pride and care for background. But his thoughts keep wandering back to the arbor and to Li's burning kisses. Never before had this recollection so obsessed him; he thought he had banished the whole scene long ago to the limbo of forgetfulness. But now he can almost feel her kisses on his lips and the pressure of her slender body against his own. He remembers, too, how his hand had trembled as he held his coffee cup, and the reaction that had followed this amorous incident.

But now he wants to think of a different kind of love, of his love for Anneliese, of her big innocent blue eyes, of her darling letters, but his thoughts keep straying back to that first experience, that·adventure of which he had felt so ashamed at the time.

Werner is trying to make out the time by his wrist watch. Then he nudges Volkenborn, and begins to remind him of how at precisely that moment

the night before they had been sitting with Eichholz and the others, but before he can finish his sentence the sergeant major lifts·the flap of the canvas
and cries:

"Fall in! The company will take over!"

In an instant, Volkenborn is off his bench. How
painful his feet are! His uniform clings to his body
like a cold compress, as he straightens himself and
adjusts his belt, holster and gas mask. All thoughts
of home are forgotten, and his mind concentrates
on the present. We are taking over. Now for it!

The trolleys are left behind; Volkenborn carries
the machine gun and Werner takes a thousand
rounds in four cases. An "old soldier" was to carry
the machine gun, but Volkenborn insists on taking it
himself. "You'll be glad enough to hand it over presently, Junker!" says Leuber, the gun captain.

"Not unless I get a bullet in my head," Hans re-
plies curtly.

He carries the gun with as much pride as if he had
just captured it. He has it on his left shoulder, and
is too proud to change sides, although his body soon
begins to ache under its weight. He clenches his
teeth and encourages himself by saying "only so
much farther to go," as one does when running,
swimming or rowing in a race. It is to be a trial of
strength: carrying through a task that he has set
himself in the pride of his physical strength. His
comrades are the spectators, the umpires; their eyes
are on him, and he must not fail. It is up to him to
show them what he can do. His ambition is to be rec-

ognized by them as their equal, to show them that he too is an "old soldier." In the old Fifth Company he has already given proofs of his mettle but here in the Machine Gun Company he still has to show what he can do, and he is determined to carry it through.

How the company commander manages to find his way up to the Front, nobody knows. It is quite dark, and firing is continuous. Just before the castle, on a height where the Field Dressing Station has been located, the Third Section again suffers a direct hit, and there are more casualties, some fatal. Nobody bothers to ask who has been killed. They do not want to know, but simply push forward with the ferocity and indifference of men running amok. To keep moving is the main idea, to keep advancing. They may run right into the next salvo! But anything is better than standing still, waiting for what is to come.

In front of the Field Dressing Station, to the right and left of the road, lie rows of canvas, from which here and there sticks out a leg or a foot wearing a torn and bloody boot, or sometimes a head, scarcely recognizable as human. No faces are visible, but all are swathed in bandages. So they lie, half buried in the mud and dirt. Hands protrude, the finger nails showing pale against the filth. Blood everywhere! On all the bandages! Blood mixed with mud and filth! Sometimes quite dark in color, but in other places lying on the ground in bright red pools.

A hundred paces farther on, a body stretches right across the road, and Volkenborn stumbles over it. There lies some poor chap in his blood! he thinks, and the thought has hardly passed through his mind when he hears a horrible crushing noise as the wheel of an artillery limber smashes the dead man's skull.

Often they lose touch with one another. Volkenborn finds himself falling into a shell crater, that lies right in the middle of the road. It has been freshly made, and so there is no water in it, but instinctively he finds himself holding his machine gun aloft, as though he were wading through a stream.

He can hardly see his hand before his eyes. How on earth does Lieutenant Sollmann manage to find his way; must have eyes like a cat? There is no longer any sign of a road, only mud and slime everywhere. Shell hole after shell hole! Occasionally they pass trees that seem to have been almost eaten away by giant insects, or a house that has been shot to pieces, its outlines standing out vaguely through the mist and darkness. Here things are busy. It is the Battalion's Battle Headquarters. Somebody shouts for "storm troops." For a moment Volkenborn stands listening and staring at the broken masonry, feeling as if something or somebody were calling to him from it. How clearly he can see the outlines, dark though it is! As he pushes onward, trying to avoid craters, making his way round them, striving to keep in touch with the file in front of him, through the mist and darkness he still seems to see the white brickwork of the house, and his tired mind centers on one problem: Why does it look so white, since bricks are red?

III

At the company commander's orders, the Third Section has remained in rear of the castle. Only the First and Second Sections are at first brought into action. The lieutenant allots their positions to them, and there is no question of regular reliefs, they are too few. They have no clear idea of how the front runs, as star shells are going up on all sides.

Volkenborn has fixed his gun in position, greased it, and covered it over. Werner has dragged a corner of the canvas over his own head. They are crouched together in a shell hole, for there are no proper dugouts here; with their four machine guns, they have simply been put forward into the infantry line. The other four machine guns are to the rear of them in the second line, which has concrete shelters.

The fire is still concentrated on the roads along which the advance is taking place. The castle and the Field Dressing Station seem to Volkenborn to be the enemy's chief objective. Then come the second and third lines. There is a continuous series of short bombardments. These wicked high-explosive shells! Their ears buzz again with the sound of them. There, where the Battalion's Battle Headquarters is located, there, half left to their rear — Volkenborn can see it from his seat behind the gun — the fire is growing more concentrated. Are there any batteries posted behind there? An unhealthy spot for a battle position!

By five in the morning, the fire on the first line has become more intensive. Volkenborn had been relieved, but cannot sleep; he sits huddled up beside Werner. It is still dark, with hardly a sign of the coming dawn, the mist is too dense. A faint streak of light shows itself in the east, but things still remain indistinguishable. It is several times on the tip of Volkenborn's tongue to call Werner's attention to the continuous shelling of the Battle Headquarters, on which he keeps his eyes fixed. But he decides to leave it unsaid, the noise of bursting shells making speech all but impossible.

Presently, he finds Lieutenant Sollmann standing beside him. This officer is not satisfied with their position; the machine gun must be moved thirty paces to the right. Sollmann helps them to carry it. The move is carried out with feverish haste, and scarcely is the gun fixed in its new position, when a shell falls right on the spot where it had stood, and blows packs and cooking utensils to pieces. For seconds, they stare with strained eyes at the spot, then the lieutenant turns sharply on his heel and spits into a puddle. Volkenborn, impressed by this action, does the same, and then stands staring at the white spittle as it floats about in the pool.

A second shell falls near them, and then a third, as though the magnetism of the earth were attracting fire to that spot. They fall with a thud, splashing mud and filth all around. An orderly is standing in front of the company commander, who rises from his knees. Volkenborn hears how the orderly delivers a message, and adds, hastily, unasked, as though eager to tell the news, "The commanding officer is wounded, and the adjutant is dead!"

He hears this at a distance of less than ten paces, and the words keep drumming in his ears, as though being repeated by some one far away.

Lieutenant Sollmann is no longer there, and the orderly has gone. The sergeant is beside Volkenborn, leaning his elbows on the edge of the crater, his binoculars to his eyes. On the right of him cowers Werner, his hands blue with the cold.

Shells scream over their heads. It is no longer simply a harassing area fire, but the curtain fire preceding an attack. It grows lighter and clearer, and the star shells can be followed as they rise from the shell holes. The ground quakes like a volcano, and it seems as though subterranean forces were at work. Great lumps of soil fly through the air, carrying shell splinters with them. Dud shells bury themselves almost noiselessly in the mud.

"Why the hell don't you fire, Junker?" cries the sergeant to Volkenborn, who is kneeling behind his machine gun with his thumb resting on the release, but has not yet opened fire. The sergeant tries to pull him away from the gun, but he resists and starts hammering away. Without a pause, he fires one full belt right off. The sergeant tries to direct him; he pays no heed, but slips the second belt in.

The attack is advancing in three waves. The

ground is in a terrible state. Jumping and crawling, the enemy advance from shell crater to shell crater. At first the barrage is too far forward, and falls behind the advancing foe. Suddenly it is drawn back, and cuts off the retreat of their own advancing in-fantry. On the right a German infantryman is stand-ing in a line with Volkenborn's machine gun, and is prevented from retiring by the German curtain fire, which has cut him off from his own base. The English continue to advance, and they attack the position in flank. The German infantryman, caught between the two fires, throws up his hands, and Volkenborn ceases firing.

"Sweep more to the right," cries the sergeant. Volkenborn sees two Tommies aiming at the Ger-mans with their rifles. His machine gun hammers out again, and the two fall. Then he sprays the ground in front of him as coolly and systematically as though it were the twenty-five metre target at the range, letting the belt travel carefully. He fires the third belt in short, sharp bursts. It is like put-ting the finishing touches to a plane, but he can hardly see what he is doing. This belt finished, his hands drop as he straightens himself. The sergeant slaps him on the back.

"Well shot, Junker!" Volkenborn is as white as chalk, and Werner can see how his hands shake.

It is noon before the third attack is beaten off. The sergeant is wounded, and Werner and Volken-born carry him back to where the company com-mander stands. It is only a matter of a hundred yards, but they can hardly keep their feet after they have placed him on the stretcher.

Lieutenant Sollmann has a talk with Volkenborn, and appoints him gun captain, and he has no strength left with which to bring his heels together in acknowledgment. The lieutenant offers him some cigarettes, good English cigarettes, and he smokes one and feels better. The sergeant lights up, too. Further attacks are to be expected. Rifles are cleaned and made ready, and ammunition is brought up.

There is much coming and going at the Battalion Headquarters. Dispatch bearers dash back and forth. Supplies of luminous ammunition and hand grenades are brought up, and the men pause for a short rest. The remains of the demolished house look quite different. There is nothing white about them. Seen in the daylight, the bricks are red or yellow. A part of one of the walls is painted a bright blue. That must have been the larder, thinks Volkenborn.

They have already taken their ammunition. Werner has sneaked a bottle of mineral water, and they share it between them.

"I say, there's Lieutenant von Kless!"

They go across. Behind a row of trees and in front of a thick hedge are rows of canvas. Werner goes ahead.

"Here he lies, Volkenborn."

His head is uninjured, and somebody has placed his service cap beneath it. Werner lifts the canvas a little and then lets it fall.

Volkenborn stands looking into the dead officer's face.

"We must be getting back."

A shrapnel sings through the air and strikes a tree.

They bring up two thousand rounds for the machine gun. The shell hole is enlarged and strengthened with stones that Werner fetches, and the machine gun is cleaned and made ready. The afternoon passes in comparative calm and without casualties. Then it grows dusk, and a mist rises. Volkenborn pulls the cover of the machine gun over his face; Werner is on duty.

Cold prevents Volkenborn from sleeping long. With his feet he shifts some of the planks that they have placed on the ground to keep the water out, but it still oozes through. He can see the face of his dead friend before him. It seems to confront him from the floor of the shell hole, lying on a muddy service cap. It looks quite peaceful, but as though cut in marble, like Michelangelo's Madonna. Withal it is the face of a stranger; so much so that he can hardly recognize it. There is something almost menacing in the expression. Then Volkenborn seems to see before him the face of the pale Flemish woman, with the intent eyes. She is putting her hand out towards him. The finger nails are white and have blue shadows. Suddenly he feels the hand around his throat; no longer one hand, but many: a chain of hands that are choking the breath out of him. In vain he tries to cry out, he can make no sound. He falls backward and with him fall the bleeding bodies of dead men. He feels blood running over his eyes and shuts his mouth tight, so as not to be choked by this hateful stream. He is suffocating. With his right arm he seeks to push off this something that is holding him down, when his hand presses against a dead mouth, from which black blood oozes. Again he falls back, and this time awakes.

The canvas is dripping, for it is pouring in torrents, and his face is soaking wet. With difficulty he staggers to his feet. His right arm is stiff with the cold. It is night, and he looks at his wrist watch. He has been asleep for six hours. The sentry hands him his flask.

"Spirits have been served out, Junker!" At first he refuses, but at last he takes a pull. The smell makes him feel sick, but the stuff warms him.

He stands beside the sentry. Through the gray mist he sees star shells floating. Here and there a rifle shot rings sharply. In the distance the big guns are still busy. His head seems empty of all thought. He tries to concentrate. How long is it since they left Bruges? They surely could not have been there two days ago! What was yesterday? An attack? Yesterday! Sergeant Leuber was wounded. The lieutenant gave us cigarettes. And then — in front of the hedge, behind the trees, the last tent!

Again in imagination he is looking into the dead face, which has beauty, but such a cold expression. He repeats to himself, "Lieutenant von Kless is dead! There he lies! In that tent! He is dead!" Beyond that, all thought fails him. All round him there seems to be an emptiness. He would like to cry, to feel, to give way to sadness, but he still stands leaning on the edge of the shell hole, staring with unseeing eyes into the night, and drinking occasionally from the flask. The taste is filthy, but it sends a glow through his body, so he drinks again. He is so frozen, so physically miserable, that he has no heart left for other feelings. The lieutenant is dead!

IV

After a week in the front line they are relieved, and Lieutenant Sollmann says, "You were to have gone on leave, Volkenborn, but all leave has been cancelled since this scrap started. But I'm going to risk granting you a week on my own responsibility in special recognition of your services. So off with you!"

Werner helps him to get his things together. "You're in luck to get away from it all for a while."

Volkenborn makes no reply. He is feeling worried about his leave. Only the day before he had written to Lothar, to say that he was not coming, all leave being stopped, and that the silver wedding festivities would have to go on without him. And now he is to get his leave after all. It seems hardly possible, and he feels ashamed to go off and leave Werner and the others behind. It seems to be his duty to remain with them. Will it not be setting a bad example to go on leave while the company is so hard pressed? Oppressed by these thoughts, he avoids meeting Werner's eyes as he shakes hands with him, after buckling on his pack.

It is already dark as he passes the castle. Left and right lie the rows of canvas. They have names on them. What for? Who wants to distinguish between those who are so alike? For one dead man strangely resembles another! Dust to dust! Earth to earth!

At ten o'clock that night he is standing in front of the orderly room. The sergeant major tells him that there is a train the next morning at seven. That means that he can enjoy a night's rest. "In your place, Junker, I should hop right off now, so that there may be no chance of recalling you!"

But Volkenborn shakes his head. He cannot do that, it will be too much like running away. No, he will stay the night.

He was awakened by the sound of knocking at his door and a voice calling his name. Instantly, he realized what it meant: a battalion order to the effect that he was not to proceed on leave.

Getting up quickly, he buckled on his kit, reported to the sergeant major — who had a hearty laugh at his expense — and a quarter of an hour later he was making his way to the Front, after a night's rest that had held only three hours' sleep for him.

The Front was enveloped in smoke, like a town in which there had been a great conflagration, and the guns were busy. At the sight of all this a shudder ran through his body from head to foot, and the realization of the inevitable fate which was to destroy so many seized on him, and gripped him hard. Fear, stark bodily fear, assailed him. Was this to be the end? Was it to be? Was it for this that he had remained, and not got away while he had the chance, as the sergeant major had advised? Why had he chosen to stay? Was it all foreordained? He had had his opportunity and had not taken it. Why? Well! Whatever fate might have in store for him, he would see it through like a man.

Thoughts of home came to him. In imagination he saw his name in the obituary column of the paper. To-day was the twenty-second, and on the twenty-fifth the celebration of his parents' silver wedding was to take place. How dreadful if it should happen just then! The lieutenant would write to them; so would the colonel. The regiment would send a paragraph to the Arnstadt paper. Anneliese would read it. "On the night of the 22d to the 23rd Hans Volkenborn, Fahnenjunker in the —— Regiment." Anneliese would cut out the notice and lay it on the top of the little bundle of letters — Anneliese who had been looking forward so to his leave.

Such were his thoughts until once more within the fire zone, but from that moment when the fumes of powder began to penetrate into his lungs, and the first shell exploded near him, these daydreams vanished from his mind, and he was once again the typical soldier, ready to take all risks without hesitation or protest, and when he reported to his company commander he spoke of his sudden recall as though it were an excellent joke.

In this mood Volkenborn resumed his duties, and ceased to wonder about his own particular destiny.

V

Three days later the company was relieved, and once more returned to rest billets. From day to day they expected to be entirely withdrawn from that line, but it seemed as though the pessimists were going to prove right, that they were likely to have a further dose of all the filth and horror. Volkenborn and Werner were billeted on the Army Medical Corps. A mail had come in with letters and parcels, in addition to which a soldier returning from leave in Arnstadt had brought Volkenborn presents from home. As their regulation rations were wretched, they were all very glad of "extras."

The only thing about his company commander that Volkenborn found to complain of, was that he did not pay enough attention to the kitchen, and was not energetic enough in his treatment of those whose business it was to commandeer the local food supplies: left to their own devices, they made money by selling the troops' rations to the highest bidder. The company commander had no share in such transactions, but he was too indifferent or slack to interfere, being one of those who always avoid all unpleasantness as far as possible. Improvement was always being promised, the food was always being tasted and pronounced unsatisfactory, but nothing ever happened. The lieutenant had his meals by himself, and his servant, a man called Pfefferle — an ugly beast with puffy red eyelids and perpetual tears in his eyes — always managed to forage extra luxuries for him. It was even whispered among the men that those who greased this fellow's palm well were sure to obtain any concessions that they might want from the company commander, and for this reason and on account of successful activities in other directions, he was known among the men as the "secret company commander." This blackguard was generally hated, and Volkenborn, who could not bear the sight of him, resolutely refused to become one of his clients.

The field railway passed the little farmhouse in which the orderly room and the lieutenant's quarters were situated; and every morning, between six and half past, Russian prisoners, who were building great concrete dugouts behind the front, passed this spot. This work was supposed to be in the nature of a reprisal for the brutality with which the German prisoners of war were treated in enemy concentration camps.

It was a pitiable spectacle. Dirty, ragged, with hollow cheeks, sallow faces, with sacking wound round their legs, in broken boots, and filthy, patched, yellowish-brown overcoats, they dragged themselves by, never looking at anything as they passed, like ghosts without eyes. If now and again one of them glanced up, it was the glare of an animal. Every noon, they came back again by the same route, and Volkenborn saw how they made a rush for the tub that stood in front of the farmhouse — a tub of swill, into which the refuse and broken food was pitched. A dozen would plunge their hands into it, pushing and jostling one another, and then hustled on by the N. C. O. in charge of them. The sight of such misery made Volkenborn sick at heart, and actual physical nausea almost overcame him at such a wretched and shameful sight.

One evening he was walking with Werner along the track of the field railway, westward in the direction of the sunset, where the sun was going down in a golden ball after a cloudless day. The permanent way seemed to be running straight into the sunset, and when Volkenborn half closed his eyes, he had the impression of looking along a ladder that led upward to the sun.

They were walking arm in arm and talking. Speaking about home, about Luise, about Anneliese. It was so good to have somebody to talk to, so good to have somebody to listen to. Every possible subject came up in turn for discussion: concerts, birthday celebrations, walking tours, tennis in snow-white flannels, elegant jumps over the net as they changed courts, running races, muscular development, training, regattas with pretty girls watching and waving them on; and then they spoke of these young girls, of their hair, their eyes, their smiles.

Once again Werner produced the photograph of

his Luise, which he always carried about with him
in a little Morocco-leather case. Once again he
described in detail her dress and her coloring, and
explained what slim wrists she had, and, with finger
and thumb, he made a tiny circle in the air. Volkenborn duly admired the photograph, the slender-
ness of the wonderful and much vaunted wrist, and
then began to speak about Anneliese, and drew from
his pocket a pale blue envelope; her spidery and
rather unformed writing provided them with further
material for conversation. From Anneliese, they
fell to discussing other girls, going into details concerning the color of their eyes, their carriage, the
smallness of their feet, and other charms that they
possessed.

As they walked along, arm in arm, telling one
another what it was that they specially admired in
feminine beauty, a dark and ugly shadow came into
view between them and the sun, something that
seemed to be coming up the rungs of the ladder that
the track of the field railway formed between them
and the sunset; something sinister that, framed by
the sunset, looked like darkness made visible. As
it drew nearer, they saw that it was — the gang of
Russian prisoners.

As the Russians come abreast, they made room
for them to pass, glancing at them casually. Suddenly Volkenborn took some cigarettes from his
pocket and pressed them into the hand of the Russian who was passing him. The man was so surprised
that he almost let them drop. For a moment Werner

hesitated, then he too followed his friend's example. Hastily the two lads turned out of their pockets half a packet of chocolate, a dozen cigarettes, a broken cigar, and handed them to the passing Russians. The eager hands that were stretched out to receive them looked like dried leather through the grime that covered them. Not knowing how else to show his sympathy, Volkenborn patted one of them on the shoulder. As they stood and watched them, the Russians turned and waved their hands, a greeting which they returned. Depressed by this incident, they made their way back in silence through the twilight.

VI

The society of the two Army Medical Corps men, especially of their N. C. O., an undersized person with a fair pointed beard and cold impudent eyes, proved none too agreeable, but there was no way of avoiding them entirely. The N. C. O. knew his job, but to Volkenborn's disgust made a poor show under fire. A great talker, he courted popularity by telling stories about himself and his adventures, but only succeeded in nauseating decent-minded men among his hearers.

In the evening, as the two Junkers were smoking their cigarettes and some of the others were sitting there listening, he would begin his yarns. He would tell his stories with many interruptions, stopping from time to time to clear his throat and spit, to pick his teeth, to crack a louse that he would catch in his shirt or in his stockings, with saliva-moistened fingers, or to fill and relight his pipe. The result was that his listeners, willing or unwilling, were constantly kept in a state of suspense and impatience. Even such unwilling listeners as Volkenborn and Werner found themselves irritated by these constant interruptions. Unpleasant as his stories were, there was something in these constant pauses that incited the listener to closer attention.

He regaled them with the history of his last leave in Berlin. In a *café chantant* he had made the acquaintance of a "decent girl." At the time she had a young man, but he was quickly disposed of. Then there followed a description of her charms: just a sentence or two, illustrated by ample gestures, a click of the tongue, and various expressions that Volkenborn had never heard before, but of the meaning of which he was not in doubt. Then followed an account of his visit to her rooms, how he hung his tunic over the back of a chair, and of how he turned back the bed-clothes, — all described in such a manner that Volkenborn felt he would like to strike him in the face, but he remained where he was and perforce had to listen to the rest of the story. Had to listen to a detailed story of the night's happenings: the creaking of the bed, her insatiable desire. Then followed a description of the morning, of how she looked, of how the room looked. Never in his life had Volkenborn had any experiences of this kind, and, despite his efforts to the contrary, he found his mind greedily sucking in all these details.

But this was not the whole of the story. The N. C. O. went on to describe how he made the acquaintance of the girl's mother. Still quite young! In the prime of life! Then followed an account of how mother and daughter shared his affections, and a description of the rival physical charms of the two. Nothing was left to the imagination; all was detailed in plain words. But it had soon proved too much for him, and he had found himself between two fires, and subjected to constant scenes and threats, until one day he had slipped away from it all as suddenly as he had come. "Hot stuff, both of them; they'd soon have made an end of me."

During this narrative the Junkers sat as if they were not listening, as if talk of this kind could not possibly be intended for their ears; as if they could not possibly be expected to understand what he was talking about.

The N. C. O. also pretended to ignore their presence, but as he finished one of his stories, he would sometimes turn to Volkenborn and say in a mocking tone, "Hope you didn't hear that, Junker," and turning away again would add; "Stories of that kind are not for innocent lads like that," and laugh derisively.

Volkenborn never commented to Werner on these yarns, each one of which was filthier and smuttier than the last, but on one occasion, as they were passing through the village, he said quite suddenly,

"There are moments when I feel like putting a bullet through that blackguard's head!" Werner did not ask whom he meant, and made no answer, but he knew very well.

VII

Towards the end of the fifth day in rest billets, the bugles suddenly rang out. The enemy had penetrated into their lines near Poelkapelle, and they were rushed up, to hold themselves in reserve at the threatened spot.

It was night as they advanced, Volkenborn leading with the company commander. The artillery fire was severe and there were heavy losses. The road was strewn with wrecked cars and dead horses. In some places the mud was so deep that only the bloated bellies of the dead animals were visible. As they were passing through a village, Volkenborn saw how two men were cutting thick pieces of flesh out of the body of a horse that had just that moment fallen, and was still living. He drew his pistol and quickly put three bullets into the poor beast's brain. "They ought to be in your skulls, you brutes!" he shouted.

Towards noon the next day, as he was marching beside the lieutenant's horse through the village, and thinking of poor little Möbius, of whose death he had learned that morning while reporting at head-quarters, he came again to the spot where he had killed the horse the day before, and found nothing there but a bare skeleton, from which all the flesh had been hacked away, leaving the ribs staring at him like the rafters of a burned-out house. He was feeling both "nervy" and tired, with the result that a sudden access of horror seized on him and there flashed before his eyes a mental picture of his comrade Möbius lying dead somewhere on the road, his bones stripped of their flesh like the poor horse's, his head on one side, staring at him blankly.

The company was again in the lines. Lieutenant Sollmann had his quarters in a concrete dugout near the road behind the castle, and Volkenborn's sleeping place was near the inlet, close behind the little stove. He had just received a packet of butter from home, and after having written a letter to his people, to say that they could not spare anything from their meager rations, and that if they sent him any more, he should return the packet to them, he was toasting bread. Although he had just written to say that he was in want of nothing, and was much better off than they were, the truth was that he was living almost entirely on bread, and that this butter was a very welcome addition. He was on such short commons that he had sent a card to his brothers, begging for some biscuits. As the result of insufficient food, the whole division was suffering more or less from dysentery, and at the Dressing Station there were pails full of lime — and opium pills with which to meet this epidemic. For a day or so these measures proved effective, but the trouble came back again even worse than before. The ra-

tions from the kitchen proved uneatable, and, if
Volkenborn had not been obliged to take over the
rations for the company, he would not have gone
near the kitchen, so impossible was it to eat the food
provided.

Lieutenant Sollmann had given Volkenborn his
map, so that with its aid he might be able to prepare
a sketch of the machine-gun positions. He was carrying out this task with the greatest care, being
anxious to show his technical ability in this direction,
and as the sketch was to be ready in an hour Volkenborn requested one of the orderlies to go and fetch
the rations for him. Almost immediately afterwards
Lieutenant Sollmann came back with the regimental
machine-gun officer, one Lieutenant Bernhard, and
Volkenborn was obliged to lay his sketch aside.

"Come and have a drink; there's plenty of time
for the sketch, and we can have a yarn together until
the kitchen comes round."

The lieutenant offered Volkenborn a cigarette,
and they began to smoke and talk to one another.
The stove in the corner was red-hot, and from time
to time the whole dugout trembled as a high explosive shell burst somewhere in the immediate
neighborhood, occasionally entirely extinguishing
the lights for a moment. The walls of the trench
however held fast, and Volkenborn felt himself in
comparative safety. His thoughts turned to Werner,
who was once again lying out in a shell hole, and he
realized that he was better off than his friend. Here,
at least, he could hear and see what was going on,

and even this constant dodging of the enemy's fire
had a something sporting in it that made it attrac-
tive. The lieutenant too was "awfully decent" to him,
and he felt that he was being treated with especial
favor. As soon as the orderly returned, he would
finish the sketch, take it to the commander, and then
write to Anneliese and his parents. He was hoping
that the man might also bring some letters for him.

Meanwhile, the lieutenant was telling stories
about garrison life in peace-time. Sollmann was a
Reserve officer, a fact which he thought it necessary
to introduce from time to time in a joking manner
by beginning every third or fourth sentence with,
"As you know, I'm merely a lieutenant of the Reserve, but — "

This struck Volkenborn as extremely comic, but he
was very careful to laugh cautiously in a constrained
manner. Sollmann had just been "pulling the lieutenant's leg," and the latter was about to reply, when
a private soldier rushed wildly into the dugout.
Capless, face and tunic covered with white dust, his
left sleeve a mass of blood and mud, he shouted,
"Herr Lieutenant . . . a direct hit . . . Lieutenant Gallatz . . . and all of them killed." Sollmann sprang to his feet. "What? Come on, Volkenborn!"

Out they rushed into the darkness, Volkenborn
carrying the lieutenant's gas mask, Sollmann leading by at least twenty yards. The path that they were
taking lay under a heavy fire, and the concussion of
a shell brought Volkenborn to the ground. Quickly

picking himself up, glad to realize that he was still
alive, he plunged onward. Having lost sight of
Sollmann he shouted, "Herr Lieutenant! Herr Lieutenant!" There was no answer; his voice was inaudible amid all the din. The road turned sharply to
the right and he followed it to the village, where
shell after shell was falling. On both sides of the
street what was left of the houses was being finally
blown to pieces. The stench of powder made it almost impossible to breathe: once he suspected the
presence of gas, stopped, and put his mask on. Then
he snatched it off again, remembering that it was not
his. Where was the lieutenant? On he rushed, right
through the village, still shouting, "Herr Lieutenant!" Still no answer but the wild roar of the bursting shells. He decided to retrace his steps, but by
this time the village street was an inferno, and it
would have been impossible to get through alive.
Undecided what to do, he stood cowering for a
while behind a lime-washed wall, which still remained
intact, his pulses beating like mad and his whole body
trembling. With an effort he pulled himself together. He had to get back somehow, back to the
dugout. They had to find the lieutenant. But where
was this infernal dugout where Lieutenant Gallatz
lay?

He straightened himself, and as he did so another
shell fell near where he stood, sending lumps of
earth and stone flying all round him. He seemed to
feel something strike him in the neck, and his knees
sagged under him. After feeling himself all over, to

see if he were hurt, he started to run for his life. He
could hear the shells coming a second or so before
they fell, but not soon enough to enable him to get
out of their way. These infernal high-explosive
shells! They deafened him: they seemed almost to
be dragging the teeth out of his head. The atmosphere was so thick that it was becoming almost impossible to swallow, and a lump seemed rising in his
throat.

His one idea was to make his way through the village street. Hearing a shell coming he sprang aside
into a house, three walls of which were still standing. At the same moment a second shell fell on the
outer side of the walls. "Now for it!" he thought,
as he seemed to feel the wall and roof about to fall
on him, but it was only a beam that had grazed his
shoulder. Without thinking, he started to run back,
keeping close to the white wall, rushed through a
garden, through a hedge, across a field, and through
a ditch. The ditch was a wide one and he tried to
jump it, but fell short. The ground everywhere was
ankle deep in mud, which seemed to cling to each
foot as he lifted it. His legs began to grow weary.
The shells, he noticed, always bounded once into the
air before they burst. To his overstrained nerves,
it seemed as if they were laughing at him, seeking to
entice him to join their own mad dance. They were
trying to get him into their clutches, trying to seize
him and break him in two like the branch of a tree.
They shrieked of hate and destruction, as, like a
mouse escaping from the claws of a cat, he dashed

onward, only to find himself caught in a wire entanglement.

Scarcely had he torn himself free, when he was
knocked down by another explosion, and he found
that he was bleeding, but could not discover where
the blood came from. On every side, more barbed
wire; and, instead of getting away from it, he
seemed to be becoming more closely entangled. He
must have stumbled on to the old German wire de-
fences. He began to feel himself growing weak, and
toppled over among the wire, and lay where he had
fallen. Shell splinters were singing round him, burying themselves in the mud beside him. It seemed to
him as if he would never be able to get up again.
He began to feel faint and dizzy, but, realizing that
it was now or never, he succeeded in pulling himself
together again. He was not going to die here like
a fly in a spider's web. Where was he trying to get
to? He was looking for the lieutenant, of course. He
had lost him; he had his gas mask, so he must find
him!

Bit by bit, he managed to free himself from the
wire, tearing his hands badly in the process and was
able once more to stand upright. The shells were
still dancing wildly round him, but he had recovered
his nerve, and ignored them. Step by step, carefully
considering every move he made, he worked his way
through the barbed wire; bending down to free his
trousers, his coat, his sleeves. He went through it all
as carefully as if he had been wearing his best suit at
home, and was caught in some thorny bushes.

When he had freed himself — after what seemed to him an eternity, — he walked on through the mud, skirting each shell hole with caution. When he came to a ditch, he no longer tried to jump it, but waded straight through it, like an animal. At last he gained the road, and recognized that he had been going in the right direction. He had not the strength to run, or was it that he no longer had the inclination to do so? He now felt no anxiety as to his own safety, but seemed rather to have fallen a prey to despairing indifference. Death could scarcely come any nearer than it had been, and he had lost all interest in the struggle. Why should he run? Why struggle? It made so little difference. Bolt upright, never ducking or turning aside at the sight or sound of a shell, he walked down the road, on which a heavy fire was still concentrated. Whether he reached the end alive, or fell dead, was now a matter of complete indifference to him.

But as he drew near the dugout, his pace quickened, and he was running when he encountered the man who had brought the news of the disaster.

"Where's the lieutenant?"

Lieutenant Sollmann stepped out of the dugout.

"Volkenborn, man alive! I thought you were done for! But you're bleeding and must go and get bandaged. Lieutenant Gallatz, and the other severely wounded must be transported at once to the dressing station. Fetch the stretcher bearers — quickly!"

Volkenborn started off. On the way he felt his arm, which was beginning to be painful. He found

that he could move it, but it stabbed from time to
time, and his hands were smarting. He rubbed the
blood off them on to his trousers.

Half an hour later Volkenborn, with a dozen
men, was standing in front of Lieutenant Gallatz's
dugout. Harms — the orderly whom he had sent to
fetch the rations — was already dead, his whole
chest one shattered pulp of bleeding flesh. Volkenborn scarcely looked at him but forced his way
through into the dugout, the entrance to which was
very narrow. How were they to get the stretcher
through? The lieutenant was lying at the back,
groaning dreadfully. The stretcher bearers were
standing there and considering what was to be done,
and the guards were staring aimlessly at the
wounded men. Volkenborn's temper blazed up.

"Don't stand there like wooden images, but lend
a hand!"

With the help of the bearers he tried to carry the
lieutenant through, but both of his legs were shattered, and he shrieked at every movement. That
would not do. Two more men took hold of
the stretcher, and the lieutenant began to whimper
like a child. His head had fallen forward and was
resting just under Volkenborn's chin. Once they
had got him out into the open, Volkenborn de-
spatched a lance coroporal to see which was the
best way to take. The road was too far off, and under fire. The only thing to do was to take a short
cut.

Four men helped to carry the stretcher, but it

proved heavy going. What with making detours to avoid exposed spots and the swampy condition of the ground, the task was almost too much for them. Slowly they made their way, constantly slipping and halting amid the groans of the lieutenant. The lance corporal came back and reported. "Quite impossible, we must get back on to the road." Volkenborn protested. "Rot! We *must* get through there somehow!"

The fire began to draw nearer and seemed already to be on their heels; shrapnel was flying all round them.

"My leg, my leg!" whimpered the lieutenant.

Some one had put a gas mask under his leg. Whose was it? They made an attempt to run, and again Gallatz shrieked. The stretcher seemed as heavy as lead. A shell burst not twenty paces from them, but no one was hit. On they pushed, mud spouting up into their faces and pieces of shell whizzing round them. They came to a ditch, and the bearers wanted to go round it, but Volkenborn made them go through the water. The bank bristled with barbed wire and the water was breast high, but they got through somehow, helping themselves by means of the wire, and tearing their hands badly. A little lower down shells were splashing into the water. One of the bearers stumbled and was nearly carried away by the stream. A moment later another bearer slipped into a shell hole and they had to put the stretcher down in order to pull him out. They arrived within a hundred yards of the castle, but the moat had concrete banks, and they had to go round it. Bits of shell were hitting the trees, motors were rushing by. At last they reached the gate and found the grass plot completely covered with tents, in which lay dead and dying. A narrow path passed between them. From one of these tents projected an arm. The hand was open, and seemed to Volkenborn as if it were reaching out to him threateningly. Where was the staff surgeon? Somehow they stumbled down some stone stairs and through some doors into a lighted room, in which there was a great table. They placed Gallatz on it, and Volkenborn watched the man who began cutting the blood-stained rags away with a great pair of scissors. He saw the little syringe with which the surgeon injected a narcotic into the lieutenant's thigh. It seemed to him as if he himself could feel the pain, the fluid spurting in, and the withdrawal of the syringe. Then he heard some one say, "Give them some water!"

He broke the neck off a soda-water bottle and drank; drank as if he would never stop again. How good the water tasted! Then they all sat down, and Volkenborn watched the shadows under the domed ceiling, as the door opened and shut. The smell of ether fell heavy on the air, a feeling of horror overcame him, and he got up.

"Stand to! We must get back!"

His limbs felt like lead, as he walked down the road. They returned, bringing a second wounded man into the castle. By this time it was already light, and they were able to see the spot where some hours before they had been caught in the wire. The devastated land lay gray in front of them. From time to time a shell fell and sent up a fountain of mud; then all would be quiet again. The morning was cold and wet, and they all shuddered as their eyes fell on this depressing scene.

When he finally got back, Volkenborn had to lie down in the lieutenant's cabin. He accepted the offer without protest. What was it I had to do? he thought. I was to finish a sketch . . . and so thinking, he fell asleep.

At noon he woke and found that Lieutenant Sollmann was not there; he got up, had a wash, had his injured right arm seen to, rubbed ointment into his legs and hands, and then finished the sketch as well as he could. At first, he thought he would write a letter to Anneliese, but instead he went out, seated himself on a luminous ammunition case and stared across at the castle, round which the mist was slowly rising. Carefully he recalled all the happenings of the night. He had wanted to finish the sketch, otherwise he himself would have gone with the orderly to fetch the rations and would afterwards have been sitting in the "arbor" chatting with Lieutenant Gallatz, and would, in such case, have now been lying dead like the orderly, or desperately wounded like Gallatz. Was it fate, and if so, what was fate? Was it not rather all chance, and are not chance and fate the same thing? And a voice within him seemed to say, No! There is no such thing as chance!

But there is fate! Everything is foreordained! Misery and suffering is all foreordained!

VIII

Once again they had five days in rest billets. Once again he and Werner went for walks along the track of the field railway, but now they had no sun to cheer them, for an early winter had fallen upon Flanders, and the days were gray and depressing.

On one of their walks they met some men of the Army Ordnance Corps; men who were still young in years, but who bore all the traces of premature age; men from whose faces the starvation rations of the home front had long since banished all capacity for cheerfulness and laughter. With their prematurely gray hair, they seemed in keeping with the general dreariness of the November landscape.

Once again they had their quarters with the Army Medical Corps, and once again they had to sit and listen to the same old stories from the non-commissioned officer in charge. Again, there were letters from home, and then one night, for the third time, they were ordered into the front line.

On this third and last occasion they were more to the south of the much-disputed Poelkapelle. Volkenborn had his quarters with the company commander, somewhere along the way from Westroosebeeke to Poelkapelle. The road was a straight one and sloped upwards towards Westroosebeeke, but in reality it could hardly be called a road, being rather a succession of shell holes littered with dead bodies. Once, Volkenborn saw a fat white cat run across the road, going in the direction of the hopper in which the concrete was mixed. His first thought was to call it over to him to feed it, to keep it, to have a pet that he could fondle. But the next morning, as with Peter he was passing along the road again at dawn, going to fetch some spirits, the man pointed to the white cat! Peter drew his pistol. "The brute's eating the dead bodies!" He fired, and the animal was gone.

"There's no ammunition better than brandy," the lieutenant had said. "Off with you, Volkenborn, or the fellows will drink half of it before they bring it back." The return journey with the bottles and casks was not such a simple matter. Along the road were a number of heavy batteries, which the enemy bombarded every half hour. This avalanche of shells was bad enough for the gunners, but it made the carrying of liquor through the shell holes and over beams and corpses a specially difficult matter, in view of the necessity for not spilling a drop from the casks or breaking one of the bottles.

After ten days they were finally relieved. Volkenborn had already heard the news at the Headquarters, but had been doubtful about believing it, and it was not till he had swung himself up into the lorry in which the last machine gun had been loaded, and the horses had begun to pull, that he felt convinced that relief was really an accomplished fact.

The driver, after lighting his pipe, began to tell stories about the horses, and to explain how, in his part of the country, more wheat than barley was cultivated, and to talk about the three fine, healthy calves that had been born on his farm that year. He spoke of how the women had to be in the kitchen, the cowsheds and the fields at the same time, and wound up by remarking that it was high time that the war came to an end.

Volkenborn found it extremely pleasant to sit and listen to all this, and only to be obliged to throw in an occasional "Yes? Really! Is that so?" He imagined himself to be listening, but all the time his mind was busy with other thoughts, and Anneliese and her tomato-growing kept obtruding on him. She was rearing ducklings too, she had written, and he found himself asking the driver, "Do you keep ducks too?" In answer the fellow grew eloquent about his poultry yard.

Then, turning round, he looked back towards the trenches, where the continuous flaming of explosives almost produced the effect of summer lightning. He could still hear the rattle of moving columns along the main road that lead to the Front; the grumbling of the guns; that continuous, dull roar, that sounds as if Nature herself were taking part in the struggle. It is a sound that all soldiers grow accustomed to, but, nevertheless, to hear it dying away in the distance was a relief and a blessing beyond all words. This increasing quietude brought Volkenborn the same relief that a sick man experiences when a cool hand is laid on his forehead. Once again he found himself able to make normal use of his ears, to distinguish the ordinary sounds of everyday life, and to realize that there were places where peace and quietude still prevail. How pleasant it was, once again to be able to distinguish the footfalls of the horses, to be able to hear the striking of a match or the sound of a human voice! To him it seemed like a new experience, one that stirred all his senses into new activity. It was as though he could smell better, and could actually taste the cigarette he was smoking. Even his eyes seemed keener; and what a relief it was no longer to see the air dancing in front of him from the vibration of the guns!

High up on a poplar a thrush was singing its throat out. At first he could hardly realize what the sound was, and it was not until they had almost passed out of hearing that he said, "Did you hear that? It was a thrush!" At their quarters they were given some sour wine, which the driver tossed off without as much as making a face. Biscuits too were produced. Volkenborn sipped the wine and nibbled at the biscuits, which were mildewed. But after all, there was comfort in the very name of wine and biscuits. It suggested jollification and happiness.

After a march of some four hours they reached a spot where a train was waiting for them and got aboard, but it did not start till late in the afternoon. By midnight they were back again in Bruges, and as they marched through the streets Volkenborn had time to observe with astonishment all that was going on. Belgian women walked beside the troops and from time to time exchanged open or secret greetings with the men; one might almost imagine that it was a regiment returning to its own garrison town. "My girl has known for a week that we were to arrive to-day," said the man marching beside Volkenborn.

IX

On returning from his morning bath Volkenborn asked his lieutenant for leave to go into the town.

"What are you going to do there?"

"I want to fetch a sketchbook, Herr Lieutenant, that I left behind me in my quarters."

The lieutenant gave Volkenborn a keen glance. His eyelids were inflamed as usual, and his eyes looked smaller and colder than ever. Then he nodded.

"All right! Go and fetch your sketchbook, but don't be too long about it, do you understand?"

Volkenborn made his way into the town, walking quickly until he came to the level crossing. He was feeling refreshed by his swim, and as he walked he was fidgetting with his uniform, which, although it had been ironed, was still damp and consequently somewhat uncomfortable. As he walked along, he looked into the shop windows, bought some Belgian cigarettes from a street hawker, and found he had made a bad bargain. It was not until he passed the railway and was walking past the various cafés, which had just opened, that the thought of his mission began to make him feel uncomfortable. Just at this very spot he had once met Lieutenant von Kless. It had been in September, and that seemed such a long time ago now. The lieutenant was dead! How long ago was it since he was killed? He had difficulty in remembering. Everything seemed to be confused in his mind.

He walked up and down for some minutes in front of the red house. Turning at the end of the square, he said to himself, "This time I really must get it over." Then he had another look at his watch, and once more found himself walking slowly past the house. A nervous dread seemed to have seized on him, and he felt himself obsessed with a ridiculous idea that the door would suddenly open and — Still laboring in this nervous crisis, he crossed to the other side of the road. All the blinds were down. As he stared at the house, he kept thinking, Why am I standing here? What am I waiting for? What I've really come for is to fetch my sketchbook — the one that the lieutenant left behind.

Once again he consulted his watch and realized that he could not delay any more, that he must get back to the company. Even then he did not cross straight over, but walked diagonally across the other corner of the square, and then turned and went slowly in the direction of the house, lighting a fresh cigarette as he went. The last one he had thrown away half finished. He hurried up to the door and seized the knocker. Taking a last puff at his cigarette, he threw it away and watched it as it lay smoking on the pavement.

The sly porter opened the door, led the way up-stairs, and Volkenborn entered the drawing-room. Then a door opened, and he realized that he ought to step forward and bow, but felt unable to move as the beautiful Flemish woman advanced towards him. Without a word she walked past him and went up to the writing table, where she stood motionless, her left hand resting on the table, her right hand hang-ing down. In silence he watched her, and felt in-capable of either speaking or moving.

As his eyes fastened on the white blue-veined hand, strange and indescribable emotions ran through him — emotions so confused that he him-self could find no words with which to describe them.

CHAPTER FOUR

COMRADES

I

He was once more passing the railway on his way back, saluting the officers whom he met, looking in at the bookshop, examining trunks in a shop window, and mentally making a note of the firm which had for sale one such as he wanted; but all this had taken place quite mechanically, and it seemed to him almost as though it were not he but another who was walking through the town.

In his thoughts, he was still facing the beautiful Flemish woman in her drawing-room, his eyes fixed on her hands, on her figure, on a fold in her gown. She was standing before him with her hand on his shoulder — such a little hand, and yet it had seemed like a heavy weight, like something burning that inflamed the blood in his veins.

As he walked through the streets, thinking over the scene in which he had played a part, thinking of the touch of that little white hand, a faint smile played round the corner of his mouth.

Sitting that evening in his quarters he began another letter to Anneliese. As was his custom, he started with a description of his room; stating precisely the position of the table and describing the head of a saint that hung over his bed, then he touched on more serious matters, gave details of their march, and added something, rather casually, about heavy losses. This led him on to the death of Lieutenant von Kless, and to a remark about how much he had liked him. Then, fearing that his letter was growing too tragic in its tone, he proceeded to finish it off with an account of the thrush singing near the farm yard, of some remarks about the sour wine and the mildewed biscuits, and finally with a description of their railway journey. But his letter contained never a word about the nights when they lay in front of Ypres, nor about the unhappy Flemish woman whom his lieutenant had loved. All these things seemed too remote to form the subject of a letter.

II

A fortnight later the six Junkers of the regiment were in a train bound for Germany, going home for a course of instruction before receiving their commissions as officers. Volkenborn's brother came to the station to see him off, and, as the train steamed out, shouted after him: "My love to Germany, and tell them that we shall all be back soon; that we shall be having peace in two months."

On the previous day Hans Volkenborn was awarded the Iron Cross. The lieutenant had handed it to him with these words: "Wear it in memory of the adventures in which we both took part at Ypres." His brother Lothar fastened the ribbon of the cross into his buttonhole. It looked distressingly new and made him feel quite uncomfortable.

In the evening, he cycled out to Leffinghe, where the Brigade Battle Position was located, and sat in the dugout for half an hour, chatting with Kurt. As before, Ursel's photograph stood between them and they often glanced at it. Once again he had seen the same affectionate look in Kurt's eyes as they shook hands. Then he cycled back again at night, his machine side-slipping often on the muddy road. Behind him lay the Front, with its constant gleams of gunfire and star shells. War, danger, fate; all these he was leaving behind for the time being, and before him lay home, peace and love.

The Junkers were returning to Germany, but their Möbius was not one of them. "Now we are six; seven was an unlucky number," said Volkenborn. As he listened to Gerhardi's conversation, he seemed to see the dead Junker before him, with his spectacles, his small, well-shaped head and the kid gloves of which he was so proud. Then quite suddenly — as had happened to him once before on the march through the village where the skeleton of the horse was lying in the road — he seemed to see Möbius' head lying on the ground before him; the face pallid as only a dead one can be.

On their own initiative, they broke the journey at

Arnstadt. At home it was a day of rejoicing, and the scanty larder was ransacked of all its luxuries. After an excellent dinner there was a bottle of good claret, and then another and still another. Over a cigar, he told them how Lothar had prophesied that they would be having peace in two months. On the strength of the coming peace they had all stood up and clinked glasses. After the meal Hans had rung up Ursel and Elma, and had been invited by them to bring his comrades along and spend the evening with them. He then rang up Margaretensee, but by this time Werner and the others were already sitting with his father in the garden. Of this Volkenborn was very glad, as he hardly knew exactly what he was going to say. It was quite a long time before he heard an answering voice, a voice that sounded quite strange to him.

"Anneliese Lengerke speaking."

He had hesitated a moment before he replied "Hans — Volkenborn speaking."

He had originally intended to say "Hans," but he had not had the courage to leave the Volkenborn out. Their conversation at an end, he returned with a smile on his face, and joined his father and his friends in the garden.

III

Arrived at Döberitz, the Junkers were posted to their units. The course was divided between three battalions, to which the Junkers of the different regiments were allotted. Volkenborn soon grew accustomed to the life.

It is an essential part of the soldier's calling to be able to deal with any situation and make himself at home everywhere. To none is this easier than to a healthy young man who is not given to reflecting too profoundly. But to such a one this life has definite dangers. All that is normal, regular and homely in him is suppressed, and, on the other hand, adventurous and nomadic instincts are developed. To the soldier in the field, every day brings some new situation, and nothing seems lasting. The morrow brings constant changes. For this reason he accepts all the day has to offer him of good or bad, and worries but little about the future. To be ready for everything is his most essential quality. But necessary as these qualities are on active service, they are calculated to unfit him for civilian life. However adaptive he may prove himself, will he ever again be able to settle down to an organized and peaceful existence. Such a transition may be easier for the older men, but for the youngster who has passed the most impressionable years of his life in active service it will prove in many cases impossible.

Among his new comrades there were some to whom Volkenborn at once took a fancy, but most of them were of such a different temperament to himself as to prove unsympathetic. Nevertheless, much as he disliked their characteristics and peculiarities, he still realized that they were his comrades, that there was a tie which bound them together, despite all personal differences.

It was this bond of comradeship which was the redeeming feature of life at the Front. This simple, sober, elementary, and yet strong tie of sympathy that united one man to another, was the one good thing that stood out like a ray of sunshine from a background of misery and horror.

But it soon dawned on Hans Volkenborn that comradeship at home was a very different thing from comradeship at the Front. Of course, the matter might be a purely individual one, and in this connection he often recalled Pietschmann and Baluschek. They were rough uneducated men, whose speech was full of ungrammatical eccentricities; in peace time one was a journeyman butcher and the other a fisherman's assistant. But such as they were, he had been able to give them a whole-hearted liking and confidence, and, despite a certain coarseness and other peculiarities that he sometimes found rather trying, he recognized that there was much in their characters that was worthy of respect. Perhaps his present comrades were too young; perhaps he had become spoilt by having been in the company of men older than himself. Or was it that they were too frivolous, did not take things seriously enough, and were lacking in manly qualities? Anyhow, strive as he would, he could find no bond of sympathy between them and him, and, under these circumstances, all he could do was to make up his mind just to accept them and to decide that their personal qualities were no concern of his.

The company officer, Captain von Cassel, was not exactly distasteful to him, but what he did not like was his stereotyped smile; a smile that his face always wore when he inspected their rooms, or when the company paraded in the morning; a smile of which it was difficult to say whether it expressed friendliness or a certain amount of duplicity. To Volkenborn, the captain was always extremely affable, and, on the occasion of the first guest evening at the mess, he placed Volkenborn next to the battalion commander, who was the guest of the evening. This, of course, was an unusual distinction. But Volkenborn was not greatly impressed, realizing that this honor was firstly due to the fact that he was the possessor of a very smart new uniform — which he had ordered from a first-class military tailor in Bruges — secondly, to the ribbon of the Iron Cross that nestled in his buttonhole; and thirdly, because he was one of those fortunate beings who readily found their tongue in strange company.

The three inspection officers were men of totally different types, but were pleasant and good fellows. Lieutenant Herting of the First Company, to which Volkenborn belonged, was rather of the stiff and dry order, but even he had to acknowledge himself conquered by Volkenborn's ingratiating smile. Lieutenant von Rettwitz was the typical society officer, elegant, amiable and good-looking; he wore corsets, played the 'cello, and had delightful manners. The third inspection officer was Lieutenant Frey, a fair man with an aquiline nose and an impertinent manner of looking people up and down. Although personally less engaging than his two fellow officers, he obtained better results on parade than either of them, and was, furthermore, an expert at all games and sports, a fact that greatly added to his popularity.

A fortnight before Christmas Volkenborn was promoted to noncommissioned rank. He had been disappointed at not having had this promotion conferred on him while he was at the Front, and he now treated this distinction with an assumption of disdain and said nothing about it in his letters home, so that his parents were only apprised of the fact by his prefixing his noncommissioned rank to his name on the outside of the envelope, as is the custom in Germany.

The burning question of the day was Christmas leave, and it was announced that only those Junkers were to have leave who lived in Berlin, or to be the guests of some one living there. This decision was received with much growling and grumbling. Volkenborn said nothing, but at once developed a scheme for meeting the difficulty. He hurried off to Eichholz, who had been allocated to the Third Battalion, and discussed the matter with him. As the result of the conference he was enabled, three days later, to show his captain a letter from Frau von Eichholz, in which she invited him to spend Christmas at her house in Berlin. At the same time, he wired his parents to send him a complete suit of mufti, and his school cap to the Central Hotel in Berlin, adding by the way of explanation, "We are planning a Christmas surprise." He was granted a week's leave in Berlin.

At noon, he entered the hotel in uniform; and, as the afternoon was merging into twilight, came out again in "civvies," and wearing the red cap that indicates a sixth form boy in a German school, carrying a light gray ulster and swinging a malacca cane. He made various purchases in the Friedrickstrasse and nine o'clock in the evening found him in the railway waiting room of the Lehrter Bahnhof. He had found it impossible to get a ticket for the express train, so he was obliged to wait for the slow train, which did not start till eleven o'clock. Perhaps it would be as well if he walked up and down the dark platform, instead of inviting recognition by sitting in the waiting room. There was a further danger: this train stopped at Döberitz, and he would have to run the risk of being seen and recognized by one of his officers. However, he was feeling in a happy-go-lucky mood, sure of the effectiveness of the disguise, and above all attracted by the risk he was running.

In the waiting room he hung his red cap up on a peg and stared about him. He was enjoying a sense of dual personality which pleased him immensely: one moment a Fahnenjunker, and the next a schoolboy. Officers came in and out; soldiers passed his table and sat down here and there, looking past him, scarcely seeming to see him. He felt delighted. "If they only knew!" he thought. What a difference clothes did make!

He smoked one cigarette after another, drank several glasses of grog, and drew sketches on the little round mats that accompanied each drink; he read the menu from one end to the other, went and fetched an illustrated paper, dipped into a novel that he had with him, and then wrote his name and the number of his regiment on its flyleaf. Then, not knowing what else to do, he ordered a cup of coffee.

Whilst he was stirring it he suddenly saw Lieutenant Frey come into the waiting room and walk towards his table! A cold shudder ran down his back and he looked in another direction, stirring his coffee mechanically. With his eyes still cast down he could see the lieutenant's patent leather boots approaching his table. He still kept his eyes lowered, and a moment afterwards the boots had disappeared.

At last, he ventured to look up and sip some of his coffee. He had made up his mind not to let this episode worry him, so he walked over to his overcoat, took a box of matches from his pocket, and lighted up another cigarette.

The lieutenant was sitting only three tables away from him, and, without actually looking at him he became aware that the officer was regarding him intently. Now was the opportunity to show how cool he could be. Everything was at stake. Obviously, the lieutenant thought that he had recognized him, so the only thing to do was to bluff it out, either make him doubtful of his identity, or failing that, impress him with his daring. If he had any decency in him, he would then feel obliged to pretend not to recognize him.

Quite calmly Volkenborn finished his cigarette, signed to the waiter, paid, thrust his newspapers into his pocket, put his novel under his arm, took his red cap from the peg, and then sauntered slowly and indifferently out of the waiting room.

The train was already standing waiting beside the platform, and he selected a second-class carriage at the far end. It had a lavatory compartment. He wondered whether he should take refuge in it; then resolved not to do so, as it would be at least half an hour before the train would start, and there was no sense in making himself unnecessarily uncomfortable. Should the danger of discovery become acute, he could always bolt in at the last moment.

Fortunately, there was not a single lamp alight throughout the whole train, for light had to be used sparingly in those days. It was frightfully cold and the windows were all frosted over, so he began stamping with his feet on the floor, and two civilians, who had got into the same compartment, began to do the same thing. The guard came along and examined their tickets. Then a lady with many trunks and packages got in. "Another food hog!" thought Volkenborn. She carried on a long farewell conversation with a lady, and by this means he learned the main facts about her family history, his ears strained all the time for the approaching footsteps of the lieutenant. But his anxiety proved unnecessary, as they had evidently entered another carriage.

The train was late in starting, and Volkenborn soon forgot all about the lieutenant. One of his fellow travellers asked him for a light, and they entered into a conversation about the scarcity of tobacco, about standing in food queues, about the perpetual artillery struggle in Flanders, about speeches in the Reichstag, and bank managers who had been brought home as indispensable. "I suppose you are one of those who have been recalled as indispensable?" Volkenborn innocently asked one of the two men — a stout person with an obtrusive watchchain and an aggressive cold in his head. To this the stout gentleman made no reply but began to talk about the wonderful deeds that were being performed at Verdun. "They are heroes," he said, "Each one of them is a hero!" and as he spoke his voice shook with admiration and emotion. A malicious answer rose to Volkenborn's lips, but he kept it back, smiled, and once more busied himself with his own thoughts. After all, what business of his was a miserable slacker like this? The next day, at the same hour he would be sitting talking to Anneliese, holding her hand, listening to her voice. He could hardly realize it.

IV

In the hall, he had exchanged a few words with Anneliese's father. The old gentleman was going

off to an important agricultural meeting, and
treated Volkenborn as an old friend with whom
one does not stand on ceremony. After Frau
Lengerke had given him tea and plied him with a
number of questions, she left him alone with Anneliese.

The long-hoped-for moment had arrived, and the
result was they both were tongue-tied! Conscious of
the sound of his own breathing, his eyes wandered
from his teacup to Anneliese's hands, which lay
folded in her lap, to her shoes, to the clock — and
still no suitable words would come to him. Then, in
despair, he looked into her blue eyes and she gave
him an answering smile.

Despite this smile, he was unable to throw off a
feeling of restraint and shyness; none of the things
that he had been planning for weeks to say to her,
would come to his tongue, and so they sat, like two
children, their hearts full of sentiment which they
lacked the experience to express. In despair at his
inability to recall any of the many things he had
meant to speak of to her, he stood up and fidgeted
with the plates on the tea table while she sat waiting for him to speak with her hands on her lap,
smiling at him. At last he sank into his seat again
and began desperately: "I can still hardly realize. . . ."

Christmas Eve in Arnstadt.
Volkenborn accompanied his parents to church.
He wore his best helmet, the ribbon of his Iron

Cross, and a new greatcoat with real buttons and silk-embroidered shoulder straps.

As always on this night, two tall Christmas trees stood one on either side of the altar. The verger was lighting the wax candles, and Hans sat watching the reflections of their light on the vaulted roof of the church and on the whitewashed walls. He saw too how they fell on the congregation, illuminating the faces of the children.

Looking round, his eyes met those of Ursel and Elma, and silent greetings passed between them. Watching the golden glow of the candles, a strange feeling of love, happiness, and thankfulness overcame him. He was back again at home! He had fought for his country and he had been spared to return again. This church, with its two tall, slender pine trees placed beside the altar, from which fell the chaste light of many wax candles, was for him a symbol of home — of that home for which men were suffering and dying; for which he had fought and suffered.

With the rest of the congregation he raised up his voice in thanksgiving, and sang with his whole heart; high above the other voices rose the pure treble of the children's voices, but disillusion came with the sermon, which seemed to him to strike a miserable and depressing note, and to be entirely lacking in that force and conviction that alone brings comfort in a time of need like this.

The text was "Lord, have mercy upon us!" What a text for a Christmas sermon in a country whose manhood had been fighting for its very existence for three years past! To wail and moan from the pulpit on such an occasion at such a time was surely not what was expected of any minister of God. Such sentiments, if expressed at all, should be kept within the four walls of the rectory. From the pulpit they were nothing less than treason, and a man, like this parson, who could so fail to rise to the needs and dignity of the occasion, who lacked the patriotism and perception to realize that strength, self-reliance and courage were what was needed; that the belief most essential now was faith in our cause and in its ultimate victory; the belief that God himself was on the side of the brave, the steadfast and the enduring — a man in whom all such feelings were wanting was surely not fit to speak to a congregation on Christmas Eve, of all days, in the third year of the war! On such a day, to utter feeble, cowardly platitudes was surely a crime, not only in the eyes of the people, but in those of the God of Battles!

As he listened to the preacher's colorless words, the blood began to boil in his veins, and at the lachrymose end of the sermon the words "stupid old bleater" escaped him involuntarily.

No sooner had he said it than he could have cut his tongue out. How tactless, how abominable of him to have so spoken in the house of God, and on Christmas Eve, of all times! But the pardonable irritation that he had felt at the wretched, depressing, cowardly tone of the whole sermon had proved too strong for him, and he had been unable to control himself.

His father, sitting beside him, must have heard his exclamation, but he hoped that no one else had done so. His father had said nothing, but checked him with a movement of his hand, and had then coughed.

He felt so ashamed of himself that he could not find courage to join in with the first verse of the hymn that followed, but gradually the whole atmosphere of the place, the Christmas trees and the candles, and the children's voices, acted as a sedative to his overwrought nerves, and by the end of the hymn he was singing with the rest of them and letting the Christmas spirit gradually enfold him.

The next morning, he stole out of the house while it was still dark. As the crisp snow crunched under his tread he looked up at the gable windows of the Villa Scholander, but the curtains were still drawn. How could he expect any one else to be up at six o'clock on Christmas morning?

The snow lay thick on the ground, the full moon was still high over the horizon, and the stars were shining brightly. The moonlight was reflected in the snow in thousands of dazzling red and golden crystals, and his footsteps rang out sharply on the frozen ground.

Passing through the village, he met one of the farm girls crossing the yard with a lantern in her hand, and he stood and watched the play of the light on the snow. The barking of a dog and the crowing of a cock awoke him from his reverie, and he hastened onward, breathing in the clear bracing air of a frosty Christmas morning.

A pale light spread over the heavens, making them seem still more remote, and in the east the sun began to rise; a red ball that gradually threw a pink shimmer over the landscape, and left the woods in violet shadow, which gave place to blue as the light grew stronger.

By the time he had reached the main road, the bells were already ringing out from Margaretensee, and a great black crow was swooping downward to a field. He watched it as it folded its wings and began hopping over the ground in little short bursts. Not a soul was to be seen along the roads, and just before he reached Margaretensee he turned off into the woods.

Even the cart tracks were snowed up, and it looked as if it had been many a day since any one had passed that way. The snow was so pure and white that he found himself walking reverently over it, but his footsteps seemed a desecration; the presence of a human being was robbing the winter landscape of its charm.

In time he came to a piled-up heap of wood, from which a hare bolted, frightened by his presence. There was something wonderful, something romantic in being the only human being afoot in this snow-clad wood on Christmas morning.

With his sleeve he brushed the snow off the wood,

sat down with his chin on his hand, glanced at his wrist watch, and then again at the woods, which lay before him. He sat listening; listening to the steps that he could hear drawing near; like a melody running through his soul; steps for which he had long been listening.

Anneliese stood before him, brown hair glinting in the sun; giving him both her hands, she wished him a merry Christmas.

Hand in hand they walked, now looking at the snow beneath their feet, now glancing shyly into each others' eyes. What beautiful blue eyes she had; in them he seemed to see the whole glory of the Christmas morning.

A deer broke cover and flashed across the road. In front of them was a clearing on which sunshine and shadow were playing with wonderful effects; like golden rain dropping from the clear vault of heaven.

His arm stole round her shoulder, and with her head bent back against his breast, they wandered on, speaking but little.

"I seemed to have so much to tell you, and now it has all gone out of my head," he said.

"What need have we of speech?" she replied. "We know one another too well for words; let the stillness of the woods speak for us."

The bells of Margaretensee were still chiming as they turned back, and found themselves again on the high road. Before leaving the wood, they stood looking at one another; then Anneliese gently released her hands, first laid them on his shoulders, and then took his face between them.

They kissed; a kiss as shy and timid as the dawn.

As Volkenborn was coming back from reporting his return from leave to his company commander, he met Lieutenant Frey, who remarked in his usual insolent manner, "So your cheek carried you through successfully, Volkenborn?"

"*Zu Befehl,*[1] Herr Lieutenant," was his reply.

He was a decent sort, after all, was Lieutenant Frey.

V

On New Year's Eve Volkenborn was invited by one of his comrades to spend the evening in the house of his cousin, Frau von Leczinsky, of whom he had often heard the others speak. As another Fahnenjunker, little Rossberg, was to be of the party, Volkenborn mustered up his courage and accepted.

Rossberg was a pleasant youth, whose complexion and eyes many a girl might have envied, and a thin small voice that also had something feminine in it. His great grief in life was that he was serving in a transport corps, but as the only son and heir of his family, he was not allowed in the front line.

In the afternoon they sat in a café, after having paid a formal call on Frau von Leczinsky, who was

---

[1] "At your service." The prescribed form for addressing a military superior.

not at home, or at least had been invisible. They wrote the usual post cards and showed each other pictures of their mothers and sisters.

At seven o'clock they duly presented themselves in the drawing-room of their hostess, rather shy and ill at ease, but the vivid and charming personality of Frau von Leczinsky soon made Volkenborn feel quite at home, and to his surprise he found himself entertaining her with anecdotes about the Front and about Döberitz.

She was in the early thirties, very dark, her striking blue eyes framed in becoming dark circles; her long lashes, and the expression of her face produced a fascinating effect. Like all brunettes of her type she had a dark, almost olive complexion and full red lips that were always slightly parted. Her emerald green gown was sleeveless and décolleté.

The rather daring cut of her gown disturbed Volkenborn, and, whenever his eyes rested on it, it seemed to bring his conversational ability to a stop; however, he had evidently made a good impression on her, for she asked him to take her into supper.

The supper was a regular banquet, and they sat long over it, drinking potent wines until Volkenborn began to feel excited, and everything to his eyes seemed to take on a changed aspect. The candles in the four-branched candelabra began to look as if they had a halo round them, the silver and glass seemed to glitter more brightly than before, and even the flowers looked strange.

There seemed to be something odd too about the

way the people were moving their hands, and their voices came to him as if from a distance. Little Rossberg was always smiling across at him and raising his glass to him.

Frau von Leczinsky, an amiable and charming hostess, kept filling his glass, and as she did so he noticed that her hand had a nervous tremor. Whenever she laughed, the sound seemed to intoxicate him even more than the wine. It was a provocative laugh, and like nothing he had heard before. It sparkled like champagne. In the course of conversation she would lay her hand on his shoulder, on his arm; she whispered some joke about her cousin into his ear; some remark about the audacious way in which he was flirting with his neighbor, or about little Rossberg, whose cheeks were looking so rosy and bright. At each touch of her hand, the blood rushed into his cheeks; he looked smilingly into her eyes, and then turned away again, for there was something in her expression which startled him.

Once she dropped her handkerchief, and, as Volkenborn bent to recover it, she stooped too, so that her hair brushed his temple and he could see her white bosom within her low gown, and inhale the warm perfume of her body. When he handed her handkerchief to her his face was scarlet.

After supper, the guests amused themselves according to their different tastes. Frau von Leczinsky's cousin turned his attention again to the wine, little Rossberg amused himself with the grama-phone, and Volkenborn assisted with the preparation of champagne cup, a task on which he rather prided himself. They danced, they drank, they flirted, but Volkenborn was too well-disciplined to let himself go beyond the normal limits, although the wine he had taken had gone to his head. As the clock struck twelve, they all stood up, clinked glasses, and drank to the New Year, and Volkenborn, as he did so, thought of Anneliese. When he danced with his hostess, the contact of her body excited him.

"Would you like to come and see my pictures?" she asked him. The walls of the study were covered with photographs and daguerreotypes of a former generation. They walked through the library and into the music room, where two pictures by modern artists were hanging. Volkenborn knew something about these artists and was glad to be able to talk about them. Frau von Leczinsky kept close behind him, and he could feel her breath upon his cheek. Once, moving clumsily, his shoulder touched her bosom, and she smiled at his apology.

"I have still one more picture to show you, perhaps the best of all." They passed into a bedroom, where some exotic perfume seemed to flood his nostrils and almost suffocated him. The electric bulbs were concealed in silk shades, and the room, which was thickly carpeted and curtained, was only dimly lighted. He had never seen such a room before, and involuntarily glanced nervously towards the door.

There were so many shadows in the room that he found it difficult to see the picture. He wanted to say that it was badly hung, that it was too high, that the light —

Words seemed to stick in his throat.

Her hand fell on his shoulder, and, as he turned as though to confront some hidden danger, he felt her arms around his neck, her soft body pressed passionately against him, his lips were closed by her kisses.

Without thinking, he wrenched himself away from her, pushed her away from him, and made for the door, but, with the handle in his hand, something seemed to make him turn towards her again, and he saw that she was standing motionless, both hands pressed to her forehead.

He released the door knob, the blood mounted to his head. With inward terror, he found himself drawing near to her again. Some power, against which he fought in vain, seemed attracting him. Was it pity, or was it passion?

Her hands fell from her forehead and she stretched them out as though to ward him off. "Go!" she said. "Please go!"

But he felt that he could not leave her like this, and that the fault must, in some way, be his, and that he must attempt to atone for it. "Forgive me!" he said, taking her outstretched hands in his. Then words failed him. He saw that she was deadly pale and he led her to the sofa, where, thinking she was about to faint, he chafed the palms of her hands, to which she submitted without a word. For a long time they sat side by side, in silence.

Suddenly she began to speak, whispering, so that her voice seemed to him to come from a great distance. Hesitatingly, with many interruptions, speaking disconnectedly, and even as though she had forgotten that he was there, as though this whispering voice were not her own, but one that she herself was listening to.

Then he felt her tears upon his hand, and although she had ceased speaking, he could still hear her whisper sounding in his ears, could still hear things that he had never dreamed to hear from a woman's lips.

Then he became conscious that she was bending over him, that she kissed him gently on the brow. Like a child, ashamed and overcome, he threw his arms around her neck.

Early next morning Rossberg and Volkenborn were on the way to the station. They had an hour's journey before them, but neither seemed inclined to talk.

New Year's day was a holiday and they were free of all military duty, so they had some coffee and decided to go to sleep for a while. But Volkenborn found sleep impossible. What was he to think of this unhappy woman? In vain he sought some solution: he could find none.

Alexander Leczinsky — her husband — had joined up on the first day of the mobilization. His marriage had been neither an unhappy nor a happy one, but there had always seemed something want-

ing, something that they both lacked. She had longed
for a child, which she thought would have filled
the gap in their lives. But their only child died,
though not before she had realized that, although
she had loved and cared for her little one, it could
not wholly satisfy this insatiable longing. Once she
had loved her husband passionately, but now there
remained nothing but a kind of friendship between
them, friendship to which they both held loyally;
but the very intimacy of this friendship became a
new source of misery to her. She knew his whole life,
his whole nature, as one knows the room in which
one passes the greater part of one's life. It was so
circumscribed, one day so like another. She always
knew exactly what was going to happen. When this
monotonous sameness seemed to be strangling her,
there came the excitement of the first months of the
war. For her, their enforced separation was like
entering upon a new life. The general feeling of tension distracted her thoughts from her own trouble,
and she devoted herself to hospital work. For a
while she was content, but the war lasted so long
and — again came that feeling of restlessness, of
longing for something unobtainable. Always there
seemed to be something lacking in her life, and she
could find nothing with which to fill this gap. Then
her husband was invalided home from the Front —
not wounded, but suffering from some troublesome
disorder that caused him much pain — she hastened
to him, nursed him, watched over him devotedly,
and he was grateful. Scarcely was he well again than

he returned to duty — and found the death that he sought.

Again she had devoted herself to hospital work. Again she sought some means with which to fill up this everlasting gap in her life. She had many admirers and loved one of them, but, as she had feared, he too was killed. On the night when he died she had clearly known what was going to happen, and took what she had thought to be an overdose of veronal, but recovered. Then a madness of passion seized upon her, a veritable dance of death; an intoxication of surrender, an insatiable longing for love. Her passion had been, above all, for the very young lads, those destined to die without ever having known what love was, those who were going to their death with the innocence of childhood still in their eyes. They attracted her; it was on such as these that she had lavished her passion, so that they at least might know what life was. And, one by one, they had met their fate. "Death had marked them for its own, and my love seemed fatal to them all."

Hans Volkenborn, although he could not understand much that this strange woman had told him, was deeply moved by sympathy for her. Nevertheless such a temperament was a mystery to him. If her husband had been such a man as she described, why had she made him so unhappy? Had she found that which she was looking for in the lover who had been killed? If she had really loved him, how could she possibly have brought herself to lead a life of wild passionate adventure, after his death? Such a temperament was quite incomprehensible to him.

In his mind he once more went over all the episodes of the evening before. It was all firmly impressed on his memory, from the strange mixture of admiration and repulsion with which his first speech with her had filled him, to the moment when she had kissed him so passionately. As though in a dream, he could still see her bending over him, could scent the perfume that she used, and feel the passion of her body.

VI

The next morning, Captain von Cassel appointed Volkenborn company leader. That all orders should be given by the Junkers themselves and the work of the Battalion carried out by them was part of the scheme of training; the officers merely stood by, to see that everything was done correctly.

As the captain passed down the line, there was something in the expression of his eyes, something in the sarcastic curl of his lips that warned Volkenborn what was about to take place. Consequently, he was not surprised when he was told to carry on.

"*Zu Befehl,* Herr Hauptmann. Attention! The company will take its orders from me! Number off by fours! Right wheel! Quick march."

For Volkenborn it was an unpleasant experience, as the captain sought in every way to catch him napping. Once he pulled his horse round suddenly.

"Look out, man, or I shall ride you down!"

But Volkenborn held his ground as the horse galloped down on him. You can ride me down if you like, he thought, but you can't frighten me!

At the last moment the charger swerved to one side. The captain blustered and brandished his whip, but Volkenborn kept cool. After all, he can't eat me, he thought.

Once he failed to speak sharply enough to a Junker who had not understood his order, and the captain began to bluster again. All right thought Volkenborn, I can play that game too! Without the slightest consideration, he shouted his orders to the company, speaking in the same harsh aggressive tone that the captain himself used, even using the exact expressions that were habitual with that officer. His comrades glanced at him, half angrily, half in delight at his reckless impudence. When one of the Junkers — podgy little Graf Klettenstein — who was a special favorite of the captain, made a false turn, Volkenborn was down on him in an instant.

"Klettenstein — man, I shall ride you down! You are going to sleep where you stand!"

Volkenborn led the company back into camp, reported, and dismissed them. Rossberg patted him on the shoulder and whispered a word of encouragement and consolation into his ear, to which Volkenborn replied, "He needn't think he's going to upset me, not much!"

He had just put his rifle in the rack and hung up his belt when the captain entered the room.

The senior Junker made his report, and the captain walked down the row of beds, beside which, as prescribed by the regulations, the Junkers were all standing at "Attention."

Volkenborn thought, Now he's going to put it across me, put it across me before the whole lot of them! If he were a decent fellow he would say what he's got to say to me privately. Anyhow, I'll show him that I'm not afraid of him!

Prepared for the worst, he waited for the officer to come to him. The captain stood before him, smiling that unpleasant sarcastic smile of his that Volkenborn hated so. Pulling himself together, he stared coolly into the eyes of his superior, but something in the situation tickled his sense of humor, and involuntarily his habitual smile came to his lips.

Whatever the cause, whether it was something really comic in the whole situation, or whether it was merely the result of that old habit of his that had so often got him into trouble in his school days, he did not know.

For a moment the captain stood staring at him in silence, then with two fingers he took hold of one of the buttons of his tunic, advanced his face quite close to Volkenborn's, then suddenly turned away, remarking in a tone which was a mixture of sarcasm and approval, "I shall hand in your name for promotion to the rank of Fähnrich," and then strode out of the room with much jingling of spurs.

There was a regimental order to the effect that

the Junkers were to be medically examined every Monday. This was the result of the appalling prevalence of a certain infectious disease among the men. Volkenborn and Rossberg had always managed to evade this extremely unpleasant examination by adroit maneuvering that enabled them to slip through the noncommissioned officer's hands, whose duty it was to call the roll. "If the commanding officer gave me the order in person, I should refuse to obey it; wild horses wouldn't drag me to such an inspection," he said on one occasion.

It was these inspections that, without his realizing it, created a new atmosphere, and in some extraordinary way seemed to react on the relationship between him and his comrades. A suspicious feeling, a feeling quite contrary to his nature, began to form in his mind. It had its inception in these medical inspections, and gradually led to his noticing things that had hitherto escaped his attention.

VII

The Sunday leave to Berlin always made a pleasant break, an agreeable relaxation from the tedium of their daily duties. Usually Volkenborn went to Berlin by himself, and only occasionally with Werner or Rossberg, who both had relatives living there.

He generally passed Sunday afternoon in strolling about the streets, looking in the windows of the booksellers, or spending an hour over a cup of coffee and a cigarette in one of the big cafés, where he had an opportunity of reading all the principal newspapers. When he had finished the papers, there were always the people to look at, and so pass an hour or so until it was time to return to his hotel, where he had supper, and afterwards went to a picture palace, or occasionally to a theater.

But the chief delight of a day or two on leave in Berlin was the hotel bedroom, the white bed, the sofa, the carpet, the telephone, and above all the bathroom. On Sundays he would sleep till nine o'clock, that is to say, he would wake up at six, get out of bed, wash, brush his teeth, and smarten himself up, and then hop back into bed again and lie dreaming, half asleep and half awake.

To him, this thinking and dreaming in bed was the happiest time of the whole day. It was so jolly to lie there, not actually asleep, but just thinking lazily about the pleasant bath that was to follow, about dressing at his ease without any necessity for hurrying. And then when he fell into a half dream, it was a dream of which he himself selected the subject. Usually on these occasions he lay and thought of Anneliese; of early morning walks with her at Margaretensee, through the woods and across the heath. Then he would recall a musical evening that he had spent in the Villa Scholander with Ursel and Elma. His thoughts would stray off to his coming promotion to commissioned rank; to his parents, to Christmas day, to his dog, to an excursion he had made a year or two ago with his father; or he re-

called all the news in the last letters he had received
from Kurt and Lothar. It was all so quiet there,
and nothing disturbed the play of his fancy but the
occasional footsteps of a passing chambermaid.

And then at nine o'clock would come the expected
knock at the door and the maid would tell him his
bath was ready. He would then jump out of bed,
put on his dressing gown, and hurry along the corridor.

There was nothing much to distinguish this bathroom from other bathrooms, but it always seemed
cleaner and brighter than any other he had ever
known. Besides, there was a great full-length mirror, which for him, after the bath, was the chief
thing.

Every morning after the bath he would stand in
front of it, doing his physical exercises and watching the play of his muscles. Often he would repeat
one exercise many times so that he might study its
effects on a particular group of muscles. At other
times he would stand motionless in front of the
glass, noting the line of his shoulders, comparing
the proportions of head, throat, torso, and legs.
He would extend his arms, watch the expansion of
his chest and the enlargement of his shoulder
muscles, and then, with the aid of a handglass, would
study the muscles of his back. From week to week
he was able to note a steady development in his
whole physique.

After the bath he would dress himself carefully,
taking his time about it; it was good to be able to

dress at leisure after being obliged to rush through the whole process in half an hour at Döberitz. He took delight in the use of *Eau de Cologne,* and a slightly perfumed face cream. He would shave himself, not that he really needed it, but because he enjoyed the process, loved to feel the lather and the keen razor blade on his face. After all, there would soon be a time when he would have none of these luxuries, when he would be back again in the trenches in Flanders, or somewhere in France, with no carpets under his feet and no bed to sleep on; where there would be constant night attacks, shells bursting around him, dead and dying men on all sides. Small wonder then that Volkenborn loved to enjoy these creature comforts while he could.

At about eleven o'clock it was his custom to take his breakfast in the coffeeroom. If officers were there, he acknowledged their presence with an easy and courteous inclination of the head that could hardly be described as a bow, and made a point of omitting to click his heels in the prescribed manner — a mode of greeting which he considered only suitable for the parade ground. It always annoyed him greatly if an officer failed to return his greeting or acknowledged it in a slovenly and discourteous manner. He was so sensitive on this point that he would worry about it for the rest of the day.

After breakfast he usually went to the writing room, where he wrote innumerable letters on his thin, pale blue paper; smoking cigarettes, pausing to watch what others in the room were doing, and adding amusing comments on their peculiarities to his letter. If a pretty girl gave him a friendly look, he would say something about it in his letter to Anneliese — but phrasing his comment carefully to show that he had neither eyes nor thoughts for any one but herself.

On the first Sunday in the New Year, after having idled luxuriously over his bath and his toilet, he was sitting in the writing room, penning a reply to a letter from Ursel, before going to his lunch. She had written to tell him that Elma and her parents would probably be visiting Berlin soon. Volkenborn was delighted at the prospect, and had just begun a reply — full of superlatives and notes of exclamation — when a waiter came to tell him that he was wanted on the telephone.

At first, he thought she had already arrived and was ringing him up, but as he followed the waiter to the telephone call box, something seemed to tell him that it was not Elma.

"Is that Herr Volkenborn? Margrit Leczinsky speaking. Can you spend the afternoon with me? Do say that you can, please! We will go for a spin in the car. Only an hour, or even half an hour, if you are pressed for time. Please, don't refuse! I'll call for you with the car at three o'clock. Good-by!"

As he went back across the lounge he wondered how Frau von Leczinsky came to know where he was staying? Had she obtained his address from her cousin? Why had she invited him? And if she wanted

to see him, why had she not rung him up earlier?
She seemed to him to have spoken hurriedly, in a
tone of suppressed excitement. What had he said in
reply? He could hardly remember; had scarcely
known what he was saying; had answered mechanically "yes."

She held his hand for a moment, and the car
started. Volkenborn recognized a street, a square,
or some building that he knew, but all the while
this excursion seemed unreal; he was chiefly conscious of the hum of the car. Through the windows
he seemed to see everything as in a dream; it was
almost like sitting in a picture palace and watching a film unfold before his eyes, a foggy, confused
sort of film that was being wound so quickly that he
could not follow it.

He threw a glance at the chauffeur, noting his
gray mutton-chop whiskers and the ruddy hue of his
otherwise clean-shaven face. With a queer sort of
mechanical interest he watched the man's hand on
the wheel, glanced at the clock, at the speedometer
with its vibrating indicator, and then stared at a
suspended crystal vase with its bunch of red carna-
tions. How the petals trembled with the vibration of
the car!

Frau von Leczinsky held one of his hands in both
of hers. She wore a fur coat, and he sensed something seductive and enervating in the warmth and
softness that seemed to radiate from her.

After a time, he removed his cap, and stole a
glance at her. When her head sank on his shoulder,

he set his lips, and stared stolidly in front of him —
at the trees of the boulevard down which they were
passing.

The chauffeur turned the car, and they were on
their way back.

"Won't you come in and have tea with me?" she
asked suddenly.

He nodded, looked at his watch, and nodded
again.

"With pleasure. My train goes at six, and I must
not miss it, but I still have time."

They had tea together, her personal maid serving them. Just as she had removed the tray, Frau
von Leczinsky rose.

"Do you want anything — shall I ring?" he
asked.

"No, thank you. I'll get it myself. She has forgotten my medicine."

How beautiful she is! he thought, as his eyes followed her through the door. How black silk becomes
her!

"I often have heart attacks, — that is what this
powder is for. They're very good," she explained,
on her return to the room.

She opened one of the little folded papers and
shook the contents out into a glass.

He would have liked to ask her if it were not
dangerous to take such a large dose, but his courage failed him.

In silence she looked at him for a moment, and
then she raised the glass and drank.

"Why did you come so late into my life? Too late, much too late!"

For all answer he bowed low over her hand. How strange it seemed! Gently she passed her other hand over his bowed head.

"How kind and gentle you are! But you must go, or you will miss your train. You mustn't lose it on — "

He had still time and to spare, and still lingered, striving to console her.

"No, dear, please go! It's better so. I'm feeling better now. See, I'm quite calm again."

She stood up, and again he kissed her hand. As he did so, he could feel it trembling.

"What is it? Are you feeling ill? You ought to go and lie down." For the first time he addressed her with the familiar German *"Du."*

"I will. I'll lie down for a little, lie down directly you're gone. I'm feeling tired—very tired."

Then she kissed him.

The next day at noon, Fahnenjunker von Rechow, the cousin of Frau von Leczinsky, received a telegram and hurried off to Berlin by the next train. As Volkenborn learned that evening, the captain had given him three days' leave. Frau von Leczinsky had had another heart attack, and it was likely to prove a fatal one, Rossberg said.

The news came as a shock to Volkenborn. He could still see her shaking the powder packet into a glass, still hear her saying, "You came too late into my life, much too late!"

Greatly worried, he avoided his comrades, and
went out. There were no stars, and all was dark
and gloomy.

VIII

There followed dull, unhappy days, — days in
which he hardly took enough interest in life to in-
quire if there were any letters for him. It was a time
of solitary evening walks, of sleepless nights, of
ugly cruel dreams. Rechow came back at the end of
his three days, but Volkenborn did not venture on
more than a casual inquiry as to his cousin's health.
The only one of the Junkers with whom he was intimate was Rossberg, and even to him he spoke but
little.

But Volkenborn was young, and youth recovers
quickly. Life calls for its rights; Hans Volkenborn
was a soldier, and the service demanded his full attention.

They had machine-gun drill, and many of his comrades were tyros at the work. He, in his turn, found
himself behind the gun. No sooner was his hand
on the lever than the officer inquired, "It's not the
first time you've served a machine gun?" Then he
fired: of a hundred rounds, eighty-four were hits,
distributed equally over the whole target. "You
shoot splendidly," said the lieutenant. Volkenborn
took a deep breath and laughed; Rossberg con-
gratulated him on his skill.

Other things occupied his attention. On the occasion of their field-service drill, one of the Junkers, Spindler, was ordered by the captain to drill the company. Spindler was a Bavarian, quite a simple sort of lad from a mountain village, where his father was the local school-master. He was poor, but a fine fellow, powerfully built, with fair hair and small dark eyes. His movements were swift, sudden, but clumsy. Always anxious to do his best, he was nervous and awkward and never seemed sure of himself. Although he was serving as a Junker, and was therefore ultimately to become an officer and the comrade of officers, he could not suppress his "inferiority complex," as Klettenstein called it.

The captain did not like him and started to bully him, as he had done with Volkenborn; but Spindler lacked Volkenborn's coolness and *savoir faire*. Without a doubt, Spindler would make a good soldier under fire at the Front, but all this maneuvering in the field ground, these unpleasant tricks of the captain, completely upset him, and he became nervous and excited. He ran aimlessly about, and did everything that an officer in command of a company — which he was supposed to be at the moment — should not do. The captain was always shouting at him, brandishing his riding whip, bullying, leaning down from his horse and pushing him on. As Spindler gave his commands, his whole body trembled with anxiety, and his voice shook. He gave one order, and the captain shouted out something different, the result being that the company fell into complete disorder.

"Potato peeling is your job, not soldiering! You'll never make an officer, you clumsy fool!" The captain sprang from his horse. "I'll show you how to use your legs, damn you! Get a move on! March!"

Spindler doubled panting across the field, the captain behind him with his raised riding whip. The inspection officers made the company fall in again with the rear rank in front. Red in the face, Spindler came back, his veins swelling out over the edge of his collar. The captain shouted at him again, and he made a sharp turn and stumbled.

"Stand up, fellow! I'll send you to the cells if you don't pull yourself together."

The company marched back to its quarters. As they did not begin to sing at once, the captain ordered them to do so. He rode close to where Spindler was marching.

"Didn't you hear me say sing?" Spindler began to sing.

The captain made his horse curvet and carried on a conversation with Klettenstein. Then he called Klettenstein from the ranks, and the two fell behind and returned together. The men were all singing.

Volkenborn turned and looked at Spindler, who was staring straight in front of him, the tears running down his cheeks.

Scarcely had the men been dismissed, when the captain came into the room, inspected the beds as usual, and halted in front of Spindler. Volkenborn was standing a few paces farther away; he was feel-

ing furious. Why doesn't Spindler hit him in the
face? But the Junker stared at his captain submis-
sively.

"What made you become a Fahnenjunker?"
Spindler did not answer.

"Answer, can't you!" shouted the captain. "What
is your father?"

"A schoolmaster, Herr Hauptmann."

"A schoolmaster! Then why the devil don't you
become a schoolmaster, or a tailor, or a shoemaker
— instead of having the impudence to imagine you
can become an officer?"

The captain turned away, laughing derisively.

"A schoolmaster! a schoolmaster!"

Klettenstein opened the door for him.

Volkenborn did not venture to look at Spindler,
he felt so deeply sorry for him.

IX

Naturally among such a large number of young
men there were cliques; those specially intimate with
one another, who were attached by personal tastes
and sympathies that united them more closely than
the ordinary ties of comradeship. In the company
there were many groups of this kind: in one there
were the cavalrymen, nearly all from titled families;
the infantry were mostly of middle-class origin, with
the exception of some who belonged to the Guards;
then came the military engineers and other depart-
mental corps; but, in addition to these military

groups, there were cliques, drawn together by personal tastes and common interests.

Volkenborn belonged to none of these cliques, he had nothing in common with any of them. He made no attempt to discover what it was that drew them together; contented himself with observing the ordinary forms of comradeship, being most careful to conceal any dislike or disapproval that he felt for anybody.

With the exception of Rossberg, the only other Junker with whom he was in the least intimate was Engelhardt. Engelhardt was in love with his sister's particular friend, and the naif way in which he spoke about his affair delighted Volkenborn.

His friendship with Rossberg caused a certain amount of curiosity among the others, but Volkenborn was too simple-minded and inexperienced to be aware of this curiosity. He made no mystery of the fact that he always addressed him with the familiar *"Du,"* was constantly making appointments with him, sat next to him at table, was always talking to him, when they were on duty in the guardroom or when they were in bed; he always helped him to clean his rifle and that, in a word, he considered him his particular friend.

For his part, Detlev Rossberg was very attached to Volkenborn, had the greatest confidence in him, and hung round him with that rather affectionate manner that a smaller and weaker youth will often show for a bigger and stronger one.

One evening, as Volkenborn was returning alone

from supper, a Junker who belonged to the Third In-
spection-Battalion joined him. He was a nice-looking
boy, not any taller than Volkenborn, but very slender; with his delicate complexion and the dark
shadows under his big blue eyes, he looked like a
girl. He always wore a well-fitting uniform, and his
hussar tunic fitted like a glove over his narrow hips.

"You seem very keen on Rossberg?" he said, and
put his hand on Volkenborn's shoulder.

"I like him very much. But why do you say that?"

"You like him, but don't you love him?"

"I don't know what you mean! Love? I'm not a
girl! You surely don't suppose I make love to men!"

Volkenborn laughed, and the other put his arm
through his and said:

"Why do you keep yourself away from the rest
of us? Rossberg is always with you, and so is that
dreary Engelhardt. You hate me, don't you?"

"But, my dear fellow — what on earth are you
talking about? It all sounds such nonsense! Why
should I hate you? Such a nice-looking chap, with
such a handsome nose! Why should any one hate
you?"

The other was silent. Then he pressed Volkenborn's arm, began to walk more slowly, and felt for
his hand. Volkenborn laughed and came to a standstill, as they had just reached their quarters.

"Good night and happy dreams!"

As Volkenborn turned away, he suddenly felt
arms thrown round his neck.

"My dear boy, I'm not your sweetheart," he said

rather angrily, and rubbed his cheek with his handkerchief. The fellow's still a kid, he thought, as he
passed on above. What a kid! To throw his arms
round my neck and give me a kiss. Even if he *is*
feeling homesick, I am not his mamma.

There were still things in this world that were
beyond Hans Volkenborn.

The celebration of the Kaiser's birthday passed
off very well. Volkenborn was delighted because the
major was so nice to him, and the captain invited
him to a dance. The theatrical performance was a
great success, and the champagne cup that Volkenborn brewed was universally pronounced to be excellent. It made him slightly tipsy, and he felt in high
spirits. Misjudging the distance between his glass
and the table, he banged it down rather hard, with
the result that he broke the foot off, and then
laughed till the tears came into his eyes. Encouraged
by all the wine he had drunk, he even took a seat in
the midst of one of the cliques, and came to the conclusion that they were all jolly fellows. The inspection officer of the Second Company presided. Smutty
stories were exchanged, and Volkenborn sat tight
behind his glass, and laughed at them all. It seemed
all quite harmless to him, and he felt sure that they
really did not mean what they said, but were only
pretending to be gay dogs, swanking in order to
impress one another, and in order to seem to be experienced men of the world. This pretended viciousness was mere gassing.

He saw everything in a rosy light, drank Klettenstein's health, and decided that he was a real good sort, and was so very vague as to what was taking place around him that he failed to notice, first that the captain, and then Klettenstein had left the mess, and that neither of them came back. Even if he had noticed their departure one after the other, it would have conveyed no idea to his brain.

The homesick Junker was sitting next to him, and kept drinking by mistake out of Volkenborn's glass, and repeating, "Shall we go out too?"

"Go? Shall we go? Why should we go, and where are we to go to? Come on, let's drink another glass to Mamma's health. Rossberg! You're going to sleep; come on, man, drink up!"

At four o'clock in the morning Volkenborn was the last to leave the mess, and as he closed the door behind him, he found the senior Junker waiting for him.

"Didn't you think it was awfully jolly, Seitz?" he asked. "The captain was extraordinarily decent, all through the show. I shall always remember how decent he was."

Fähnrich von Seitz was three or four years older than Volkenborn, and had studied for a year or more at the University before the war broke out. He was a very quiet, serious young man with a rather troubled expression and a gentle sympathetic voice. Volkenborn liked him, but thought him just a little cold and reserved.

At first Seitz did not answer him. Then, without looking up and as though in thought, he said, "Well, you know, Volkenborn, it all depends on how one looks at it all. The best way perhaps is not to think too much about it, to close one's eyes — or," and he laid his hand on Volkenborn's shoulder and his voice sounded warmer and more affectionate than Volkenborn had ever known it to sound before — "or to get. as delightfully drunk as you are — but unfortunately that's a gift that all of us don't possess."

CHAPTER FIVE

THE SHRINE OF THE VIRGIN MOTHER

I

It so happened that Elma arrived in Berlin at
the same time as Volkenborn's brother Lothar, so
they all went to the theater together. The musical
comedy was very bright and gay, and, carried away
by the excitement of the evening, they were in the
highest of high spirits. After the show, old Mr.
Scholander invited the two Volkenborns to supper
at Kempimsky's restaurant, where they remained until late; talking, telling yarns about the war, and recalling former incidents out of their common experience, while from time to time Hans would smile
across at Elma, raise his glass, and drink to her.

But afterwards, as he sat in his bedroom at the
hotel, — full of this meeting with Elma, whose
presence seemed to have brought with it something
feminine and soothing — he suddenly thought of
Margrit Leczinsky. He almost seemed to feel her
presence in the room. Nervously he glanced round
him, got up, drew the curtains, locked the door, and
then sat down again, staring in front of him.

Margrit! What was it? Was he dreaming — a

confused, terrifying dream? Had he fallen asleep?
Was he really awake now?

He seemed to see Margrit coming towards him.
They passed through many rooms, looking at the
pictures as they went, pictures that covered all the
walls. When he put his hand on one of them, he
found that it was not a picture, but tapestry, and
she laughed and said: "How surprised you look!
Put your hand on me! I'm softer, and more beautiful
than that." Then they kissed, and Margrit was lying on the sofa, and he threw his arms passionately
round her. Then suddenly she was still, and, when
he looked into her face, it was white, and when he
touched her, she was so icy cold that he withdrew
his hand in fear. And there was Lieutenant von
Kless standing in the doorway, and asking, "Is she
dead?" After saying that, the Lieutenant sat down
at the piano and began to play, and Volkenborn went
across to Elma, who was leaning out of the window,
and took his place beside her. Beneath them flowed
the canal, and they leaned still farther out of the
window, and he found himself shouting, "Take care,
Elma, or we shall be out!" And as he spoke they
began to fall.

II

The course of instruction was finished, but there
was still some delay about his promotion to the rank
of Fähnrich. At first he felt hurt at not having the
right to wear the sword knot while he was still on

leave, so that he might return to his regiment with this outward and visible sign of rank, but this feeling of disappointment and annoyance soon passed.

A fortnight's leave! A fortnight in Arnstadt, at Margaretensee, with his parents, with Ursel and Elma, and above all with Anneliese! Fourteen days of delight, days of love and kindness, days during which they would all unite to spoil him and make much of him. Days full of sunshine and happiness, of peace and home delights, but alas, days that would pass all too quickly.

When the time came to part from them all, he realized — quite unexpectedly and without his being able to explain to himself why — that he found it hardest of all to say good-by to Elma. As he looked into her eyes, he saw something there that moved him deeply, and his heart was saddened with a presentiment that this might be good-by for ever. They were standing at the door, and Elma went into the house, to fetch some cigarettes that she wanted to give him. As he listened to the sound of her footsteps dying away as she disappeared into the house, a feeling of profound sadness came over him. Dreading the scene of their final parting, he ran down the steps and hurried off without once looking back.

III

He had taken his seat in the brake van. Werner and Kerksiel, who were remaining behind at the

Recruiting Depôt in Bruges, had supplied him lav-
ishly with books and biscuits, and he had started
feeling very comfortable and in excellent spirits.

The brake rod took up rather a lot of space, as
it ran right down the middle of the van, and inter-
fered with his legs; but he enjoyed the compensation
of having a whole compartment to himself.

He nibbled at his biscuits, dipped into the maga-
zines that Werner had bought from the bookstall,
looked out of the window, jumped out and
stretched his legs every time the train stopped, inspected his men, gave them cigarettes, sat for a
while with them in their compartment listening to
their jokes — and then got out again at the next station and went back to his own van.

The journey lasted all day. The regiment, which
since Ypres had been detached with two other regiments and divisional artillery from the old corps,
was now converted into a "Flying Division" and was
lying in the north of France. That it had suffered
heavy losses was about all that was known of it at
the depôt.

It was "chance," — as the sergeant major had
said — that had decided that Volkenborn, and not
Werner or Kerksiel, should be sent to rejoin it.
Chance! How often he had heard this word! Was
there such a thing as chance?

No! Once again he declined to believe it. It
seemed to him at the moment quite as it should be
that he was going to join the regiment, and not one
of the others. It was not chance, but destiny, and it

was no good thinking about it; no good asking why.

Perhaps he really was about to meet his fate this time. How often had he heard about forebodings of this kind? As he thought the matter over, it seemed to him that Lieutenant von Kless had definitely known that he was going to be killed in the advance to Ypres. He thought too of Margrit, and of that last afternoon that he had passed with her in such strange circumstances. At the time he had not realized it all, had not understood, but now, recalling how she had looked at him, remembering the expression of her eyes, and her smile, it seemed to him that she knew then what her fate was to be.

Such thoughts followed him through the long journey. He recalled the strange presentiment he had, when he said good-by to Elma. Was that a premonition? What was such a premonition worth? At Ypres Werner had been convinced that he would not come out of it alive. In fact, they had all thought so, but they were still living. No! Such a thought was not necessarily a premonition of death.

From his seat in the built-up part of the brake van, he could see the whole train and the landscape in front of them through the window. The roofs of the other carriages looked like the scales of a snake crawling slowly and steadily over the country. The weather was simply perfect, and the peasants' cottages looked white and clean in the sunshine, whilst all along the line hedges and trees were already in leaf. When he half closed his eyes meadows and fields looked like one unbroken carpet of green reaching to the line of the horizon. It was spring, with all the wonderful colorings of that season. The buds of the poplars were already bursting into leaf, and meadow and field seemed to be anxiously awaiting the moment when they too could put on their spring attire. How different trees look at various seasons of the year! In the autumn, before Ypres, they had seemed uncanny, wretched, depressing, the picture of melancholy; but now they spoke of hope and happiness and appeared bright and eager in their youthful dress. At the next stop Volkenborn alighted and picked forget-me-nots from the slope of a ditch.

Towards noon, the train was running along behind the front line and the noise of the guns could be plainly heard. Many airplanes were up, Volkenborn recognized the spot. To the left lay Ypres and there was Poelkapelle and Westroosebeeke, and farther to the right Shap Balie, Staden, and Houtholst.

What a long while ago it seemed! Pictures rose before his eyes, and again he seemed to be looking at the road in front of the castle at Staden. He had seen it for the first time at night, and then in the morning had come the attack. How quickly the line of English infantry had advanced. As though some unseen hands were drawing them on. And as one pulls a weed up, flings it down, and lets it lie there and wither. . . . The dead lieutenant!

And then had followed all those terrible nights, — the details of which he could hardly remember.

He could only recall them as some terrible experience of long ago.

In the afternoon, the sound of the guns grew fainter. Volkenborn wrote a letter, a bright cheerful letter, to Anneliese. He rather exaggerated the comfort of his brake van. As he wrote, he thought of the famous story of the Postillion of Eichendorff, who traveled into the land where the orange trees grow.

Who knows, he thought, what sort of orange trees we may find here? Those "oranges" that come flying through the air, hitting some and missing others!

As he sat smoking, watching the country through which they were passing, a mist began to rise, and he had queer thoughts about the death that might be in store for him. His mind toyed with the idea, not so much of death and dying, but of being dead and what comes after; and not so much with the idea of what the great adventure would prove to him, but rather of what was the present state of those whom he had loved and who had gone before. In his mind's eye he could see them; they all passed before him.

Round his own picture — the one that was hanging over the sofa, in a small oval gilt frame — his mother had draped crape, and every time she looked at it she burst into tears. He seemed to see her trembling fingers as she draped his picture. Then he saw his father, talking with somebody, discussing the latest news from the Front, or arguing about

the war loan, and saw how suddenly he excused himself and pleaded urgent business. And he knew that
this was because his father was thinking of his son,
Hans Volkenborn, who had been killed, and could
no longer bear to talk of other matters with ac-
quaintances. Then he saw Elma, looking out of the
window with that strange distant glance of hers, and
he seemed to hear her say, "I knew it! There was
something in his face that told me so! I knew he
would never come back again!" And then Anneliese!
He saw how she received the letter containing the
news. It was written in red ink. Oh, don't cry so,
Anneliese! Be brave! It is all over. I was glad to
die! To die for you; for all of you; in gratitude for
so much love that you have shown me. Be glad that
I have died for the Fatherland! Never forget that!

Then he could hear Lothar saying: "The youngster! Our poor little youngster! That he too should
have to die!" And then he saw him walk to the telephone rather uncertainly, stumblingly, heard him
ring up Kurt, and then he could see both brothers
at the telephone. Kurt had not yet heard the news,
and he suddenly took a step nearer and supported
himself with a hand against the wall. "What! What
do you say, Lothar? I can't hear you plainly. Good
God! It can't be!" Yes, Kurt, it is true. Don't stand
staring at the wall, but pull yourself together. It *is*
true! It's true and nothing can alter it, so what's the
good of being sad about it. After all, there's no
better death than to die in face of the enemy. Don't
you remember what we used to sing about it at

school? When you think of me, think of me only
with happy thoughts! Promise me that you will do
that!

Twilight fell and the French frontier lay behind
them.

Wonderful dreamland! Marvelous phantasma-
goria! The pictures that you show are not always
terrible ones, and not always do your passing scenes
and visions give pain. Sometimes you are gentle and
clear as an evening at sea, when the waves murmur
soothingly of slumber. When in such a mood, you
show us nothing ugly, and both life and death seem
easy, and beautiful as a cloud on the distant horizon. Easy and beautiful, but sad too. Magic of
dreamland! It banishes all earthly care.

The Junker folded up his letter and addressed it.
To do so he had to get nearer to the window, as it
was rapidly growing dark. At last it was finished
and he placed it in his pocketbook ready for posting,
but he did not hand it out when they came to a station, for he always made a point of posting these
letters himself.

Nightfall found them at Cambrai, where they
walked about the streets for a long time, seeking for
some instructions as to whether they were to spend
the night in quarters or to march straight off on account of an expected air attack. Volkenborn walked
up and down in front of the anti-aircraft guns,
watching the searchlights from the batteries as they
wandered across the sky. Yes! Here was the War
again, right enough!

IV

They spent the next two days on the march, the
sun blistering their faces. Water was scarce owing
to the absence of all villages and towns. The guns
seemed to have left nothing standing; from time to
time they saw a signpost lying on the ground, which
bore some name that was familiar to them from
the newspaper reports from France. Stragglers began to fall out and remained sitting by the wayside,
especially the younger men of the latest reserve that
had been called up. War is no game for children,
thought Volkenborn.

There were very few trees, and consequently no
shade, which made the heat very hard to bear. They
seldom came across water of any kind; the whole
district seemed one mass of brown, dried-up fields,
with a feeble crop of grass here and there. The
only objects that relieved the monotony of the
landscape were the many white crosses that they
kept passing. They seemed almost like dusty, withered, dead flowers. They all bore inscriptions, but
by this time they had all become more or less illeg-
ible. But how could it possibly be expected, here
amid this desolate, ravaged district near the Somme,
among these ruined pastures and corn-lands that
had drunk so much blood, been ploughed with so
much iron, that time could be found to trouble about
the names and regimental numbers of those who
were buried there, or about the date when they

had met their fate? War, that had singed and bleached the countryside, that had torn the branches from the trees, scorched and withered the grass, and rent and shattered the very surface of the earth until its goodness had dried up, did not pause to spare the inscriptions that marked the spot where humble men had died.

The young soldiers passed by the graves of their comrades and, many of them, without knowing it, were drawing nearer to their own.

Volkenborn was conscious of no fatigue. He felt no thirst, and consequently drank nothing, so that his water bottle was full at the end of the day's march, and he was able to share its contents with his comrades. So well had he borne the heat and fatigue that he made up his mind to take part in the great army marching competition after the war. He seemed hardly to feel the weight of his pack, although at one time he was carrying two rifles. When the column halted, he was feeling so fresh that he performed all sort of evolutions with them, to amuse his comrades. He displayed feats of strength and did tricks that required great agility; then he ran a race with his batman, Schuster. All this cheered the men up, kept them in good spirits, and made them forget their fatigue. Then once again they were on the march, plodding doggedly on, scarcely lifting their eyes when they met a returning column, coming back along the blazing, dusty road. As they marched, the dust rose like flour from the ground, so that they seemed to be marching knee-deep in a

white cloud. Their lips were dry, black and cracking; a bitter taste filled their mouths.

For the first time in his life, Volkenborn slept under canvas. The idea had always sounded romantic
and adventurous, and he tried to grow enthusiastic
about it. For a long time he walked up and down in
front of the low tents, until, beginning at last to
feel fatigued, he sat down in front of his own and
thought over what he was going to say to Anneliese
in his next letter: he prepared poetic sentences in
which he described himself sitting in front of his
tent and gazing up at the dark sky, now shimmering
with stars. Far away to the west he could see the
flashes of the guns, and hear the sound of their discharge. There lay the Front, less than a day's march
away.

He tried to grow enthusiastic about this new experience, but found that sleeping under canvas was
but a prosaic affair after all. It began to grow cold,
and the damp of nightfall chilled him. For a while
he talked with Schuster, who was also feeling sleepless, and then he crept out of the tent again and
tried a pipe of tobacco — to bring him into the right
mood for sleep.

When he finally lay down again, he thought of
what Schuster had been saying to him, and realized
how young the man was. The actual difference in
age between him and Schuster was only a matter
of a few weeks, but Volkenborn, with all his experience of war, felt himself to be many years his
senior.

As he was reflecting on all this, it occurred to him that Schuster was very like what he had been once. He used to ask the same questions, had been just as restless and nervous during his early days at the Front, — when he was "green." It was the uncertain feeling of expectation — waiting for one's baptism of fire. How unlike the real thing were all these expectations! In reality, everything was so unheroic, so elemental. One ran like a madman, as though the seat of one's trousers were burning, you flopped down, flung yourself somewhere down in the dirt and shut your eyes. Yes, my good Schuster, that was what I really did, and there was no getting away from the fact. The day after to-morrow, or whenever the occasion arises, you too will do the same; but if I were to say so now, you would feel yourself insulted, as I should have done in the early days, when I felt as young as you do. What a long time ago that seems!

V

The next evening they reached the camp where the regiment lay. Officers and noncoms. reported to the major in charge of the Reserve Battalion — which happened to be the Second Battalion. On the way Volkenborn met the company sergeant major of his old Fifth Company, who called out to him:

"So you've come back to us, Volkenborn?"

"*Zu Befehl,* Herr Feldwebel, naturally!"

In reality, he had known nothing about the battalion he was to join, but replied without thinking.

As he walked on, talking with the transport driver — an old captain of Landwehr, who was quite excited about making this little excursion to the Front — he thought: Fate made me meet Sergeant Major Peterson and decided me to join the Fifth Company. Well, so be it! When Volkenborn, with his sixteen young recruits, reported to the company leader of the Fifth Company, an inexplicable feeling — to which he could give no name but which was very definitely disagreeable — took possession of him. Lieutenant Algermissen was no longer there; he had been killed during the attack on Longueval, and a young lieutenant led the company; a tall clumsy man with a deep but rather shaky voice, and a very long receding chin, that gave his good-tempered face a feeble and undecided look. All this rather depressed Volkenborn, who realized that the gulf that had formerly separated him from his lieutenant no longer existed. In those days the lieutenant had embodied for him his conception of the company, had been its actual symbol, but this young, inexperienced officer was quite a different thing. He was — a substitute, just as the sixteen boys that he brought with him were substitutes.

The sergeant major was one of the old lot, and as for Pietschmann — Pietschmann gave him a delighted and hilarious welcome, which reconciled him in part to all these other changes. And there were still others left from the old days: those two smart soldiers, the brothers Herkschröder, and Pollmann the sprinter, and Schomberg of the pallid face, the carefully trained moustache, and the tired gray eyes. Lance Corporal Köhler of the shiny boots and the carefully parted hair was still there, and Wulff, who had also become a lance corporal. There were, of course, others as well, but alas! many were missing.

As he sat that evening talking to Pietschmann by the light of a solitary candle, and they had told each other all the news and were at last silent, Volkenborn began to feel how greatly everything had changed, both in the "Old Fifth" and in himself. As the candle began to flicker out, they lay down to sleep.

"It's like this, Hansy. The show ain't what it was and I sha'n't be sorry when they put the shutters up. All the same it's fine to have you here again. It's quite cheered me up to see you. And now let's have a sleep."

It was a long time before Volkenborn could sleep: his thoughts were busy with recollections of the former lieutenant of the company, of Baluschek, who, scarcely healed of his wounds, had been returned to the Front and been killed, and of many other comrades whom he would never meet again. He felt like a wanderer, a long time away from home, who had enjoyed many strange and delightful experiences, and who, back in the home for which he had been longing, found everything changed and strange. The death of so many of his comrades seemed almost to reproach him for his absence, and even the presence of well-known faces and their hearty greetings could not entirely remove the feeling that everything was different from what it had been when he left them.

The next day at noon he met the lanky Fähnrich Benninghoven of the Third Battalion.

"Hello, Benninghoven; I thought you were in the front line! What are you doing down here?"

"I'm acting commissariat officer; come and see me. I'm to be found over there, behind the anti-aircraft battery. I can give you a glass of something good to drink."

In the evening Volkenborn looked him up. He found Benninghoven quartered in a comfortable English tent. But there was something about him that suggested dissipation and degeneracy; something that made an unpleasant impression on Volkenborn. They drank sherry and talked about things in general; of the course of instruction Volkenborn had just completed, of regimental news, of the officers who had died; of those who had been promoted, and of their present position in the woods before Aveluy.

Benninghoven kept filling up their glasses rapidly, and soon they were beginning on a second bottle. Volkenborn felt that the wine was beginning to affect him.

His first thought had been not to stay long, but, although he still was painfully aware of something unpleasant about Benninghoven, he remained drinking glass after glass until Benninghoven's face began to assume distant and hazy proportions.

The wine was beginning to cheer him up. What sense was there in returning to his own cold, solitary tent? He did not feel in the least like sleeping, nor was he anxious for any more conversation with Pietschmann. After all, the sherry was good.

"Have a slice of Gruyère with it?"

Volkenborn accepted the cheese and enjoyed it thoroughly.

"By the way, Benninghoven, where on earth do you get all these luxuries from? Do you always live in style like this?"

Benninghoven explained.

"My dear fellow, I have got my own source of supplies. You have to! It is no easy matter to see that nothing goes astray. The whole band of them here — the noncoms. who look after the kitchen and all the fellows who contract to supply the food — they are all a queer lot. They get hold of the grub and sell it to the highest bidder, and, although we know it's going on, it's almost impossible to prove anything against them, as they all hang together as thick as thieves. Besides, it's bad policy to interfere with them, for if one does, one very soon finds oneself on short commons. I don't mean to say that I exactly run with the hounds, but I'm too wise to do anything to interfere with their sport. Perhaps it would be different if I had my commission; then I might be able to take a firmer stand. But as it is I make the best of a bad job. Prosit, here's luck!"

So that's it, said Volkenborn to himself after

a pause, and put a great hunk of cheese into his mouth. After all, what's it got to do with me? To-morrow we are going to the Front, among the nettles in the wood of Aveluy; what's the good of worrying about trifles? The wine is good!

It was very late when he left Benninghoven's tent. It must have been nearly midnight, and star shells were dancing over the Front. The whole horizon seemed trembling under the roar of the batteries, and airplanes were cruising overhead amid the glare of the searchlights.

The quick-firing guns were blazing away rapidly, and the flash of the shells was visible on every side. After all, war had something vivid and brilliant about it, and the main thing was not to think too much, not to worry. What was the good of worrying? It only made life harder and altered nothing. Nothing that any one person could say or do would alter matters, and there was no good in worrying and getting scared about what was going to happen.

VI

Volkenborn was put in command of the second squad of the Third Section. It was composed chiefly of the new recruits, and he was greatly relieved to find that Lance Corporal Pongs and Schuster were also posted to this section.

Their march into position went off smoothly and without any losses. The nervous tension that Vol-

kenborn had been feeling relaxed the moment that
they came under fire, and he had no difficulty in
pulling himself together. The moment that shots
began to fall round them, he felt at once the necessity for concentrating all his attention on defence,
and realized that he must make active use of all
his physical powers. Again he felt how boots, gas
mask, belt, pack, and steel helmet were a part of
himself, their wearer, as one fighting unit, and the
thought inspired him with fresh courage.

Still more inspiring was the thought of the tie
of comradeship that bound him to his fellows, to
his platoon; the thought of how they would fight
side by side and willingly risk their lives, one for
the other. Once again it was up to him and to every
one of them to give an example of coolness and
determination, of devotion to duty and soldierly
smartness.

Their position lay some hundred meters on the
far side of the Ancre. The dikes of this river had
been completely destroyed by gunfire, with the result that the whole valley was under water, and the
stream appeared to be some three to four hundred
yards in width. Narrow pontoons had been thrown
across this flooded area, but they were being constantly destroyed by the incessant bombardment to
which they were subjected. The position was rendered particularly difficult, owing to the incline on
the other side of the river being encumbered with
undergrowth that extended halfway up to the sum-
mit. It was a regular mousetrap, as, in the event

of the enemy bringing off a successful push, no German retreat was possible. The English and French had only to throw a heavy curtain of artillery fire behind them to render a retreat across the river impossible.

As soon as they had taken over, Volkenborn, with his section leader, made a careful inspection of their position. It was nearly midnight, and they were obliged to crawl on all fours, feeling their way before them with their hands, and carefully brushing from their path the dry twigs which would otherwise have betrayed their presence by cracking. A shudder of uneasiness passed over Volkenborn, as, through his field glass, he watched the enemy's outposts, which were placed just beyond the spot where the undergrowth began to thin out, and he realized how plainly he could see the men's faces and observe all their movements in the bright moonlight, which threw dark shadows from every branch and twig, against which faces and hands stood out quite clearly.

At one moment it seemed as though one of them was looking straight at Volkenborn, staring straight into his binoculars, and so clearly could he see him that he could even distinguish the whites of his eyes. The man's eyes reminded Volkenborn of those of a deer that was being stalked; they had the same startled, vigilant look. The distance between them was hardly more than thirty paces, and the tension was so great that the glass shook in his hand, as he realized that the only cover that separated him from his enemy was a fair-sized thorn bush, which threw a heavy shadow in front. Seen through the glass, the distance between them seemed much less, and the danger more imminent. Still keeping his eyes fixed on the foe, Volkenborn felt carefully and noiselessly for one of his hand grenades. It is just a matter of who gets one in first, he thought; and then the man shifted his gaze, glanced carelessly in another direction, and began to say something to his comrade behind him, whom Volkenborn could hardly see at all.

The sergeant major gave him a sign, and they began to make their way back, crawling on all fours as they had come, and it was not until they had nearly reached their own lines that they ventured to stand upright and walk. As they did so a twig cracked under their feet, and the sergeant major muttered something under his breath. An instant later a bomb fell near them with a dull thud, and apparently buried itself somewhere in the mossy ground. "Down for your life!" Hans cried, and as he spoke it burst, and the sergeant major uttered a groan.

VII

"You've made a bad start, Junker," said Pongs, as Volkenborn walked down the trench next morning. He was returning from the field dressing station, where he had been helping to get the sergeant major into the motor ambulance. He himself had

come off with nothing worse than a shell splinter
in his calf, and he had not even known that he was
hit until he had reached the dressing station. His
wound was rather painful, and the bandage in-
convenienced him.

No, it was anything but a good start, to get
hit by one of your own men. For one of the raw
recruits had got "nervy," and without any warning
call, and without making sure whether the sergeant
major and Volkenborn were back, had seized one
of his grenades and thrown it at them. Pietschmann
had given him a clout over the head, but that had
not helped matters. It certainly was a bad start.

Volkenborn slept until noon. The sun woke him,
scorching his feet, for which there was no room in
the shallow shelter that had been scooped out from
the side of the trench. He could see the blue sky
between the branches of the trees, and hear the
twittering of birds. Butterflies were winging lazily
to and fro between briar bushes and wild straw-
berry plants.

For the moment Volkenborn could not remember where he was, and then he recalled what had
happened, and knew that he was near the Wood
of Aveluy, and that the enemy was scarcely a hundred yards away. His eye fell on his bandaged leg,
and his thoughts turned to the wounded sergeant
major.

All was still and calm; hardly a shot was to be
heard, and no airmen were up. It was so quiet as
to suggest that there was a shortage of ammuni-

tion. To Volkenborn there was something ominous
in this unnatural stillness; it seemed suspicious.

At nine o'clock that evening they were withdrawn
from the trench. The sentries had their instructions, and only Volkenborn and Schuster remained
behind to reconnoiter. They had discarded their
belts; Volkenborn had the sergeant major's automatic and binoculars, and Schuster had a couple
of hand grenades with him. He carried these only
for use in an emergency, as this was to be a reconnoitering expedition only.

Half-past nine, and nothing moved. Volkenborn
and Schuster were lying side by side within reach
of one another. Ten o'clock. Still no sound! Not a
shot! All the guns were silent.

Why were the troops not firing? Last evening,
at that hour, the bombardment had begun, and the
heights above the Ancre had all been under fire.
Why were they not shelling the approach roads?
Why did they hear no shrapnel flying across the
stream, trying to destroy the pontoons? This awful
stillness! The swine have got something up their
sleeves!

Yet this stillness was in a way a relief to overwrought nerves; the men reclined at full length on
the moss that smelt cool and damp with the night
dew. Now and again a slight rustle would come
from the trees, as though the leaves were being
brushed together; one could almost imagine that
they were made of glass, thin glass, so sharp and

brittle was the sound. The clearing lay in the bright moonlight, and as the breeze swayed the top branches of the trees lightly, their shadows seemed to be dancing in the moonlight. A spider had thrown its web across, between the branch of a bush and the stump of an old tree, and they could see it shimmering in the pale, fantastic light; dewdrops hung suspended from it, flashing many beautiful colors, like the facets of some rare gem. Volkenborn watched it through his glasses and noted how delicate was its tracery and yet how strong it was, and how it withstood all efforts of the breeze to dislodge it.

A sound broke the stillness! What was that? Could it be? For a while he listened, then touched Schuster on the shoulder, and whispered, "A nightingale!"

Again he took a long look through his glass, and again withdrew it from his eyes, looked at his wrist watch, and saw that the time was nearly half-past ten. Nothing to be seen, and still that menacing silence. He began again to grow uneasy. The enemy's reconnoitering parties never started as late as this. And why was the artillery silent to-night? Farther away to the south, some four or five miles distant, he could hear that an irregular harrying bombardment was being kept up, but on this sector all was quiet. Why?

Then, lying with his ear to the ground, he heard the sound of footsteps. Schuster had heard them too, and turned and gave him a look.

They were coming!

At first there were only two of them; then, a moment later, two more. They were whispering together. Presently a fifth joined them, evidently an officer.

Volkenborn lay motionless, close to the ground, and kept his glass on them. He could see the officer's face quite plainly — a young, handsome face. He had a map in his hand and was explaining something to the men. He held a silver pencil, with which he pointed to spots on the map. Then he laughed, and Volkenborn could see his white teeth. Two of the men had disappeared, and then, suddenly, there were ten or twelve more there. They began to talk, but the officer ordered them to be quiet. They remained where they were.

Slowly Volkenborn crept back, followed by Schuster, both on all fours. Then, as they got farther away, they stood up and ran as quickly as they could, without making any noise.

"Look out!" cried Volkenborn, as they reached the trench.

Schuster alarmed the Third Section, whilst Volkenborn was reporting what he had seen to the company officer. Orderlies were soon raining in every direction: to the C. O.; to the neighboring companies. "Attack coming! Stand to! Man the trench! Hold your luminous ammunition in readiness!" The news was 'phoned through to the Regimental Battle Position and to the batteries. The moment that the artillery attack began, the mo-

ment that the first volley of mines fell, up went the
rockets! Attack! Barrage! And then hell broke
loose.

Volkenborn put on his steel helmet as a protection against the fragments of shell and shrapnel
bullets that were flying across the trench, striking
against the trees, tearing the branches down and
sending them flying among the men. He saw that
the sentries were at their posts. Suddenly he found
himself stumbling over a body. It was the sentry
he was looking for.

The mines did their work well, and in a few minutes they had swept the trench clear. But the men
could still breathe and see what they were doing,
which was a good thing. They could use their ammunition sparingly, because they could see what
they were firing at. Pietschmann held his light machine gun in readiness. The mines were smashing
everything into bits. With a constantly increasing
fury, with a horrible clamor, they swept the trench,
biting into the earth, sending it flying in every direction, and then exploding and spreading death
around them.

Their noise fell deafeningly on the ears, and had
a paralyzing effect on the senses, sending the blood
rushing to the head and setting a strangle hold on
the throat. The men stood or crouched against the
rear wall of the trench, holding their rifles and
hand grenades tight, and staring wildly at the parapet in front of them. The bombardment had already lasted fifteen minutes, and Volkenborn, de-

spite the horrible noise and uproar, could still note
that the curtain of fire was shifting and was beginning to fall behind the trench. Now it was coming! He shouted orders to the sentries and ran
down the trench to Pietschmann. At the same moment a mine fell, the last one to reach the trench;
it struck the spot where he had just been standing,
and the concussion almost dashed him down at
Pietschmann's feet.

"They are coming! They'll be here in a moment!"

This was the first of many nights; nights that
varied in their details, but were very similar in the
terror which they inspired. The methods with which
the enemy prepared his attack would vary; the attack itself would develop sometimes on unexpected
lines, but the result was always more or less the
same. And it seemed as if there was to be no inter-
mission in these offensives. They did not always
advance right up to the trench, as on this first
night, but usually there was a longer preparatory
machine-gun fire; a clearing had to be mown for
the infantry by artillery and mines, and a way made,
for the advancing waves.

There were not always so many dead lying in
the trench and near the parapet as on this occasion, when Volkenborn made three packets of the
dead men's belongings: watches, rings, and pocket-
books. The sergeant major made a list of these arti-
cles.

Such was the first of many similar nights.

VIII

An orderly brought word to Volkenborn that the company commander wanted him.

"You were going to take out a raiding party to-night?"

"Yes, Herr Lieutenant!"

"Further attacks are expected, so you had better postpone your attempt. There's no sense in running risks as things are at present."

Volkenborn hesitated before going out of the door.

"Anything you want?"

"No, Herr Lieutenant."

What should he want? Nothing. So there was to be no raiding party! Right! The men would be glad enough, and — well he would not have to go either.

When he had hesitated in the door and the lieutenant had asked him what he wanted, he had felt inclined to say that, in his opinion, raiding was very important, in view of the coming attack.

Raids of this kind made the enemy nervous, and gave him an unpleasant foretaste of what was to come. Besides, it was very important to take prisoners just now; prisoners from whom we could get information.

Volkenborn had wanted to say all this, but he failed to do so. He had even felt that the lieutenant had waited for him to say it, but still he remained silent and went away as though everything were in order, as though he had been convinced by the lieutenant's arguments. Schuster looked disappointed when he told him that the raids were to be discontinued for the present. Volkenborn did not stay to discuss the matter, as his conscience reproached him with having failed to stand his ground when he had received the lieutenant's order.

Pongs was sitting in front of his own special hole, which was opposite the dugout occupied by Volkenborn. He was unraveling an English bandolier, which, unlike those worn by the German soldiers, was not of leather but of webbing. He said that his wife would make a dress of it for his little daughter, or perhaps a shawl or a bonnet.

"Well, Junker, what's the latest? You've just come from the lieutenant?"

"The raids are to be discontinued, as further attacks are expected."

Volkenborn sat down on the hand-grenade case and watched the thread being unraveled, marvelling how quickly and easily Pongs did this work.

Pongs was smoking a pipe, so Volkenborn, to bear him company, lighted a cigarette. It was growing dusk, but he could still see how the bandolier was growing smaller and smaller and the ball of yarn bigger and bigger.

What's one man's meat is another man's poison, he thought. We attack each other like brigands, and the winner steals all that he can get from the loser. Perhaps we are not exactly murderers;

we do not fight with the sole intention of robbing, but the loot serves as some sort of consolation for all we have to endure and makes the whole horrid business more endurable.

We no longer share the common feelings of civilized humanity. A dead man is a dead man, and is of no further importance to any one. We no longer think of him as some one who was once alive, but just as a lump of lifeless clay, and, consequently we look on his belongings and his equipment as common property — as a lucky find for some one.

Volkenborn remembered how Pietschmann had once told him that, when he first saw him, his first thought had been that he would have his breeches and his automatic whenever he should be "done in."

Yes. These had been Pietschmann's very words, and yet he was a decent, honest fellow, a good comrade — one of the very best.

Were the dead really dead? Did nothing concerning them matter any more? Were only the living of account?

Volkenborn found his eyes fixed on the ball of yarn that Pongs was winding off the bandolier, watching it grow gradually bigger. Would it be the same with us, he thought? Should we be wound off from one phase of existence into another, of which we know nothing? Were we in God's hands — and did He watch over some, and let many escape Him? Was that what one meant by Fate — by destiny?

Pongs wrapped his full ball of yarn up in paper and put it into his haversack.

"You would hardly think that there was so much yarn in a bandolier, would you?" he said, as he lighted his pipe.

In the meanwhile it had grown dark; the moon had a halo round it, but there were few stars to be seen.

Schomburg, one of the burial squad, came along, and stopped a minute beside them. He had just been reading the *Kölnische Zeitung,* which reached them fairly regularly, and was in a rage about the report of a session of the Reichstag that he had seen. "A month here in the trenches would do the swine good! That would put a stop to some of their jaw!"

When he had passed on, Pongs said:

"Politics is a matter of business, and for the matter of that, so is war. Only the man who owns something, or who hopes to acquire the ownership of something, is really interested in either. Property or power, that's what they're all fighting for. War is nothing more or less than a Stock Exchange speculation. That's all it is."

Volkenborn made no reply, but looked at his wrist watch. It was a quarter past nine, and he wondered whether there would be any attack to-night? Would it be earlier or later than the night before? He hoped that the moon would be out by then. He was going to place Schuster away on the right; in that windy corner where the path ran through the wood. There ought to be a second ma-

chine gun there, but nobody seemed to know where
they had mounted the heavy machine guns. One of
them might be of good service at that particular spot.

What had Pongs been saying? Politics and war
were both business, both speculation. Who were
the speculators then? The capitalists? But then, he
was a Socialist, and believed in Liberty, Equality
and Fraternity. Were we not all standing shoulder
to shoulder — fighting for the Fatherland, for our
homes?

"I don't agree with you, Pongs, that war is a
business. I cannot imagine this dreadful war, this
world war, as a mere business undertaking. We are
all out to defend our homes, and that is the only
thing that we here are interested in."

Pongs sucked at his pipe until the reflection
lighted up his face. Then he answered, "Well,
Junker, you may imagine that that's what you are
fighting for, and I admit that that is the traditional
idea — fighting for the Fatherland. It makes an
excellent slogan; so full of pathos! But don't let's
talk any more about it."

Volkenborn got up. It was getting late, and the
listening posts must be stationed.

"I must go over to Schuster and tell him to take
up his position on the path through the woods. If
only we had one more machine gun!"

IX

Every night there was a "stand-to" in the
trenches, and every night there came an attack.

Every night they carried other sheets of canvas down the road, and the lorries carried the dead men away.

This time it was Schomburg's turn. A mine had torn his head completely off, and Schuster dragged the canvas along so carelessly that the head rolled off it, and went cannoning down the road.

Their faces were beginning to grow pinched and small, and although the spring was fine and sunny, even the beauty of the weather could not remove the dark circles from beneath their eyes, nor could it put blood into their lips, which were dried up and pale.

The rations were becoming steadily worse. Every day they had dried vegetables, and every day they had the same watery soup, although sometimes it had another name. The kitchens had been put up down by the railway embankment; at the same spot where they washed their pots and emptied their refuse into the Ancre, they also drew their drinking water, which in consequence was dirty and stinking. In order not to notice how unpleasant it tasted, they were obliged to drink their tea and coffee as hot as possible. Both of these beverages tasted exactly the same. At Ypres they had spirits, but here they had none; they felt the lack of them severely. Their only luxury was tobacco, but two cigars and two cigarettes a day did not go far. The day was a long one, and the night formed part of the day, or rather it was the most important part of the day. Bread was very scarce, and had a rotten taste.

They never knew what it was to enjoy a meal, but were always hungry; sometimes they felt too tired even to be actively aware of hunger. The jam served out to them was made chiefly of carrots, and was more or less rotten. The beef was dry, but nevertheless they swallowed it eagerly; their greatest luxury was a lard substitute which, unappetizing as it was, at least contained a certain amount of fat. But this particular luxury seldom came their way. The black pudding was as gritty as if it were made of sand, and its skin was slimy. Volkenborn felt sick even when he touched it, and it was his task to divide the rations out among his men. He generally left himself out on these occasions and only took his share of bread. Lothar kept him supplied with butter, and he used to give each man of his squad a sufficient quantity to cover a slice of bread. His brother Kurt would send him a sausage from time to time, and from this he would give Pietschmann and the others a slice or two. Once he received a package from Anneliese, which contained half a sausage and half a cake. They were packed in quite a large box, and rattled about impressively, but when they revealed themselves for what they were, his spirits fell. It really was rather depressing to be the recipient of half a sausage and half a cake.

The days passed, one like the other; the only things that they knew were hunger and fatigue, and the only thing that cheered them up was the arrival of the mails. That is to say, it was cheer-

ing for young people like Volkenborn to receive
letters, but for the older men, for whom letters only
meant the story of how wives and children were all
suffering for want of food, their arrival merely
added to their natural depression. Their people
were starving at home just as they were starving
at the Front, and they were tied down in this God-
forsaken France, in this mousetrap near the Aveluy
Wood, and could do nothing to help them! The
most that any of them could do was to save up
a few marks from their miserable pay and send
them home; and even then it was doubtful in most
cases whether the money ever got there. Beyond
that, the only thing they could do was to write kind,
bright, cheerful letters, and say nothing about the
miserable nights they were going through, and
nothing about the hunger and filth.

When were they going to be relieved? When
was this hell upon earth going to come to an end?
They could not even write and say when they were
likely to be home on leave. Each letter they wrote
seemed to bear on its envelope an invisible note of
interrogation as a sign that what was written in
the pages it contained was untrue.

Nevertheless they would speak vaguely about a
coming leave, and the more optimistic among them
would begin a sentence: "When peace comes" . . .
and then would go on to discuss plans and pros-
pects, and talk about various undertakings which
they had in view. When they were writing these
letters they almost succeeded in convincing them-

selves, for the time being, that these hopes really existed. The word "to-morrow" had long been banished from their vocabulary, and they only thought and dreamed of some distant, wonderful period when all would be well with them again. But every time that a mine came flaming down amongst them, this huge note of interrogation flashed before their eyes. Every night the lies they told were falsified and took their revenge by claiming more victims. Day by day their lot became unhappier and more threatening. Dreams and hopes for the future were their only combat, and the only solace that offered itself to enable them, for the moment, to forget the unendurable present.

Volkenborn would think of Anneliese, of her violin, and of how she would play to him when he returned. He liked to imagine that he was sitting in the drawing-room at Margaretensee, and that on the occasion of his next leave he would be taking tea with them in his officer's uniform. He would choose narrow shoulder straps, without any padding under them, and elastic, such as Lieutenant von Kless had worn. Like that, they looked very smart. Then he would need patent leather boots. And then, when peace came! The return of the regiment! The flowers, the laurel leaves and the colors! The young girls all dressed in white! There would be great dinner parties, speeches, universal joy everywhere. And then he would be back in Arnstadt, on leave. What a joyful day for his father and mother! It seemed almost inconceivable.

Such thoughts were but dreams; he never spoke about them to anybody, but sometimes in his letters he touched on these thoughts of the future, since there was nothing more cheerful to write about.

One evening, he was standing with Pongs in the trench, their elbows resting on the parapet, watching the shells from a new battery as they fell on the heights of the Ancre. The guns had not yet found the range properly. Halfway up the height stood a shrine dedicated to the Virgin Mother, and past this ran the road of the German advance. The English gunners were now busily engaged in bombarding this spot, and after each discharge the shrine disappeared behind the cloud of dust. The air was white, and occasionally black smoke rose from it like a pillar. The sound of the guns echoed and reëchoed throughout the valley of the river.

For a long time they stood watching the little chapel, as it disappeared and reappeared through the smoke. The deeper the twilight fell and the darker it grew, the clearer the outline of its white-washed walls stood out; just as though they had collected and were holding all the light that there was to cheer them amid the loneliness of the ruined landscape.

"Do you believe in God, Pongs?"

Suddenly, and quite casually, Volkenborn asked this question in a low voice, and without even looking at his comrade. The Virgin's shrine seemed to him like a candle that all the guns of the enemy could not extinguish. After each fresh bombardment it still stood there, apparently unharmed, bathed in the moonlight, confident in the darkness of the falling night.

From the river below rose the croaking of frogs, a high metallic sound that one seemed almost to feel as well as hear; a sound that vibrated continually through the mild air. Crickets were chirping, and a thrush uttered its frightened note. In the distance the sound of marching columns could be heard. Now and again there was a rifle shot, and somewhere far away to the south of Aveluy there was the rat-tat-tat of a machine gun. All these sounds were muffled, which made them seem at the same time nearer. Like a smothered cry they came through the great stillness; like a sad, uncertain, frightened question.

"Do you believe in God, Pongs?"

They hardly knew which of them had asked the question, but they both heard it; to each of them it came differently and had a different meaning. To one, it was an anxious imperative question and one full of care and unrest; to the other, it was full of bitterness, doubt and resignation.

Never before had Volkenborn heard this question asked, but now it confronted him inevitably. The mere fact that he repeated it to his comrade, that he formulated it in words, was merely the result of a wish to free himself from an oppressive thought; to find some one to share it with him. His own doubts, his own fears, of both of which he had but a vague perception, he passed over to his com-

rade in the form of this question. Was not his own
faith firm? Had not God often enough blessed and
protected him? Wasn't he keenly aware of this debt
at this very moment?

But what about the others? Those who had
fallen, who had not been protected, whom God's
hand had not spared? Why must they die and not
he? In what way was he worthier than they? What
guided God's selection? When Death overtook one
of these, did it mean merely that this one had accomplished one phase of existence quickly, and that
another needed longer to reach the same point,
to fulfill his destiny and accomplish God's will?
But what was fulfillment? What was God's will?
Who should say? But did we not feel Him speaking within us? Was He not waiting His own good
time? Patience and faith! There was nothing but
that to hold to.

Pongs replied himself.

"I don't believe in God. I can see no reason why
I should. I have never known Him. The rich have
a good time, and the poor are wretched. Is that
a reason for believing in God? We are now in the
fourth year of the war, and hundreds of thousands
of men have been dying in the course of each of
those years — without any cause, by chance, just
because they happened to be at the spot where a
shell fell. Who shall say why they happened to be
there? Are we to be grateful to God for such meaningless chance? If there be a God who sees everything, and takes no steps to prevent evil things from

happening, I, for one, have no use for Him."

Mine-throwers had been placed in position in the road below, and throughout the day they had been engaged in getting the range. They could hear the mines rising, could detect the strange noise that they made: a noise that at first seemed to die away and then to increase until it was howling and shriek-ing like a steam whistle growing louder and more violent. On the left, where the Front curved back from the river, there were signs of activities. Ma-chine guns were rattling away and hand grenades exploding; the detonations were punctuated by single rifle shots.

The moon hung high above the trees, casting mysterious shadows into the trench, so that Pongs' face looked as though it were behind bars; so strange was this effect that Volkenborn hardly rec-ognized him.

"If the gunner over there finishes smoking his cigarette, and doesn't throw it away half finished, you will still remain alive; just because you will have time to walk away before the shell falls. But should he throw his cigarette away a second or so earlier, and pull the lanyard, you are done for. And he, the gunner over there, what does he know about it? He lights another cigarette afterwards and is glad to see that his case is not yet empty. I can take hold of this gun here, fire off four rounds in any di-rection that I like, or I can omit to do so, just as I feel inclined. It may be that I shall hit somebody; it may be that all four shots will go astray. What has God with all His omniscience and His omnipotence to do with *that?* Fate? I don't believe in that either, although as an abstract idea it seems to be more sympathetic than God. But why should I call that which I don't understand, all that which to me seems senseless and disconnected — why should I label that chance? In what connection does it stand to me, to my being, if, in the course of the next half-hour, the fellow standing over there should pull his lanyard and I am blown to bits without his even knowing what he has done, without his even *wanting* to hit me? Can you answer me that? Why do we call such a senseless proceeding Fate? It's just derision and mockery! Derision and mockery of all our hopes and plans; of all order and justice, of all sense!"

The airplanes were up, so high as to be almost invisible. To judge from the noise of the propellers, it was a heavy bombing squadron. They seemed to be making for Cambrai or Lille.

"They'll drop their load and buzz off again as soon as they've got rid of the bombs. What do we know of the people we're fighting against? What do we see of them but just a glance during one of these night skirmishes? Are we sane at the time? No! It's a sort of fever; an ecstasy of fear, rage, and madness. I ask you, Volkenborn, would you, in cold blood, shoot down men whom you do not know, have never even seen, and who have done you no harm? That English officer the other day! If you, who are a Junker, had met him in times of peace, you would perhaps have become his friend. But to-day you would shoot him down — just as Pietschmann did or whoever it was, — would shoot him down without thinking, in the madness of the moment. No! I can find neither reason nor right nor Fate in the whole thing. It is just a cheap, stupid joke: no other explanation is possible."

Volkenborn passed down the trench to Pietschmann's machine gun. The sentries had already been posted, and Pongs was sitting on the case of hand grenades and smoking as Volkenborn came back.

"Everything all right? Have you heard anything?"

"No. Pietschmann is asleep, but the lieutenant will soon be coming through the trench."

For a while they sat on the case, Volkenborn making a deep hole in the clay with his stick, turning it round.

"If, as you say, Pongs, it's all so meaningless, all so impossible to understand, isn't there perhaps something behind it all; something that we cannot grasp? It seems to me that just there, where we fail to understand, where our mind refuses to act, that is where God comes in, and God's purpose is something different, something higher than ours." Pongs made no reply, and they sat on in silence, listening to the shrapnel bursting on the other side of the Ancre. Their wrist watches showed that it was ten o'clock, and the listening parties were getting ready. Volkenborn walked up and down, whilst Pongs, one leg crossed over the other, nursing his elbow with one hand, sat staring in front of him and smoking. Volkenborn was still waiting for his answer when the lieutenant came along, and so he reported to him and accompanied him on his rounds through the trench.

X

Pollmann, the "Sprinter," the "Burying Sergeant Major" had had the Iron Cross conferred upon him. It was the first class; other classes were no longer considered worthy of mention.

"It don't really worry me who gets the Cross," said Pietschmann to Volkenborn, "and I don't say as how he ain't deserved it. They've all damned well deserved it, as the colonel used to say. But what I do say is that it's a bloody shame that a beggar like that who's always lickspittling should get it before the likes of me. My name's been sent in seven times, at least. There ain't been a dirty bit of mucky business that I haven't done my share of. Me and my machine gun had a go at everything that was to be done, both on the Somme and at Ypres. And just because I'm not one of the sort that knows how to butter people up and pretend to agree with all they says, I don't get no further than having my name sent in. It's a bloody shame, Junker, and I don't care what you say about it."

XI

They had been held in reserve for the last four days, and were in an open camp in rear of the heights of the Ancre. There were air raids every night, bombs raining down on them. Some had found their mark and there had been casualties.

Each new morning the sun shone down cheerfully, as though night had never been, and before its warmth could make itself felt the landscape was wrapped in dew and mist that softened all the contours. But these fine mornings passed quickly; so quickly that they were gone before the men had time to realize them.

One morning Volkenborn turned out especially early and left the camp before sunrise. He passed down the treeless road and turned off on to the grass. Slowly he made his way across the field, which was honeycombed with shell craters. The grass was long and, although the dew still lay upon it, looked gray and withered. Occasionally he stumbled as a thick clump of weeds caught his foot. He paid no attention to what lay under his feet, feeling a dull indifference to everything around him. He hardly even saw the dirty white crosses, of which there were so many, but mechanically made his way round them without feeling any interest as to who lay buried beneath.

The sun was rising, but he was walking away from it westwards and saw nothing of its splendor. Then, suddenly aware that it was above the horizon, he turned, as if suddenly aware of some one walking behind him.

Like a tree spreading its branches to the sun, he spread his hands out to it and bathed them in its warmth. It seemed to pass into his body and he breathed it in with long deep breaths, until he felt that its brightness entered into his being. . . . As he walked along, he sang songs that Ursel used to sing, songs he had heard from Elma one evening in the garden, in those days so long ago, when everything seemed so different. These last four weeks with the regiment had seemed more like months, and he longed again for leave, if only for a few days. How the idea of baths and clean linen appealed to him! How pleasant to lounge again in an armchair and to take books from the bookcase, turning over the pages with fingers that had been manicured, smoking a cigarette the while. How he would like to spend an afternoon with Ursel, who would be playing the piano; to sit in the little armchair with its gray cover, and perhaps to stroll over to Margaretensee! How he longed for leave, if only for a day!

That evening the company was ordered to the Front again. And just when the men needed a little rest before their departure, when they all wanted to write post cards and letters, or to have a last chat with their comrades of the other companies, there came an order: the battalion was to stand to for Divine Service.

This always entailed such extensive preparations as to make church parade unpopular. First there came an inspection, and boots and belts had to be cleaned. This meant being nagged at by the sergeant major. Then there followed a long march into the valley. Why couldn't the Padre come to them in the camp? Was he afraid of being a mile or so nearer the enemy? Why should they be put to all this trouble and inconvenience?

The battalion was drawn up and waiting when the Padre arrived. Why did he come in a motor car? Why, at least, didn't he get out before, and cover the actual advance to the camp on foot? The method of his arrival had already prejudiced the troops against him, had already deprived them of all confidence in him. What had he got to say to them? What could a man who rode about in a car know about poor devils who had to cover long distances on the tramp, and who, to-night, would be among the nettles in the trenches? What did a superior person of his kind know about them? He shook hands with the officers. Naturally, he could not shake hands with the whole battalion, and if he did, he'd get damned dirty fingers. What a bang-up coat he'd got on! Evidently made of pre-war cloth. Look at the violet bands round his cap and at his silken brassard! And then the silver cross hanging from his chain — and then — by God, yes! The Iron Cross! First class!

"Look! If the old devil-dodger ain't got the Iron Cross, first class too! Must have got it for saying Grace at the general's table, and playing the clown. Can't have done anything else to get it!"

"See it? The Iron Cross on his fat guts! Got it for all the big dinners he's been stuffing into his belly way back behind the lines."

"Isn't he pleased with himself!" grumbled Fritze Pietschmann, who was standing a few paces behind Volkenborn. "Get on, Padre, get on with the praying business! What the hell are you waiting for? Can't you see how delighted we all are with the sight of you? Now comes the surplice round his neck! So that's what we've been waiting for. Now you're a real nut! I wonder you're not ashamed to show yourself — all dressed up and nowhere to go." Volkenborn felt disgusted.

The Padre began to speak about the war — the same things that he was accustomed to say to a congregation of women and children at home. Again, as on the occasion of the Christmas sermon at home, Volkenborn was growing angry. Only too well he realized how such feeble, unintelligent words, such a smug, pedantic manner were irritating the men and doing infinitely more harm than good. Could he not realize that he was talking to men who had spent four years at the Front, — not to schoolboys, who might be moved by mere empty words about enthusiasm and undying valor. Only too well Volkenborn realized the gulf between the preacher and his congregation; the gulf of class and education; a gulf that he made them feel and resent by every word that he spoke; the gulf that stretched between the men and their officers, to whose caste he aspired to belong. Volkenborn himself was painfully conscious of belonging to the class whose representative the Padre was, and he bitterly resented the hypocrisy, ignorance and stu-

pidity that was being thrown at them in place of
warm and heartfelt words of comradeship. Did the
Padre and those of his class really believe that the
common soldier was so dull and unintelligent as to
need no other mental and moral food than a few
half-baked pious platitudes? How could such a man
dare to drive up in a motor car, flaunting the Iron
Cross of the first class on the breast of his tunic,
and talk such condescending drivel to worn-out
troops with years of misery and suffering behind
them, and with many more stern days to come?
Wasn't it sheer mockery?

"Thank God, he's come to the end of his cackle
at last! Now for the benediction, and it'll all be
over. Look! Now he's taken his surplice off and
has folded his podgy hands over his belly. Now,
then! Off with you! You've done your bit, and it's
time you hurried off to your steak and chips, now
that you've done God a good turn. Hurry up, man!
Hurry up, man! The car's cranked up and the officers have already lighted their cigarettes. I'm going to have a smoke too. The only sensible one
among them is the captain, who doesn't give two
hoots for the whole bag of tricks."

Captain Helstorf, the battalion commander,
formerly the company leader of the Sixth Company,
was very popular with the men, who held him in
the highest respect and thought a great deal of
him. He was just the sort of officer the soldier
needs; the kind of man that he can admire and look
up to. The soldier likes to have men over him who

are better educated, smarter, better bred than himself; who belong to a world of which he knows nothing and which therefore impresses him. There must be a great social difference between him and his officer, but his superior must be one for whom he can feel enthusiasm, must be "a real man," who knows his troops, understands them, and who shares all their hardships and sufferings at the Front.

Such a man was the captain. He was not by any means a fine figure of a man, and he carried himself carelessly and had tired, glassy eyes, the result of heavy drinking. He always wore elegant blue breeches and a tunic, a soft silk cap, and patent tops with spurs, and no one had ever seen him without his silver-topped riding switch. Just as he stood there beside the Padre with a cigarette between his lips and his riding switch in his right hand, so he had stood, grasping his automatic in his left, at Longueval, where he had led his battalion to the attack; always well ahead of his men and risking his life recklessly. For all the fear that he showed of them, the English machine guns might have been peashooters.

This was the type of man that impressed the men; the type of officer they wanted. The fact that he was almost always more or less drunk was scarcely a failing in their eyes; indeed, it seemed only to add a personal and endearing touch to their respect.

Although there was that in the captain's life that Volkenborn did not approve of, he felt quite clearly that he too admired him and envied him his drunken, careless indifference to danger and his capacity for sharing all the risks of life at the Front with his men. He felt that the captain's personality, his handling of his men, the very way he looked at them out of his glassy eyes as he stood coolly puffing his cigarette at the moment of greatest danger, was worth more respect and confidence than a dozen like the Padre, who, with his pride and his motor car, had only succeeded in rousing all that was worst in the men. The supercilious way in which he had addressed them had made them bitter, plunging them still deeper into a hopeless recognition of the fate that lay before them.

That evening the company went up to the Front again.

Volkenborn was asleep when the orderly brought the order and he had just had a disagreeable, crazy dream. This had probably been caused by the fact that he was lying in a pool of water, having slipped while asleep from his sand sack. His hips and thighs were cold as ice, and his saturated clothing clung to him.

He had been dreaming of Albert Schulze. They had been sitting in a café together, apparently in Berlin, and his melancholy friend had been dancing and had then introduced him to a girl. To Volkenborn's surprise she seemed to be Margrit von Leczinsky. They had tea in her drawing-room, which led out on to a great terrace, and he had been standing with her by the railing. Then Schulze had called up

from below that the regiment was already standing to, and that an offensive was about to take place.
They marched away, marched off through the rain.
Presently they found themselves under fire, and were
driven into the river, right into it. Margrit was
there too, smiling, her teacup still in her hand. The
water kept rising higher and higher, and a fiery ball
came towards Schulze. Twice it struck his forehead,
making a queer sort of singing noise; and then he
fell and the fiery ball flew towards Margrit, who
caught it in her golden cup and drank it. As, still
smiling her wonderful smile, she sank back into the
water, he felt the ball suddenly strike his own forehead. Then it grew red and blue and green round
him, and he found himself sinking deeper and deeper
down, drowning.

It was at this moment that Pollmann, the orderly,
arrived. Feeling stiff and frozen, Volkenborn got
ready. His dream had assumed very hazy proportions in his mind, and the only thing that he could
remember clearly was how the fiery ball had hit him.
He was feeling very low and depressed, and only
stopped to address two post cards and to add just a
line of greeting to them; then he paraded his men.

CHAPTER SIX

THE VIOLET SPHERE

I

At five minutes past seven the patrol was to go over the top, and Volkenborn was disappointed to find that two of the men who had always volunteered on these occasions omitted to do so this time. However, he made no comment, but just passed those by who did not at once nod and say "yes" when he asked them.

Schuster was the only one who showed enthusiasm. Pongs, when asked, had said, "If you want me, Junker, you must order me to come; I'm not going to volunteer this time." To this Volkenborn gave no answer. But he found Pongs standing beside him in the trench, at ten minutes to seven.

Volkenborn had his watch in his hand and was thinking the matter over. Either they would be mowed down the moment they stepped on to the path, or they would get through; once across this forest path, there would be no very great danger.

The whole company was standing to in the trench ready for the attack. As soon as the patrol advanced, an entrenching party was to follow, and an outpost trench was to be dug at once.

The company leader explained exactly what Volkenborn was to do, and where he might expect to come on to the enemy's line, but Volkenborn's attention wandered.

The hand of his watch went steadily onward, until it only wanted five minutes to seven. Another ten minutes, he thought, and then the fiery ball will get you in the forehead, and you will roll over and be dragged back again into the trench. That will be the end of you. After all, it will be just one blow on the head, and you will scarcely feel it. You will simply fall backwards and know no more. There will be no pain. Ten minutes more — eight minutes more — five minutes more —

They were seven all told: four with rifles and three with hand grenades, but all without belts. They carried their cartridges loose in their pockets and the hand grenades were slung in sacks round their necks. Volkenborn carried his automatic and four hand grenades. I shall not want them, he thought. Pietschmann will get my pistol. He'll miss me more than the others. We are growing fewer every day.

Four more minutes! Three more minutes! He whispered something to Schuster, who was standing on his right. He noticed that Schuster's eyes had a bright eager look in them, a look that was encouraging. Volkenborn was thinking it out; they must try to cross the path in two or three rapid rushes — The letter which he had written in the brake van was still on him. He placed it in front of all the papers in his pocket, so that it would be found at once.

Then Pietschmann came along and touched him on the shoulder.

"I'll keep an eye on you. If you get hung up, Fritze Pietschmann will haul you out."

Two more minutes! One more!

Volkenborn felt that the whole company were staring at him. They would all see how he was the first to fall. They would talk about it. The major would hear of it and so would his brothers, his parents and Anneliese. He would be the first to fall! They would be proud of him.

Five minutes past seven!

Volkenborn started; a mad fear seized hold of him. Forward! Jump! They are all waiting for you, All looking at you! You must jump! You must be the first! Forward! Up on to the parapet! Over you go! The whole company's watching you! You *must!*

A dreadful paralysis seized on his whole body: a heavy weight was dragging on his limbs; all the blood in his veins seemed to have mounted to his head and to be pulsating in his ears. Then, shame and honor both spoke to him, and with desperate haste he mounted the parapet, and with two quick leaps found himself in the wood, which closed over him like a wave.

The fiery ball had missed him, had spoken to another with its singing sound, and that other was poor Pollmann, the ambitious Pollmann, who had been only one pace behind him. Volkenborn rushed onward, reeling like a drunken man through the wood. With a hysterical laugh he began throwing his hand grenades as though they were snowballs. When he returned two hours later, his knees were still shaking under him, and he smiled shamefacedly at the company leader, who gave him a friendly nod.

That night he was on outpost duty. An enemy raiding party had been driven off, and Helstorf had sent out a ration of rum. They all drank his health, passing the bottle from mouth to mouth. Volkenborn, who usually was very particular in matters of this kind, did not even wipe the neck of the bottle with his hand as Pietschmann passed it to him. They all drank their share so seriously and solemnly that it almost seemed as if it were sacramental wine, and the fact that they all took their drink out of the one bottle accentuated the comradeship that existed between them; comradeship for life and death. As he passed the bottle on to Pongs, he laid his hand on his shoulder, and as he did so, for some inexplicable reason, his thoughts went back to Lieutenant von Kless. He looked at Pongs, and, so confused was his mind, that for a moment he thought that the dead lieutenant was before him. "What are you staring at me for?" asked Pongs, but Volkenborn gave him no answer.

II

Another night attack! They stagger about and clutch at the parapet while the earth quakes as though being beaten by giant steam hammers. From all sides: from front, rear, either side, come shell splinters, clods of earth and branches of trees, and the air that they are breathing is thick with the fumes of powder.

Volkenborn finds it hard to keep his feet, the wall of the trench against which he is leaning, clinging, begins to give way. As he makes a grab sideways, to pull himself farther along to the right, where the trench is deeper and seemingly safer, the parapet falls in on top of him, and it seems to him as if he were slapped in the face with an open hand. Red lights dance in front of his eyes; he feels the earth falling on to him and becoming tighter and heavier every moment, until it forms a complete crust over his body. He tries to stand up, to force this mass of earth aside that is holding him down, but his arms are pinned and he cannot move them. He is in such pain that he tries to cry out, but he is being strangled and cannot utter a sound. His chin is being forced down against his chest, a weight lies across his forehead, and a red-hot iron is searing his temples. The heat and pressure are so intense that his eyes feel as if they were melting, running away in red-hot drops of liquid. They seem to him to be red, red as fire, and stars and sparks flash from them.

Suddenly the pressure on his head relaxes, the weight by which he is being held down gives way, and, as his shoulders work free, he writhes in acute pain.

Somebody takes him firmly by the chin, and his neck seems to crack. Then he feels himself raised and thrown forward. Somebody is holding him up by his shoulders, and he leans against this somebody, who pushes him forwards. At first it is a great relief. And then he resists with all his strength and tries to move sideways, remembering that he had thought he would be in greater safety there. Suddenly he remembers no more.

He woke up from a dream. He had been standing on a high cliff, and the sun had risen and had shone into his face; at first its rays had seemed red, then deep violet and blue. He continually tried to draw his face away, because the sun was so near to him. Suddenly he had found himself falling over backwards, with the sun following him; a loud explosion in the sea then woke him.

He got up, felt his way before him with his hands, and lifted the canvas from the entrance of the dugout. Outside it was night and quite dark. He wondered where he was and what the time was. This was not his dugout; he had got into the wrong place somehow.

Then he heard somebody who stood quite near, clearing his throat, and he pushed himself backwards out of the dugout. His chest was hurting him and his numbed legs felt as if they had been cut off. Then he thought, I am on outpost duty! What on earth has happened?

But he was no longer on outpost duty. Schuster

explained matters to him. They were back again in the old first line. Their own barrage had chased them out of the outposts. Owing to some mistake, the artillery had not been informed of their position. What a ghastly business, thought Volkenborn!

"But tell me, Schuster, what happened to me? I was standing near the parapet. Did I get buried? Where are the others? What has become of Pietschmann?"

Volkenborn had no patience to wait, but went in search of Pietschmann, who was lying below the path across the wood. But he seemed to have some difficulty in finding his way, seemed hardly able to recognize the trench again. Again and again he stumbled, collided with obstacles, and cursed the darkness. Violent pain, that he thought was rheumatism, was stabbing through his limbs. If there's much more of this, I shall soon be a fit case for a sanitorium, he thought.

Pietschmann patted him on the back and shook him so heartily that he cried out in pain. Then he told him the same story as Schuster.

"The boys said you were done in! 'What!' said I, 'What? The Junker done in? Not much!' And off I dashed, and began pounding you until you came round. But I got scared at first; you looked like a stiff'un — that you did!"

Volkenborn tried to grasp his hand, but somehow he did not seem able to find it. "I'm grateful to you, Pietschmann — "

"What's that about being grateful? Here! Just light one of these fags, and you'll feel better. But, man, you're in luck! Bad job about Pongs, isn't it?"

Volkenborn, who had stooped down so as to get a light for his cigarette, straightened up.

"What about Pongs?"

"He's dead."

For a moment Volkenborn stood still, then he turned to go away. But he had not gone many paces before he stopped and leaned against the parapet. As he stared into the darkness, smoking, tiny white spots danced before his eyes, and then he saw the violet ball, but it was very small and far away. Above his head, a thrush was calling, and somewhere its mate answered. Other birds began to sing. Somebody passed behind him. But Volkenborn noticed none of this; nor did he hear the thrush. Everything seemed still and empty and dead within him. He had lost all capacity for thought, and his whole mind fixed itself on the dancing stars before his eyes, and on the little violet ball, which gradually grew more distant, until finally it disappeared.

It was morning and he returned to his unit, got his writing materials together, made up a packet and wrote another letter, which consisted of only a single page. Then he read it through several times and felt unable to take it all in. How stupid it all sounded!

III

Who remembered how many days and nights they had been lying in the trench? How often the English had attacked and been beaten back? Who bothered to keep any record of days or hours? Who paid any attention to the coming of the morning? Who watched the birds as they flew over the trench? Who even knew that it was spring, that violets bloomed and there were wild strawberries; that the sky was blue, and that fleecy clouds by day and stars by night were over their heads? Who bothered as to whether a moon was shining high above the trees? Which of these tired, pallid, hollow-eyed men had any other thought than the one that constantly haunted them as with dry lips, staring eyes, they waited for one thing — relief!

The commissariat men brought fresh rumors each day about the coming relief. One day they had the news directly from the Staff; another time the rumor came from the Division, and then there was a report that originated in the Forage Department, vouched for as accurate. But despite all these hopes, night succeeded day, the bombardment continued, the machine guns spluttered, and the hand grenades were always held in readiness. All this went on automatically, like any other habitual act that one performs without thinking. It had become a deadly routine that self-preservation forced them to carry out.

Again the commissariat men brought the news that they were to be relieved that night. Volkenborn hardly paid any attention to it, although Schuster, this time, seemed very sure that it was really true. He had already seen some of the advance guard of the relieving force, who were on their way. And in reality, this time, it *was* true! On Volkenborn fell the duty of showing the relieving noncommissioned officer over the trench. He carried out this task with all haste, as though he feared that something might crop up at the last moment to prevent relief being carried out.

By midnight, the relieving troops had taken over, and Volkenborn's company crossed the Ancre in three sections. All told, they were now but sixty men, although they had originally been one hundred and twenty.

They marched until noon, and entrained in the evening. The trucks were open ones, and the night was very cold.

The journey continued all through the night, but there were many interruptions, as the whole line was being bombarded from the air. Volkenborn was so exhausted that the noise of the falling bombs did not wake him up. He pulled the canvas of his portable tent over his head, and fell to sleep in a corner of the truck, feeling neither the coolness of the air nor the constant jerks of the locomotive, which was continually stopping and starting. His sleep was deep and dreamless: the result of many nights of broken rest.

IV

Peace and quietude! Really and truly peace and quiet! No shells, no mines, no flying clods of earth, no blood, no airplanes, no machine guns, and not even the sound of a solitary shot. Peace! Once again, day and night have their separate functions. At night one lies down to sleep, and in the morning awakens, and everything is orderly and normal. No more shell holes, no mud, no ditches, and neither worms nor rats. A roof over one's head, brick walls, plank beds, and clean straw. There are real windows, two or three chairs, a table, clean water in which one can wash oneself every morning and at any other time when one feels inclined. No longer need one use dregs of tea for shaving water; why, you can bathe twice a day if you like! There is clean linen to be had, and one wears one's best uniform. There is even a mess room with tablecloths, china plates, knives and forks. Peace and comfort at last!

The little French village seemed like a fairyland. Every morning Volkenborn lay on the bank of the canal, and never tired of watching the lime-washed walls of the houses, the blue shutters, the elm trees and the hedges, and the stumpy little church tower that watched over the village like a hen over her chicks. There were other things to look at too: the blue sky, the golden sun that touched roofs, trees and the little squat tower with its golden rays; and then there was the fresh grass, which was full of buttercups and red clover. Stretched lazily on his back, he looked through his fingers at the telegraph poles, at the swallows; and then turned over and buried his head in the grass, took a blade in his teeth, let the chafers crawl over his face and hands, and, when the spirit moved him, dived into the canal, and swam.

One day a draft arrived from the recruiting depôt, and with them came Werner, Kerksiel and other old comrades. There were many questions to be asked, and they had all news to tell one another. Volkenborn had to go into details about what was happening at the Front, which he did with a sentence or two and an explanatory wave of the hand. "You haven't missed anything. Nothing has happened of great importance; it was simply a mousetrap in which we were all caught."

V

Volkenborn was promoted to the rank of Fähnrich, and was given command of the Third Platoon. When he reported to the captain, Helstorf received him as a comrade, was most friendly, and, when it came out in the course of conversation that he knew Lothar's commanding officer, and was in fact, a great friend of his, he asked Volkenborn to tell Lothar to give him his kind regards. Then he gave him three days' leave.

Although he enjoyed his leave, his mood was not altogether a happy one. It was, of course, a delight-

ful feeling to be free again for a time. His meeting
with his brother was a joy, and Lothar did not know
how to make enough of the "youngster" who had
been through hell. It was a sheer delight to find
himself once again in the officers' quarters of the
great hotel; to have the use of the splendid rooms
with their marble walls, red carpets, wide mahogany
beds, mirrors and electric chandeliers. It was a treat
to have one's meals in the great dining room and to
have one's health drunk by the C. O. But best of all
were the hours spent in Lothar's room, talking together over a bottle of Burgundy. Then what a delight it was, after saying good night to Lothar, to
find himself again in clean, sweet-smelling sheets.
These were the pleasures of being on leave, and
Hans Volkenborn enjoyed them to the full; but behind all this there was some disturbing element: a
feeling of strangeness, even of bitterness; a feeling
for which he could find no name but of which he was
distinctly aware. Between him and the officers in
their smart uniforms, with their easy-going manners
and their gay, careless, elegant assurance that held
something automatic and artificial; between him and
those who entertained him with such hospitality,
there seemed to be growing up an invisible wall
through which they smiled at one another and shook
hands, but which was there all the same. Even the
lights and the carpets, the vases, the decorations,
the beds, all these luxuries made him feel that he
was not quite at home among them; he felt an in-
capacity to adapt himself to all this splendor; a

consciousness that there was too much of it, that it was almost a reproach to him.

The same feeling obsessed him on the return journey, when, stopping for two hours in Brussels, he walked through the town, past the splendid houses and the palaces and churches of which Kurt had spoken to him, pausing to admire the wonderful Town Hall, to look at the mansions of the patrician families and the Halls of the Guilds. He crossed one of the great boulevards and entered a *patisserie*.

As he sat at the table this sense of disillusionment seized on him so strongly that he left his cake untasted, put on his cap again, the old, faded service cap with its new cockade, and hastily left the café; passing with unseeing eyes by sunshades, flowers, beautiful women who smiled at him as they walked beside men in smart new uniforms and carefully pressed trousers, patent leather boots, and military decorations of all kinds. On he went, glancing neither to the right nor left at this parade of prosperity and indifference, carelessness and viciousness, this mob of over-fed, over-dressed, weary, blasé, impertinent people, all of whom seemed to him to be laughing at him, until at last he found himself in the waiting room of the station, sipping a cup of black coffee.

Still in this black mood, he got up and looked through the window at the square that he had just left until the whole scene faded away into a haze before his eyes, and he sat down and waited until his train arrived. As it started on its way, he

watched the passing landscape from his window, his
brain busy with some obscure idea that had no definite meaning but nevertheless obsessed him and
would not leave him; the only thing that he was
really conscious of was a dull aching pain over the
eyes that never lifted.

But when he was back again at Fleuricourt, back
on the canal, when he lay in the long grass looking
up at the swallows, swam in the canal with Werner
and on into the little bay where the water lilies grew
near the moss-clad steps; and when he paraded in
the morning in front of his section and reported to
his new commander; or when he sat at the window
in his quarters and covered the thin blue writing
paper with his thoughts, stopping sometimes to prop
his chin upon his hand and to look out into the courtyard, at the fountain, and the hedge near the church
tower, he no longer remembered that last journey,
those bad moments in the café, along the Boulevard
and in the waiting room, the terrible depression that
had accompanied him during the whole of his journey back to the regiment; and he no longer dwelt
on the dreary thoughts that had filled his breast.
Once back again amongst his comrades he was the
old Volkenborn at whom Kerksiel smiled with his
kindly gray eyes, before whom Schuster never
clicked his heels without grinning from ear to ear.

There was much talk of a new offensive, and
every day the company was trained in attack
maneuvers. A new method was being introduced and
Volkenborn was quite enthusiastic about it. At last

there was again to be an offensive, a forward movement, victory, and a speeding up of the war to a
victorious peace. There were to be no more of these
intolerable weeks on the defensive. The defensive
that demoralizes the troops, and means a slow
bleeding to death, physical and moral. No troops in
the world can stand more than a certain amount of
that. It gnaws its way into the toughest nerves and
makes the strongest men brittle to the point of
breaking.

He paid no great attention to a curious experience that befell him one evening as he was visiting
Werner in his quarters.

Werner had procured a bottle of good Burgundy,
and they sat rather later over it than usual. Here in
Fleuricourt he had once again acquired the habit of
going to bed at an early hour, thus making good the
loss of sleep in the past months and preparing for
future eventualities. As they sat over their wine, it
gradually grew dark, but nobody thought of having
a light. Suddenly Volkenborn noticed that he could
no longer see the window when he looked straight
at it, though he could still see Werner, who was
sitting opposite to him, to the left. He tested this
illusion carefully and then mentioned it to Werner,
but without taking it seriously, thinking that it was
but a passing illusion. On the way back, however,
as he was crossing a narrow bridge over one of the
streams running into the canal, he ran right into a
soldier who was coming towards him, and did so
for the simple reason that he had not seen him.

Werner, who was a little ahead of him, turned back, took his arm and led him to his quarters.

When Volkenborn lay down on his bed and again tested his eyesight by looking sideways at his window, he found that he could see nothing, that all was dark. When, however, he looked straight across over the foot of his bed, he could see light falling from the window. It was a moonlight night and he rubbed his eyes, but they still played him the same trick. He got up and plunged his face into the washbasin; then he tried keeping his eyes shut for a while, but still the window remained invisible. A violet spot rose before his eyes, a beautiful yet terrifying round sphere of color with radiating circles. Strange! he thought, this sphere again, this ball! That's what I saw some time ago. Anyway, it can't be anything much, for I feel perfectly well.

In the night he awoke suddenly. Some one was knocking on the window. It was the orderly room clerk, with orders to move. An hour later, he was on his way back into the position near the wood of Aveluy with the advance guard of the company.

For awhile they marched along the towing path of the canal, and Volkenborn found that when he looked down at his feet, everything seemed dark; when, however, he looked away to the side, over the fields or across the canal, he could clearly see the path, which was lying in the moonlight. He had exactly the same experience when he looked at the back of the file in front of him; if he looked straight at him he could see nothing, but if he looked beyond he could see him.

When day broke, they were marching through the Somme district. Here there seemed nothing but sunshine and dust, dust and sunshine. They covered part of the distance with the help of the field railway, and the smell of the oil fuel remained with them long after they had left it. At Fremicourt, where they entrained just a fortnight before, he bought some gingerbread at the station canteen, and at the field bookstall he managed to find a copy of "Marler Rolten" by Mörike. He spent all the money he had on books; mostly cheap editions of popular works: and one he bought because it was bound in linen and had gilt edges. He was quite astonished to find such good books there, and delightedly ran his hand over the binding and turned the pages.

More sun and more dust, more Red Cross ambulances; the reek of petrol and the distant roar of artillery, which gradually grew nearer. The usual procession of columns, ammunition lorries, and men of the Ordnance Department. Pinched and gray of face, they none of them looked up as they passed, nor did they answer any remark that was made to them. At last, as evening fell they came on the old field encampment at Pozières, and settled down to sleep in the tin hutments. At sunrise they were again on the march, crossing the heights of the Ancre, passing the artillery positions, descending to the river, crossing it until they once more entered the woods of Aveluy.

Volkenborn inspected the trenches under the guidance of a lieutenant of the Saxon Company from which they were taking over. He was shown where the listening posts were and where ammunition, hand grenades, and rockets were stored. He informed himself shortly concerning what had been happening during the last fortnight, how the bombardment was affecting them, when attacks were to be expected, what patrols usually went out, and how the airplanes were functioning. He listened to all this, much of which was new and some familiar, and merely said, "Yes, I know, we've been through all that."

Here, in the wood of Aveluy, he felt quite his old self, and no longer experienced that wretched sensation that had overcome him the night before in the corrugated iron hutments depressed by that inevitable reek of dust, decay and sweat, of damp earth, and of explosives that seemed to make his flesh creep, and almost to deprive him of the capacity to breathe; that nausea that overcame most of the fighting men when they once again came within the beaten zone of exploding shells, humming airplanes and ammunition lorries pounding along the road —when they again came into touch with all the horror and ugliness of war at the Front. Once again he was his own man, and even though he was in the same wood which he had so hated, where he had endured so much, where he had passed through so many desperate nights that he had longed for the risks of a new offensive — though he again found himself there and seemed likely to remain there for an indefinite time, he accepted the fact cheerfully — as an order to be obeyed, a duty to be done.

In the afternoon he walked down to the river, to the railway embankment. The company was expected to arrive at midnight. The two noncoms., who were to lead the first and second platoons in their sections, had thrown themselves down for a sleep. Volkenborn decided to meet his own platoon. For an hour he strolled along the bank of the river, listening to the croaking of the frogs, looking at the ruins of the little chapel on the opposite slope, and thinking of Pongs. Then he stopped and on a tree trunk addressed a field post card to Anneliese, and finally, as it grew dusk, he too joined the other two and fell asleep.

When he awoke it was quite dark, and he could not see the time by his wrist watch. The two noncoms. were no longer there, and he could hear the footsteps of an advancing column coming across the bridge. Was that the company? He jumped up but it was so dark that he nearly walked into the river. It was impossible to see anything. Damnation! Was it going to be the same thing all over again as yesterday? Then he found himself running into a tree, colliding with a group of men who were passing. Hell and damnation! "Company Number Five!" he called out, but there was no answer.

For half an hour, or perhaps an hour, he groped around. His eyes were playing him the same trick as when Werner led him to his quarters. He could only

see objects when he looked at right angles past them,
and even then could only see them very indistinctly.
It was a moonlight night again, and he could see
the moon clearly, but when he tried to look at his
watch, it was invisible. Only when he looked up and
over it could he just catch a glimpse of its dial. A
feeling of desperate uneasiness grew upon him. Some
platoons had already crossed but he could hear nothing and see nothing of his own company. If they had
already arrived, what was he to do?

He tried to make his way back to the spot where
he had crossed the railway embankment, but he
could not find it. Branches of trees switched him in
the face, and in trying to get out of their way he
lost his stick and had great difficulty in finding it
again. He felt in a strange mood, half frightened
and half furious. He stumbled and almost fell into
the water; in getting up he cut his finger badly on
the old bully beef tins that were lying around.

Obviously the only thing to do was to stand still
and wait, so he held on to a tree and called out from
time to time when he heard the sound of footsteps
on the plank bridge, but there was no answer. He
had waited like this before now; had stood waiting near Ypres, on the road between Westroose-
beke and Poelkapelle, but then he had been in possession of his full faculties, and that had made all
the difference.

The more he stared in front of him the less he
could see. By now the only thing that his eyes dis-
cerned was the moon. With difficulty he calmed his

excited nerves, and let his eyes sink downwards from the moon until they reached a spot which must be the horizon. The heights were over there, and there was the water, which he could still see, and could even detect the reflection of the moon in it. But when he turned his gaze where he knew the embankment must be, to the spot from which the company must come — if it had not already passed — when he tried to make out the plank bridge and to see the bank at his feet, everything was black.

His fear and excitement began to increase, and realizing how necessary it was to keep his head, he made another effort and pulled himself together.

At the worst the company had already arrived while he was asleep, and that would mean a bad wigging for him and would stand in the way of his promotion. Why hadn't the swine waked him? Perhaps, after all, only the first two platoons had arrived.

There was a clatter on the plank bridge, and the sound of footsteps. Volkenborn called out and there was an answer. This was his platoon. Thank God!

"Lange, for some reason or other, I can't see properly; come to my side and we'll walk together. You must tell me what we are passing, and I shall then be able to guide you. Come on! I'll take your arm. Forward!"

To guide them in this manner proved harder then he had thought, but he made a great effort, and tried hard to follow the road as Corporal Lange described it to him. He knew the position so well,

was so familiar with the approach that he would
have sworn that he could have found his way blind-
folded. But somewhere between the embankment
and the road, on the thickly wooded slope, they must
have gone too far to the left, for they missed the
path through the wood and found themselves near
the Seventh Company in the trench. The men began
to curse; they had been more than an hour on the
way. By this time Volkenborn was shaking all over
and was in a bath of sweat. A sort of desperate rage
overcame him.

"Hold your row! If I could see better, I shouldn't
have led you astray. Do you suppose it gives me any
pleasure to be wandering around with you damned
fools?"

That night things were tolerably quiet in the front
line and only the heights above the Ancre were under fire, so Pietschmann came across to him.

"Hans, what the hell have you been up to to-
night? What's this yarn that the chaps are spreading about you? Can you make out my old phiz? You
can, can you? That's all right then. What's gone
wrong? I can't think what can be the matter with
you. You always had eyes like an eagle. What's it
all mean?"

VI

Volkenborn and Schuster occupied the dugout near
the "ravine," which lay behind the first line. There
were only two platoons of the company in front of

them, and Volkenborn's platoon held the so-called
reserve trench, the second line, which extended about
thirty yards behind the first one. This reserve trench
did not run right through the ravine, which was only
a few yards deep, but passed to the right and left
of it, and consequently was broken for a distance of
about twenty yards, so that the men were divided
into a right group and a left group. The dugout was
shored up in a primitive manner with corrugated
iron, but in comparison with some of the other dugouts, was tolerably comfortable.

Early in the morning Schuster had fetched water
from the Ancre, in an English steel helmet and they
washed, brushed their teeth and enjoyed their coffee. In front of the dugout there was a bench, and
Schuster was busily occupied in rigging up a table.

It had rained during the night, and drops were
still falling from the branches, but the sun was already beginning to steal between the leaves, the birds
were twittering, and the air was delightfully fresh
and cool. Volkenborn was inhaling it and lying with
his legs stretched out. He was of the opinion that
the best thing to do would be to sneak a hand
grenade case somewhere from which to make the
table. Having given his views on this matter, he
passed down the trench on his way to Pietschmann,
and came across Werner who had been on duty the
whole night and was just taking his morning coffee.

Volkenborn leaned on the parapet, dug holes in
the clay with his stick and began to ask Werner what
sort of dessert they had had in the mess on the last

night, how the march had gone off, whether they had found it very misty at night, and what they thought of their present position in the wood. Werner was smothered with clay, and was spreading jam on his bread and scraping the dirt off his leggings with the same knife.

"Can't you imagine yourself once again on the tennis court — in white flannels, jumping over the net? Don't you wish we were jumping over the net again?"

Volkenborn nodded and smiled. On his way back he began to think there wasn't much jump left in any of them. They were all growing too stiff and old for that sort of thing; elegance and activity seemed a thing of the past for the lot of them. The very idea of being able to jump with these heavy boots and in this beastly mud seemed ridiculous. The only activity they had left was shown when they chucked themselves down somewhere to sleep.

Then he began to think of the unfortunate affair of the night before, and of his crazy eyes. For the moment he had no trouble with them, could see perfectly, could distinguish each blade of grass, each dewdrop, and could even see quite clearly the tiny clouds away in the distance behind the heights. It must have been a passing weakness, something that would not come back again. He remembered to have heard once that such symptoms were purely nervous, that flickering and spots in front of the eyes really meant nothing and were things that went away again by themselves. Besides, what should there be the

matter with him? He enjoyed perfect health; there
couldn't possibly be anything in it.

The captain came through the trench, and Volkenborn reported. Helstorf put his hand into the pocket
of his tunic and produced a bag of biscuits.

"Met a fellow in Brussels. A comrade of your
brother, and he asked me to remember him to you.
He gave me this for you. Getting on all right?
As good as being away for a change of air,
isn't it? Well, take care of yourself. So long! Remember, I didn't forget the message. Delighted.
What? Yes, I know! Take care of yourself! So
long!"

Then Volkenborn, Pietschmann and Schuster
(who had managed to procure the bomb case) sat
down in front of their villa, nibbled biscuits and
talked. Volkenborn recalled his brother's comrade,
one Lieutenant Lornfeld, whose acquaintance he had
made at the Staff Headquarters, and thought it was
very nice of him to have remembered him; he felt
grateful to the captain for bringing him the message
and the biscuits, and he smiled as he remembered
that he was, as usual, half-seas over. At the moment
he felt quite touched by all this feeling of comradeship, and thought he was never so happy as when
among them all. Then Fritze Pietschmann chipped
in:

"That's what I call being good pals! That's what
I call comradeship! Helstorf would lug me out of
a hole just as I'd do for him — not as I'd like to see
him in one. You'll soon be a lieutenant now, Volken-

born, and I shall still be a noncom. and have to salute you, but we'll still be comrades, and don't you forget it. That's how I feel about it."

That evening Schuster and Volkenborn were both writing letters in the dugout. Outside everything was remarkably quiet, and the usual bombardment had died down. Not a shell had fallen between ten and midnight.

Volkenborn had his greatcoat on with his belt over it, and so had Schuster. They had dropped the canvas flap of the tent, for the nights were still cool and it had been raining again.

"I don't like this quiet, Schuster, and I have a sort of inkling that we're going to get it in the neck to-night!"

He had just put his pocketbook back and was clearing his writing things away when somewhere outside, and not very far off, four or five mines exploded, one after the other.

"I thought so, Schuster; here it comes!"

He seized his gas mask and steel helmet, threw the flap of the tent back, and, just as he stood upright, a mine fell on the slope close beside him at about the height of his own head.

It seemed as though a hundred electric arc lamps suddenly flamed up and burst before his eyes, as if night itself were exploding in his very face and the darkness were melting into one white, blinding blaze, as the flash of the mine seared his eyeballs. It was as though he had been hamstrung or as though the ground had been suddenly withdrawn from beneath his feet. As he fell forwards, Schuster caught him and felt him all over to see if he were wounded, but he seemed unhurt and had not lost consciousness. For a while he did not move, and appeared to be waiting for something, to be thinking that the explosion was not all, that there must be something more to come. Then, without warning, he jumped up, tore himself free from Schuster, and plunged forward into the trench, his comrade close at his heels.

Volkenborn could see nothing. More mines came hissing across the trench; howling, spitting, sobbing, whistling, whizzing, clanking, shivering, they swept over the trees like a scythe through dried reeds. That wildcat, War, was using her claws with deadly effect, and the men listened in terror to its cries of rage, waiting and expecting to be the next victims of its fury, playing their part in that dreadful, senseless game, unable to help themselves, ducking their heads in nervous terror, clenching their teeth, and pressing their bodies tightly to the walls of the trench, waiting despairingly for an end to be put to their sufferings.

Volkenborn could distinguish nothing, although his eyes vaguely recorded the continuous flashes that preceded each explosion, like lightning before the thunderclap. This shadowy form on his right was Schuster, who had discharged his last grenade just before they were both bowled over by the concussion of the mine, and was now laughing hysterically, as though his overstrained nerves were giving way.

Somewhere near by the company commander was shouting out a question.

"Where were you just now? Why were you not in the trench? The platoon leader's place is at the head of his men!"

Volkenborn made no attempt to answer. His mind was in a maze; a maze of shadows — shadows that all wore steel helmets. What answer could he give? The words seemed to scald him. It only wanted *that!* That he should be called upon to answer such a question! And no answer was possible. Then the company commander passed on, out of sight.

The terrors of that night knew no break. Volkenborn kept tight hold of Schuster's arm, and together they made their way through the ravine, into the other half of the trench, and then back again. In the ravine they met a stretcher bearer, who shouted "Blume's done for" as they passed him, but Volkenborn's mind hardly took in what the man said. What was Blume to him? The question was why should the lieutenant have said that to him — to him of all others? Could he really have used those words; could he really think that of him? He ought to have been looking after his platoon. That was as good as saying that he, Volkenborn, had been funking. That's a fine thing to have said about you! It only wanted that! That such a thing should happen to him! That was the limit. . . .

Stung by the reproach, he plunged recklessly onward through the trench, past where the French mortars stood, across shell holes, over shattered duck boards, masses of twisted corrugated iron, knocking into breastworks, against tree trunks, running into orderlies and finally into the lieutenant himself, who did not recognize him. He hardly knew what he was doing, so completely was he possessed with blind, unthinking rage. The fact that he could hardly distinguish one object from another no longer troubled him, his only feeling was that he must do something, must keep moving; if he were to split his skull open, so much the better! He clambered somehow on to the parapet, digging his fingers into the earth, branches swishing across his face. To him it felt as though they were cuts from a whip, and the idea brought him comfort. His efforts to keep his balance failed, and he slid back into the trench.

Schuster was somewhere behind him all the time, and he now again passed his arm through his, and Volkenborn offered no resistance. He was just like a child who was going to do something naughty and has been restrained. Then again he started to walk down the trench.

The fire was dying down, and the attack had fizzled out. Night passed and dawn broke. They were standing near the parapet, smoking, when Volkenborn remarked to Schuster, quite casually, without even looking at him, and without special emphasis, "I had lost my way, Schuster; I wanted to find Pietschmann, but suddenly something went wrong with my eyes, and I could see nothing. Now I'm all right again."

But he was far from all right, and only said this

in a vain hope to obliterate the recollection of that
dreadful hour in the night, to thrust it into the limbo
of forgetfulness. He was ashamed, and so sought to
pass it all over lightly, but he was far from well.

Even now in the full daylight, when he looked up
at the sky, which was overcast, a thin veil continued
to flicker before his eyes. It was like a thin spray of
raindrops on a window pane. Here and there appeared bigger spots in a sort of irregular meshwork
of spots and stripes. This was something quite new,
and had formed no part of his former symptoms,
but he determined to disregard these warnings, to
pretend that he felt no anxiety, to take no active
steps, to resist this something that was developing,
to refuse to believe it. It was sheer nerves, and must
be fought against; he mustn't give way. He was
quite fit, had always been healthy, had eyes like a
lynx; eyes that had never failed him through all
the fumes and flames and smoke of those nights at
Ypres, so why should they go to pieces now? It
would all pass away in time just as it had come, and
was simply a passing trouble like that singing in the
ears which had afflicted many of them so often.
There were fellows whose hearing was affected by
the noise of some explosion for days after it had
taken place; and this eye trouble was a temporary
disturbance of the same nature.

VII

Volkenborn fought passionately and obstinately
not only against this eye trouble, but against the gen-

eral physical distress under which he was laboring, declining to admit that he was feeling ill, refusing to allow even to himself that his nerves had suffered badly.

What troubled him most of all was the stain on the shield of his honor as a soldier, that hasty remark that the lieutenant had let fall on that unhappy night. It was something that he could not banish from his mind for a moment, a thought that fretted and worried him during every waking hour.

He had refrained from asking the lieutenant to explain the matter to him; more than once he had decided to do so, and then at the last moment his courage had failed him. It was chiefly his pride that held him back.

Then followed an event that, for the time being, relaxed this tension. A battalion order appointed Fähnrich Volkenborn to be the leader of a patrol that was to reconnoiter the whole sector, with a view of ascertaining whether the enemy were constructing gas mines. At eleven-thirty at night they were to leave the trench.

On receiving the order, Volkenborn at once went to his company commander.

"I will only undertake the patrol either before nine in the evening or after five in the morning. I can't take the responsibility of night work on account of my eyes. Something has gone wrong with them, and I see very badly at night."

The lieutenant, who was a reasonable man, told him to report at once to the commanding officer and to have his eyes examined by the regimental surgeon.

Volkenborn felt rather like a silly child when it came to describing his symptoms to the lieutenant-colonel. Quite involuntarily he found himself making his symptoms appear much lighter and unimportant than he had done when speaking to the company commander. However, the commanding officer thought the matter should be gone into, and sent him on with many good wishes and a message to the regimental surgeon — a certain Doctor Ellrich, of whom Volkenborn had heard s. ne unpleasant rumors. At Ypres he was said to have treated a wounded man with such brutality — it was even reported that he had kicked the man — that Sergeant Major Fritsch of the Fifth Company, a steady old soldier who happened to be present, had lost his temper and threatened to strike him; there were even those who said that he had done so.

This story came vividly before Volkenborn as he presented himself for examination. He approached the doctor with dislike and mistrust.

He delivered the commanding officer's message, and then described his trouble with military brevity.

"See things dancing in front of your eyes, do you, young man? So do I, when there are shells bursting near me. If you're to be an officer, you must show a little more pluck than that, and that's all about it. Can't see in the dark, you say! Oddly enough, neither can I, so you needn't worry on that score. Anything else? No! Good! When you come into rest billets, we can go further into the matter.

We'll get some one else to look you over. That's all!"

All the way back to the company, as he crossed the railway embankment and then the road, and passed along the woodland path to the trench, one word rang through his head: The swine! Why did I put up with it? Why didn't I swipe him across the face? Why didn't I put a bullet into him? The swine! What a cur I was! I've no pluck; he was right when he said that. I'm a cur — that's what I am.

He passed down the trench and threw himself down somewhere. The cool feeling of the grass on his forehead did him good, and he plunged both his hot hands into it. How cool and damp it felt.

As he lay there, he regained his composure. What did it all matter? What was the staff surgeon to him? He would pull through somehow, in spite of him, just as he had pulled through everything else.

He reported to the company commander, discussed the matter with him, and then wrote to Lothar to tell him all about it. It had been arranged between him and the lieutenant that for the time being he should only lead the reserve platoon, which was occupying the second line. This would meet the difficulty, as they hoped to be relieved in eight or ten days.

Despite the lieutenant's consideration, the kindness that Schuster showed him, the tie of comradeship that attached him to Pietschmann, Werner and the others, he found it almost more than he could do to brace his nerves to meet the night attacks.

Strive as he might, he felt that he was nearly at the end of his endurance, and it was only a fanatical will power that kept him going at all.

After a dreadful night which had torn his nerves to shreds, Volkenborn was lying at noon in the meadow that lay beyond the road at the back of his dugout, and led into the wood.

He had been asleep for some hours, dreaming all sorts of confused things which he could not remember on awakening — staring up at the sky, which, after many days of rain, was again blue. From this sunny spot he had been watching the thin fleeting clouds that were moving away eastwards, gradually melting into the blue of the sky. Supported on his elbow, he had looked over the gently waving grass at the blue and violet foxgloves, hemlock and the Aaron's rods which were growing up the slope among the trees. He noted how a chafer tried, by running feverishly up and down the smooth stalk of a plant, to get over its disappointment at finding that once at the top there was no possibility of getting any higher, nothing else to do but to descend and begin all over again. Each time as the little insect reached the top, holding fast by its back legs, it made desperate efforts with its front antennae to find something in the air to grasp, and then, failing in this attempt, once again began its monotonous descent. He felt his heart go out to it in pity at its disappointment and for the hopelessness of its quest.

The untiring energy of this little thing moved

Volkenborn, and its renewed attempts, its obstinate persistence, and the fresh courage with which it began its work all over again, filled him with sympathy and gave him fresh hope.

Pluck! That was the one great virtue, and so thinking, he took the little thing and placed it on a longer stalk that gave it greater possibilities. No good getting down in the mouth!

Then he lay dreaming in that dreamland that needs no sleep, in that wonderful state that knows no limits, but is nevertheless under the dreamer's control, thus enabling his fancy to follow the track that he desires. A feeling of pleasant tiredness came over him as he lay basking in the sun, listening to the twitter of the birds, and hearing in the distance the hum of something that might be an airplane or was perhaps only the buzzing of insects. It was delightful to lie there, to bask, and not to be obliged for the moment to strain one's eyes in an endeavor to see what was passing in the distance.

His dream was of Anneliese, of home, of Elma, of the school that they all used to attend. With his mind's eye he saw it all more sharply defined than it had ever been in actuality. A feeling of thankfulness came over him, gratitude to the Power that had so far brought him through it all, and a recognition that, despite the sufferings he had gone through and all the uncertainty and anxiety that this trouble with his eyes was causing him, he had lost nothing in the process, but was spiritually richer and stronger than he had been before.

This assurance of having gained something deeper, something for which he had been fighting and struggling all the time, something that alone could atone for a destiny that he could not understand, that seemed to him incomprehensible and senseless, became so strong in him that he was deeply moved and found tears running down his face.

He sprang up, stretched his arms out, took a deep breath, walked quickly through the trees, stepping lightly over leaves and grass, looked round him as though to convince himself that he was really awake, that sky, sun, trees, all the wonders of this lovely summer day, were real. And then he descended to his dugout, where, after searching indefinitely for something, he gathered his writing materials together. Schuster gave him a grin; perhaps he said something to him, but Volkenborn only smiled vaguely at him, and it was not until he was in the meadow again and Schuster was no longer there, that he suddenly seemed to see his face and to hear what he had said.

I was going to write a letter to Anneliese, he thought, and smoothed the thin paper, the corners of which had curled up, damp, and rather dirty. At first he sat looking at the paper, pen in hand, then he wrote the date, and put a note of interrogation beside it, for he had long since ceased to take active account of the calendar. He found it hard to make a beginning; formerly he had known exactly what he was going to say, and just how he was going to word it all, but now it all seemed to have escaped him. There lay the note paper blankly staring at him. He sat contemplating it, until its blank surface seemed to be hypnotizing him. Again he looked at the date, added a full stop beneath the note of interrogation, which he traced over again with his pen. Then he looked up, saw the blue sky and the sunshine outside, abandoned the blank sheet of paper, stretched himself out on the grass, and interlaced his hands over his eyes.

How good it was to lie thus, to give his imagination full play, and for the moment to worry about nothing! Presently he drew the writing materials to him again, wrote a couple of lines, stopped, added a few words, scratched something out, wrote something over it, sometimes hardly able to see anything at all, at others seeing but a blur of lines running into one another, for his eyes were full of tears.

He found himself writing verses; childish, imperfect, foolish verses, but his soul was so full of exaltation that he had to write down what came into his mind.

> Passed is the dreadful night of war;
> Peace in her barque has reached the shore.
> As the spring flowers follow rain,
> What seemed my loss has proved my gain.

These were the words with which he endeavored to embody the strange elation that was entering his soul at the moment. Each time that he read the verses over, they seemed to him exactly to express his thoughts, to say just that which was at the moment exalting him.

That was how it happened, after nights of despair, of deadly tension and desperate resolve, that he sent Anneliese a letter with a poem in it, the keynote of which was steadfastness, faith and the will to victory.

He received a letter from Elma; it moved him deeply; it contained words which put fresh strength into him and gave him renewed courage. Elma, who had known nothing but comfort and luxury, was working in a munitions factory — not in the laboratory or in the office, but with the workers in the factory. She was turning shells, working at the lathe like any ordinary worker, standing day and night among the noise and dirt and dust, taking it all in a day's work. He was filled with admiration and respect, and imagined her small white hands shifting the levers hour after hour, day after day hollowing out and polishing shell cases. He saw her with her hands black and oily, her slender figure in a blue overall, saw the wooden shed in which they all slept, saw her sitting at the uncovered wooden table at which they ate, saw her writing this letter. As he pictured all this to himself he marveled at her courage.

Unaccountably he began to think of a conversation he had once had with Pongs. . . . No! a thousand times, no! He felt his faith strong within him, was more convinced than ever of the justice of the great cause for which they were all fighting; for which those at home, like Elma, were toiling, for

which those at the Front were suffering and dying.
They were all making great sacrifices for the cause,
the women at home not less than the soldiers. How
proud he was of Elma!

Then came the last night before the company
went back into reserve for five days. He reported at
the Brigade Battle Position, and Schuster guided
him into the trench, where somebody, whom he could
not recognize, announced that he was taking over.
Then he made his way back, but could see nothing.
Familiar as he was with the way, and carefully as
Schuster tried to understand his directions and to
carry them out, they finished by losing themselves at
a spot where they came on the old English trenches,
where they lay down to sleep.

No bombardment disturbed them; but this search
for places that he could not find, this blind groping
hither and thither, this helplessness, this constant
proof that he was no longer fit to lead his men —
despite any determination that he put into it, and
despite Schuster's constant help — bore heavily upon
him, and was in no way lessened by the discovery
the next morning, that they were lying right in the
middle of the company and therefore had not lost
their way.

At noon Volkenborn was ordered to report to
the regimental doctor, and by the evening he was in
Cambrai, with orders to report himself next morning to the oculist of the field hospital.

CHAPTER SEVEN

HOME AGAIN

I

The woman on whom he was billeted was at first by no means friendly. The room was furnished with only a sofa without any cover to it. There was no washstand, no jug and basin, no pictures, only a table and a chair. It looked as though everything had been purposely removed. He reflected for a moment and then asked very politely and in the best French that he could muster, for a basin and some water. The woman was going to bring the water into the room, but he stopped her. She was very fair, and he came to the conclusion that she must be a Frisian. He was standing looking out of the window when she again knocked at the door and came in, bringing a pillow and a coverlet for the sofa. He gave her to understand that they were not necessary, that he was not used to such luxuries.

"Le soldat dort à sa capote," he managed to say, and smiled at her. He had just remembered a French story that he had read at school in which a similar sentence occurred. The woman remained standing in the doorway.

"Vous êtes très jeune, Monsieur, n'est-ce pas?"

Volkenborn was standing near the window, his hand on the back of the chair. Twilight was falling and the room was in semi-darkness. The woman's face was framed in the doorway, and her strong, plump white hand was resting on the handle of the door. By looking away past her Volkenborn could just make out her figure.

"J'ai vingt ans!" he replied.

He did not know himself why he said twenty, instead of nineteen, which was his real age. He could not see well enough to make out the expression of the woman's face, but he felt uncomfortably aware that she was looking at him sharply.

"Ah, si jeune et déjà à la guerre! C'est un malheur."

Volkenborn replied in short, broken sentences, which he often illustrated with a gesture when he found that he could not finish them, and wound up with *"Comprenez-vous?"* While he was struggling with the French sentence, he remembered that he still had a candle in his bread bag which he would like to light. But the strap from which the bread bag was suspended was on a chair behind the door, and he did not like to go looking for it while the woman was still standing there. He found that he could not see her at all now, though he peered at her from all directions, but he could feel that she was still there, even when she was not speaking.

"Ah, qu'est-ce qu'il sera, la guerre c'est un mal-

*heur pour nous tous, un grand malheur, un malheur
terrible!"*

They remained silent, Volkenborn standing motionless, leaning on his chair. He could hear her
breathing, could hear a slight noise, as though that
hand which he had seen but now could see no longer
was twisting at the door handle, as though her
fingers were fiddling with it. So acute was this sensation that he almost fancied that he could see her
hand.

He imagined that he could see her coming towards
him with her hands outstretched. A feeling of
danger came over him, and he realized how helpless
he was.

Once again he heard her voice, that floated darkly
across the room to him.

"Si jeune!"

He grasped the back of his chair until his knuckles
turned white. Had she gone? Had she closed the
door after her? He felt that he dared not leave go
of the chair, that he dared not turn his head away;
it seemed to him that any movement would be a
danger, that something was menacing him.

Somebody was passing below in the street. The
klaxon of a motor sounded in the distance, but these
louder noises hardly reached his ears, so acutely was
he listening for sounds that were nearer to him;
listening to the sound of her breathing at the door,
for the movement of her hand on the handle, for
some danger that seemed threatening him.

Then he heard the sound of the door being

closed, and, without realizing what he was doing, hurried across the room and turned the key. Then he lay down to sleep, just as he was, keeping his overcoat on for warmth. He pushed the pillow off the bed for no particular reason, and pulled the chair over to him and laid his automatic pistol on it, ready to hand. Once or twice he felt for it uneasily as he was dozing off, and then got up again and convinced himself that the door was locked.

Then he fell asleep and dreamed — dreamed that he met Lieutenant von Kless down by the canal with a girl on his arm. He followed them into the red house, and on the steps he saw Elma, who waved her hand to him, but had no time to talk to him, as she had to get off to the munitions factory. Then as he was watching the factory girls as they passed on their way to work, one of them nodded to him, clutched his sleeve and took him with her. Together they passed through a great room and then into a smaller one; and last of all, after going through endless passages and other rooms, they reached a small office, where it was very dark, but where he was just able to recognize the girl. He could see her face shimmering in the darkness, and could see her white hand on the door knob. Suddenly she bolted the door and came towards him.

He was wide awake and could hear somebody trying to open the door; quite distinctly he seemed to hear a hand fumbling with the knob, heard it being turned back and forth. He lay quite still, hardly venturing to breathe, filled with some unknown dread. He put his hand out and laid it on his pistol, and the cold touch of the steel reassured him.

Then he heard quiet, cautious steps moving away from the door of his room and passing down the passage, and then came the sound of another door being gently closed. He slept little for the rest of the night, and each time that he dozed off, his rest was disturbed by uneasy dreams.

When he left on the next morning, he shook hands with her; half-afraid to look at her. What strange eyes she had, he thought, as he just glanced into her face! How strangely she looked at him, half smilingly, half mockingly, but behind it all lay unutterable sadness.

II

At the field hospital he was received by a German nursing sister, who took him to the staff surgeon. As he followed her down the dark corridor with his eyes on her white dress, on the movements of her arms as she walked before him with her head slightly bent, something alluring and feminine in her whole bearing attracted him, something that moved him so strongly as to make him forget for the moment the purpose for which he was there.

Noon found him again on the road along which one endless stream of troops and cars moved incessantly. Getting occasional lifts, jumping from one car and into another, walking part of the way, he pushed on through the dust. The trees seemed dried

up and old; caked with white dust, the countryside seemed dead, lifeless, blistered by the sun
which blazed fiercely down on the devastated landscape.

The fierce glare pained his eyes. The staff surgeon
at the field hospital had not made a thorough examination; he lacked the necessary appliances. It
appeared to be a case of night blindness, he had said,
and there seemed to be something wrong with the
retina; Volkingborn was no longer fit for service at
the Front.

He reviewed the situation with all its possibilities,
and when the regimental surgeon, to whom he reported at the encampment that evening, sent him on
with a few ironical comments to the commanding
officer, he determined first to discuss the matter with
his company commander. He decided not to leave
the regiment at present, and so they arranged that
he should take charge of the reserve platoon when
they again went into line.

Although Volkenborn did not actually keep anything back from the commanding officer, he chose his
words in such a manner as to give the impression
that his trouble was not to be taken seriously. When
the commanding officer asked him how he felt in
general, he replied:

"Splendid, Herr Oberstlieutenant. The whole
thing doesn't trouble me in the least; in fact, I hardly
notice it. It will disappear very shortly."

As he left the tent, he stumbled over the step.
Think what you're doing, you ass! he said to

himself, and stopped and lighted a cigarette. It was quite dark and his hands were shaking badly. When the match died out, he could see absolutely nothing.

Pretending that he was feeling for something that he had dropped, he prodded the ground in front of him with his stick, staring all the time straight in front of him, as though he were so interested in something as to forget to look at the ground under his feet, and was for that reason stumbling so often. Talking to himself the while, he stood still, clearing his throat, taking a puff at his cigarette, and endeavoring by every means in his power to seem quite at his ease, but he could see nothing.

Somebody was coming towards him, and he carelessly turned his head away, so that the oncomer might not notice that he could not see him. At the same time he kept prodding the earth with his stick as though he were trying to assure himself what the object was that was lying there.

"I've been waiting for you a long time, and was afraid that I had missed you, so I went back to look for you." So saying, Schuster slipped his arm through Volkenborn's.

"That was very kind of you, Schuster, but I'm getting on famously, I was only just looking."

When he lay down in his tent, he was too exhausted to sleep. That uncanny sphere of violet fire kept floating all the time before his eyes. Then it would suddenly turn as red as blood. Fear gripped him. I'm going blind, he thought. This is the beginning of the end! In fancy he saw himself being led about by Elma, and heard people saying, "Poor young fellow, how sad!"

Feeling that he could bear it no longer, he hunted for the little oil lamp and lighted it. By its feeble aid, he could once more see and recognize objects, and he felt relieved. The fiery ball had disappeared. He began a letter to Anneliese, and then laid it aside, blew out the lamp, and lay down again, but his thoughts kept him from falling asleep for quite a long time.

III

The next evening, at seven, came the alarm, and they had the order to stand to. The enemy had broken through the front of the neighboring division, and the Third Regiment of the division was to counter-attack. The battalion was to be in reserve and occupy an artillery position on the heights of the Ancre. Volkenborn's platoon was to lead. That was the company commander's order.

The counter-attack was to be launched at midnight. By nine o'clock Volkenborn was already on the way; he wanted to see the position while it was still daylight. To save time, he took a short cut, but at the pioneer park he was held up by a heavy fire, and they had to lie low for half an hour. It was growing dark when he pushed hastily onward. Fortunately they had suffered no losses so far. Again they found themselves under fire, just as it was growing quite dark. The men scattered, and

Volkenborn was no longer able to see what he was
doing. Corporal Lange succeeded in getting a dozen
fellows together, and they pushed on, Lange leading
the way and Volkenborn following, arm in arm with
Schuster. The increasing fire drove them out of their
way, and they were impeded by shell craters and
barbed wire. In their efforts to get away from the
fire zone they only succeeded in getting more into it,
and Volkenborn had completely lost all sense of
direction. The enemy's fire was raking them from
all sides, and shells were falling and bursting un-
pleasantly close; the noise of the explosions was affecting the drums of their ears, jarring their teeth,
and the concussion almost swept their legs from
under them.

Lange had disappeared, and Schuster and Volkenborn were alone. They must push on at all costs. A
shell hole brought Volkenborn down, and then he
was caught in a wire entanglement; his steel helmet
fell off and rolled away from him; his pack grew
unbearably heavy. With an effort he made another
start.

"Can't you make out the road? Have you no idea
where we are, Schuster? We ought to be somewhere near the road now. Damnation!"

They both lay still where they had tripped, even
Schuster making no effort to rise. A fresh battery
had come into action, and shells were falling all
around them. Volkenborn was lying head downwards in a crater, and Schuster lay with his chin
across his comrade's legs. Volkenborn lay quite still

and felt no desire to move; where he was he seemed
to have slipped away from it all, to be burrowing
deeper and deeper into the earth; to be reaching
some spot where there were no shell splinters flying
about, some place that would be the end of everything.

Schuster was shaking him, but it was a long time
before he became conscious of the fact; then he
thought some one else had fallen on top of him, or
that some one had thrown something at him. Why
couldn't they leave him alone? Schuster took him
by the shoulder, and raised his head. When he saw
who it was, he said, "Let me lie where I am! Make
your own way to safety! I can't move any more, and
if you try to drag me along, we shall both be killed,
and there's no sense in that. Try and find Lange;
don't bother about me! Don't you understand? I
can't go any farther. I'm going to stay here."

But Schuster would not leave him. "Why can't
you let me alone, leave me where I am?" Again they
were pushing on. He began to laugh; he laughed
until his voice cracked. Then he fell again, got up,
staggered onwards, trying all the while to free himself from Schuster's arm, trying to sink to the
ground again, but Schuster held him on his feet
and pushed him steadily along, as though he were
his prisoner. Suddenly realizing what his comrade
was trying to do for him, he tried to run; his legs
seemed all of a sudden to be as light as feathers,
and all in front of him the ground appeared flooded
with light; then blue circles began to rise and dance

around him, and he felt himself being borne away on them, being carried into the air, floating like thistledown, feeling supreme happy.

The next thing that he was conscious of was that he was staring at a candle, which had been stuck with its own fat on to a piece of wood and then forced into the wall. The candle seemed to make the place feel quite warm. With curiosity, he examined the wall, and saw that it was of white earth, and seemed to be crumbling in places. No explanation of where he was occurred to him, and he shut his eyes to think the matter out. Then he opened them again and saw that the candle was still there, quite near him.

Presently the flap of the tent moved, and he became aware of Schuster staring at him. He didn't want to be stared at, and turned over on his side with his face to the wall. How cool the earth felt! Suddenly he sat bolt upright.

"Schuster!"

Schuster gave him an encouraging smile.

"It's all O.K. We've got here somehow, and Lange has brought his lot along too."

Volkenborn continued to stare at the candle. He asked no questions; made no inquiry as to whether they had suffered any losses. He felt terribly exhausted and completely indifferent to everything; nothing seemed to concern him save that he was terribly tired. Counter-attack losses: it all meant nothing to him. All he wanted was sleep, rest, and to know nothing of what had taken place. All that interested him was the candle. It was pleasant to be able to open one's eyes and see it burning there.

The next thing that he knew was that the adjutant of the battalion was sitting beside him. Volkenborn knew exactly what he had come for, and he nodded and smiled at the lieutenant.

"I know! I failed in my duty, but I don't care."

The lieutenant patted him on the shoulder and that brought tears into Volkenborn's eyes.

Schuster was helping him out of the dugout and they were making their way along the trench when they came on the company commander. Schuster duly reported, and Volkenborn neither moved nor said a word.

Then he found himself being helped on to a lorry. It was full of machine guns, and there seemed to be no soft spot on which he could lie. Schuster was telling him to hold tight onto one of the iron rings that were let into the side of the lorry, and he clutched hold of one of them obediently. He became conscious of people shaking his left hand, which rested on one of the machine guns. He let them do so, but did not return their pressure, for he was hardly conscious that it was his hand that they were shaking. He vaguely heard voices speaking to him, and thought that he recognized Pietschmann's among them. Then the horses started.

There was no one there to hear him sob; nobody to see the misery of the look that he cast back into the darkness; nobody to note the tragedy on his face, as, feeling himself dishonored as a soldier and with no belief left in anything, he was carried onward.

The hoofs of the galloping horses seemed to beat out the rhythm of one sentence only: "This is the end!" The rattle of the wheels, the crash of the shells that were still falling seemed all to form one cry: "This is the end!"

IV

"Feeling quite comfortable?" asked Elma.

He felt for her hand and patted it as it lay half buried in the warm sand of the dunes. She had laid her shawl over his eyes, and the fresh, slightly perfumed smell of it filled his nostrils. He knew the scent well, for it was the same fragrant aroma that permeated her hands and clothing, a faint scent that delighted him each time that she bent over him: something fresh and wholesome that was part of her. He lay nestling in the sand, the endless sand of the dunes that had neither beginning nor end, his eyes feeling cool and shaded. When he opened his eyes a little for a moment, he could just catch a glimpse of golden sand from beneath the shawl.

How good it was to rest here on the soft sand; to bask in the sun and to know that he was at home again at last!

The lapping of the waves came up to him from the distant shore and sounded like the gentle breathing of a sleeping child.

Sea gulls were flying lazily on outspread wings, breaking the stillness with an occasional harsh cry.

He could not see them, but could follow the evolutions of their flight, their curves and glidings, from the varying beats of their wings as they maneuvered in the sunshine. With delight he lay and listened to the soothing sound of their wings, to the rustling of the pines behind him that were being swept by the breeze. The wonder of it all was, it seemed to him, that he could lie there and enjoy it for ever!

How remote all the past appeared! Was it possible that only four weeks before he had been in the trenches, ordering his platoon to stand to for the last time? To him it seemed as though all that had taken place years ago — or else it were nothing but a vanished dream.

The little excursion steamer had just come alongside the landing stage. She gave just two or three blasts with her hooter. Then he could hear the passengers tramping as they passed along the gangway. Only yesterday he had arrived by the same steamer, with Lothar, who was on leave. At the moment Lothar was still in the reading room, looking at the papers, but he would be coming along presently, and then they would all go back together for a meal.

It seemed hardly possible that he had only been there one day; that only yesterday he had met Elma; that all this already so familiar only dated from yesterday. Past events were as remote to him as the smoke curling from a chimney somewhere on the distant horizon, and all his being was concentrated on the present — a delightful blend of sunshine and sea air, of hovering sea gulls and golden sand, of warmth, love, confidence, stillness, quietude and peace, perfect peace.

To think that he had only arrived the day before, that a month before he was at the Front! In vain he tried to establish some order in the chaos of emotions that his return had given birth to; in vain he tried to realize this wonderful change. Sometimes he feared to think about it all, lest it should prove to be only a dream.

He was six days in Ghent, where the chief surgeon — who was due to start off on leave — quickly decided to send him back to Germany to the depôt of his regiment. He had done his best to remain in the field hospital, not to be sent back to Germany, not to leave his comrades; but orders are orders.

He came across Murafsky, as stretcher bearer of the second platoon; met him by chance, standing in front of a cigarette shop, and happened to glance at his shoulder straps. Why was Murafsky there? He must have deserted, bolted. The man merely laughed. He was fed up with it all. Wasn't he ashamed? What would his wife say when he returned to her as a deserter, a traitor to his country? No! He wasn't ashamed in the least. Were all the officers and men who were careful to find a job behind the line, who were to be seen in swarms, both here in Ghent and elsewhere, ashamed? Not they! He wasn't really a deserter. He knew where the division would go into rest billets, and he meant to go there and rejoin. But wild horses shouldn't drag him back to the Front, not into the firing line again!

What would his wife say to him? She had written
to say that the chief thing was to come home quickly
with all his limbs. Nothing else mattered to her.

They shook hands and parted. For long afterwards, Volkenborn sat alone in his hotel bedroom,
trying to piece this puzzle together, trying to understand how a man like Murafsky, a fine soldier of the
old type, could have reached his present frame of
mind. It seemed to him a piece of desperate folly
that the man would regret for the rest of his life;
nevertheless he could almost understand his view-
point, could almost find excuses for it. After all, he
too was fed up with it all.

Then, suddenly, he was obsessed with the idea
that he had abandoned his comrades, left them to
bear the brunt of all the horrors of war. He felt
that he too was a deserter; that he too had run
away from it all. He could not escape the idea that
he had wilted in face of a trouble that was really
nothing, that had already all but disappeared. He
was a shirker, had neither pluck nor endurance,
had let himself go, given way, shown the white
feather. He, Hans Volkenborn, the Fähnrich, had
been glad of an excuse to get away from all the
fighting and danger, and had no desire to return
to it! What a stain on his honor as a soldier! He
who had been able to hold his head high was now
disgraced and dishonored. He had betrayed his trust.
He was a traitor to his comrades and his country.

The longer he thought about it all, the more
miserable he grew. He kept away from everybody

and wandered about alone, where there were neither
houses nor people. He walked until he was tired and
hungry, but he had not the heart to go and get a
meal at the officers' mess of which he had been made
a member. He decided that he would eat nothing,
he would fast, as a penance. He was walking in
beautiful gardens full of flowers; the sight and scent
of them would at another time have delighted him;
but he was unconscious of their beauty, too obsessed
with his own miserable thoughts. Too tired to walk
any further, he sat down to rest in a field, and lay
gazing at the sky. His eyes began to ache badly, and
that brought him some comfort, and he welcomed
the return of all the old troublesome symptoms, the
constant flickering, the brilliantly colored specks.
Carefully he noted each recurring symptom and felt
heartened. It was not true, after all that he was a
slacker. He was really ill. Nobody could deny that
his eyes were seriously affected. He knew how bad
they were. The doctors might not know what was
the matter with them, but that they were affected,
no one could doubt.

How he longed for the dusk, for the night! What
a relief it was to find all the old trouble coming
back with the fall of the darkness! He walked up
and down the square in front of his hotel, and although he had made an exact mental note of where
the trees stood, where the street lamps were, and
just where the next turning began, he found himself
running against a tree and unable to find the entrance
to the hotel. What a relief, the realization of his in-

firmity! How overjoyed he was to be freed from the tormenting doubts that had been besetting him all the afternoon! When at last he reached his room he sank to his knees by his bedside and buried his face in the pillow, relieved by the knowledge that he had not failed in his duty, yet he was terrified at a thought of what the future had in store for him.

One morning he received a telegram, ordering him to return to a German garrison. The eye specialist at the hospital was a kindly, sympathetic man, and once more made a thorough examination of his eyes, but without any definite result. A nervous disturbance! Trouble with the blood vessels of the retina, great limitation of the field of vision! Total night blindness. But what did all these medical phrases amount to? The chief thing was that there was no definite treatment; nothing but rest and absolute quiet. He was quite unfit for field service, must give up all idea of following a military career. To his astonishment, this verdict brought with it but little regret. Could he take up painting? His eyes would make that impossible too. He would have to study for some career; take up philosophy, economics or something of that sort.

He was on leave in Arnstadt, but he was depressed by all the consideration that was shown him, the well-meant efforts to treat him as an invalid. Once he stumbled and fell on the staircase in a theater; he was not hurt, but Ursel was dreadfully upset about it. All this sympathy, this anxiety to help him, began to get on his nerves. Was he always

to go through life with people round him, watching
that he did not come to grief? The thought of such
an existence overwhelmed him with a feeling of
melancholy that nothing could dispel.

For some reason that he could not himself explain, he seldom went over to Margaretensee, and
that too, added to his unhappiness and depression;
but an indescribable feeling of discomfort came over
him every time that he found himself with Anneliese.
To such a height had this aversion reached that he
carefully avoided ever being left alone with her.
Ursel expressed surprise at this, but he had no answer to give her.

Then there arrived a letter from Elma and almost at the same time his brother Lothar came
home. Elma was at the seaside with her youngest
brother Walter, so Lothar and Hans Volkenborn
decided to pay them a surprise visit. It was only
yesterday that they had arrived; they had come
by the same little steamer that was just blowing its
siren down there at the quay.

He found it difficult to realize that he had arrived only yesterday. To him there seemed never to
have been a yesterday. He could only imagine a to-
day, and possibly a to-morow that might have much
in store for him. Here, at last, was the peace that
his stricken nerves so sorely needed.

V

His leave came to an end, and he was once more
alone, living in the doctor's house that was attached

to the barracks. In the morning he attended lectures, passing from one lecture room to the other and sitting somewhere at the back, or near the window, with a notebook in his hand. There were no notes in this book, but only a few pencil sketches and some much corrected attempts at versification.

In the afternoon he was sometimes on duty, superintending the gymnastic course; when there was nothing else to do he would go for a walk or read. His eyes were often very painful, but he was glad of that, as this suffering eased his conscience.

But the evenings proved deadly, and he would often stand with his head pressed against the window panes, looking up at the roofs as they grew darker and gradually disappeared from his vision. Then he would once again turn to his large, bare room and sit down at the little writing table, where he would smoke furiously, looking round from time to time as if afraid that some one might be behind him. Then he would write letters, letters and verses to Elma, but he never sent them. Sometimes he would sit for hours with his burning head in his hands and let the tears fall from his eyes on to the paper.

Letters came from Werner, Kerksiel, Schuster, Pietschmann and other comrades at the Front; all of which he answered. But his letters grew shorter and shorter. What was there to write about? Again, his conscience began to trouble him.

Gerhardi and Eichholz had been missing since

the last offensive, and Kerksiel and Hartwich had
fallen. This he learned by chance at the mess from
an officer who had just had news from the regiment.
At the moment the mess waiter was just serving him,
and he sat silently looking at his fork, glancing at a
spot on the tablecloth, at the glass with the tooth-
picks in it, the label on the mineral water bottle,
and then back again at the spot on the tablecloth.
Suddenly he got up, made the customary bow to the
mess president, and left the room with uncertain
footsteps.

That night he wrote to Elma, wrote a letter full
of self-accusation and despair. The pain in his eyes,
which was now becoming almost unbearable, no
longer salved his conscience. He became calmer, but
it was the calmness of exhaustion and resignation.

In his prayers, which became every night shorter
and more menacing, he repeated one constant sentence — a sentence that entreated the safety of his
comrades in the field, and was almost worded as
though it were an ultimatum from him to God. He
now thought: Come back alive, all you whom I love!
I don't care how you come, as long as you return
alive and well! He did not express this wish in his
letters to his friends, as Murafsky's wife had done,
but the idea itself was with him night and day. Day
by day he waited for news of some definite and
decisive act that should end the war.

The retreat of the German army from Flanders
had begun, and he received letters from Kurt and
Lothar. Werner also wrote from somewhere near

Cambrai, but his communication was confused and
depressing. One more such engagement, he wrote,
and there would be an end to the whole division.

Volkenborn often encountered in the morning
at the stopping place of the tram, an officer who
had formerly belonged to the Seventh Company,
and who knew Werner well. This officer had been
wounded in the summer, had not yet completely recovered, and was still attending the hospital for
treatment. One day towards the end of October,
Volkenborn met him again, and they began to talk
about the latest news from the Front, and about the
battles that the regiment had taken part in and
its losses. The officer alluded to Kerksiel and Von
Hartwich, the two Fähnriche who had fallen, and
after a pause, passing without explanation as people
sometimes do, from what was remote to something
that lay nearer, added, "Poor old Werner! He's
gone 'west' too!"

Volkenborn was so dazed that he got out at the
same place as the officer, although his destination
was farther on, and accompanied him as far as the
gate of the hospital, keeping a stiff upper lip until
his superior passed out of sight; then something
within him seemed to give way.

For a while he leaned against the gate, as though
he were waiting for the officer, then he began to drag
himself away. The porter, who thought he must still
be suffering from the effect of a wound, watched him
as he crossed the road, saw him stop as if he had
forgotten something, then turn round and recross,

and then stand still in the middle of the busy road, as though he did not know how to get over the tram-lines. The driver of an on-coming tram rang his bell violently; Volkenborn looked at him vacantly, and, after the tram had passed, continued to walk be-tween the tramlines with his eyes fixed on the ground, as though he were looking for something that he had lost.

It had been raining, off and on, all day, and water lay on the lines. To Volkenborn's terror, his eyes began playing him a new trick, and the harmless rain water looked to him to be dark red, the color of blood.

In the evening, as it was growing dark, he came on a noncom. of his company, who was sitting on one of the benches in the Castle Gardens. As they made their way back together to the barracks, Volk-enborn did not utter a word until they passed the great machinery works where armored cars and air-planes were being built for the War Office. Here there was the constant din of electric hammers.

"That sounds just like machine-gun fire," he said, and then asked, "Did you ever come in for any street fighting?"

In his room he found that two of his letters to Werner had been returned. On each of them was stamped: "Fallen on the field of honor!" There was a cross in front of these words, which were under-lined in red ink.

Mechanically he read these announcements, and gradually began to find comfort in the thought that his friend had done with all suffering and agony and was at last at peace.

On the field of honor! He walked over to the window and opened it. A fine rain was falling, and from the town there came a sound of endless hammering and the continuous purring of the machines at the works. The trams even seemed to be making more noise than usual, just as though they were making their way with difficulty uphill. Motor omnibuses, electric bells, the sound of horses' hoofs, and the heavy noise of passing lorries could be heard in the distance; but just where he had his quarters, all was so quiet that the footsteps of passers-by were quite audible.

For a long time he stood listening to these sounds. All thought seemed to have become impossible; his brain had lost all activity, his capacity for feeling was dulled. One sentence, and one sentence alone, rang complainingly, menacingly, despairingly, through his head: "Fallen on the field of honor! Fallen on the field of honor!"

VI

November came in warm and sunny, so that Volkenborn was able to spend much time in the Castle Gardens, and even to go much farther afield. On these walks he was always alone; he had no desire for any comradeship. One day he received a letter from Luise, the girl to whom Werner had been engaged. It began with many conventional expressions

of regret for the dead man — such expressions as
could be read daily in the obituary notices of the
press. Then there followed sentences that Volkenborn had to read twice before he could grasp their
meaning. Some long time ago he had exchanged a
few jocular picture post cards with her; but that
did not explain to him why she now wrote that she
had always felt attracted to him, had constantly
been thinking of him, and that the photograph they
had taken, in rest billets in Flanders — the one in
which he was standing arm in arm with Werner —
had always been her most cherished possession and
had the place of honor on her writing table. With
difficulty he grasped her meaning, but when he at
last understood what she was hinting at, he tore
her letter into shreds and threw them out of the
window. But as he followed the pieces with his eyes,
and could see them vaguely floating down to the
courtyard beneath, where they were tossed about
by the wind that always caught this space between
the two wings of the barracks, it seemed to him that
he had not merely torn up a stranger's letter, but
that he had also destroyed something delicate and
rare in his soul; something that was but a shimmering net as fine as gossamer, but which had been a
protection from the ugliness of life. He closed the
window, but the coldness was within himself.

The only compensation that he had was the correspondence with his brothers, his parents, and occasional letters from Elma.

Sometimes his thoughts would turn to Anneliese,

and he had to admit that she was as pretty and amiable as ever. But did he still love her? Had he any capacity for loving anybody? He could find no answer to these questions.

"I no longer know myself," he wrote to Elma. "Anneliese seems slipping from me; I have lost her, and she was such a dear good girl. Do I still love her? I am so tired that I have only one wish, and that is for rest and quietude. The only longing that I still have is for you, for your sisterly love. The future seems so hopeless that the only comfort that I can find is to live in the past."

Too clearly he realized that he did not know his own mind, for when Anneliese wrote and asked him to spend part of his Christmas leave at her father's villa, he found himself looking forward to this visit with delight.

With the exception of such news as his letters brought him, he knew little of what was going on; but, cut off as he was from all news and intercourse, he still dreaded to open his letters, for fear that they should contain bad news. On one occasion, when a telegram was brought to him, he trembled from head to foot. As he snatched it from the orderly, his brain was busily imagining that either Kurt or Lothar had been killed or were wounded, and that he would have to start at once, start by the next train, that he would have to obtain leave of absence, that he must hurry off to his C. O. Not venturing to open the telegram until he was alone in his room, he then found that his anxiety had been uncalled for, and that the message was an unimportant one.

The life around him seemed to be growing more strange to him. Every morning as he passed up and down the corridors and round by the rifle racks, he felt himself more and more out of touch with the life he was leading. When the sentry saluted him, he found himself growing red as though there was something shameful in this recognition. To such an extent had this obsession grown upon him that he often found himself waiting until the sentry had turned and was walking back, before he ventured to pass the gate. He spent much of his time in the battalion library. The lance corporal in charge had lost his son, a youngster of about the same age as Volkenborn: this made his own fate seem such a little matter. Then he listened while the noncom. — Robert Bergmann was his name — told him all about his family, about his occupation; explained how happy and contented he had been until the outbreak of this terrible war. He could hardly bear to listen to all this and got up quickly, nodded and said, "Yes, yes, the war, Bergmann, the war!" Then, after standing still for a moment at the window and looking across to the parade ground, he turned and left the library hurriedly, as though he had some important appointment to keep.

Bergmann had already spoken to him about trouble in the Navy, had told him that things could not go on much longer as they were; that there was general excitement and discontent which it would be impossible to suppress much longer.

He had not given this talk about coming trouble much consideration, in fact he avoided as far as possible all discussion of such matters, which he felt to be both dangerous and painful. He had long since discontinued reading the newspapers carefully, merely glancing at the official war news and occasionally reading some details about the retreat from Flanders, where his brothers were. His only thoughts were with them, with the regiment, and of what might have happened to Schuster, and where Pietschmann might be, who had again been wounded for the fourth or fifth time. He paid but little attention to all that was said in the mess about the general political situation — peace proposals, the retreat, and the new Cabinet. Occasionally he would listen for a time and watch the serious faces, but in general he felt that he had lost all interest in the matter. He felt shut up in himself, too indifferent and too tired to take interest in anything. Everything that was going on around him seemed remote, overshadowed by the storm that was raging in his own restless soul.

All this was but a passing phase which vanished one morning as he saw the Red Flag being hoisted over the barracks and learned that he was to be arrested.

Revolution! So the revolution had come! In the barrack yard were motor lorries with machine guns and riflemen. Wild-looking figures were running about, armed to the teeth. In the distance he could hear single shots. There was a crowd of agitated women in front of the gate, louts were rushing up and down the street with rifles in their hands; children were rushing screaming into their homes. Red flags everywhere! Were there still flags that were not red? Flags that did not drip blood? Hateful rags that looked as if they had been dipped in the blood of thousands of wounded men. Red flags everywhere, flaunting defiance to the sky. The whole town seemed alive with them. Wherever he looked, his eyes fell on nothing but red, red that to his unhappy fancy looked like blood.

At noon Volkenborn mounted the steps, and, seeing somebody coming towards him he made way without looking up. What was it to him who this man was he was passing? There seemed no individual faces to be recognized now, but all faces looked alike; all wore the same expression. He could not bear to look at them, but he could feel them glaring at him on all sides. He was even beginning to fear his own reflection in the looking glass.

Feeling two hands on his shoulders he looked up.

"Pietschmann!

"Volkenborn!"

They wrung each other's hands until they ached, and then they passed along the corridor, through the groups of soldiers and women that were hanging about, down the steps and across the yard.

"Feel as if I were being choked, I do, Volkenborn, when I see the likes of this! Is this the sort of beanfeast we've been shot to pieces for? A pretty wind-up! I don't think! What a damned disgrace!

Enough to make a decent soldier man put a bullet
through his skull."

And Volkenborn replied gently and quietly, thinking of every word before he uttered it.

"No! not for that, Pietschmann! It can't have
been for that. I know as little as you do what we
really were fighting for; I have often enough worried my brain to think that out and could never find
a satisfactory answer, but it wasn't for that, be sure
of it. Things were bad enough before in some re-
spects, but neither you nor I wanted to see anything
like this happen. No! We didn't suffer and risk our
lives to bring this about."

Pietschmann bit at his lip, unable to find words to
express all that was passing through his simple, un-
trained mind. With his right hand he kept a tight
hold on the buckle of his belt, as though it were a
sacred symbol, something to be clung to at any cost.
It seemed as though in this common soldier's belt
buckle were centered all the loyalty and comradeship
of the trenches; as though it stood for all that had
made life at the Front endurable for his simple soul.

They were neither of them in the mood for many
words, and so they parted with a long, firm handclasp that seemed to both of them to stand for a
promise, a vow — a dedication to something for
which neither of them could find words.

VII

The home-coming was something quite different
from anything he had pictured. There was neither

excitement nor enthusiasm about it, but just a creeping back to the privacy of one's own four walls. He felt almost like a prisoner as he stood at his window amid the silence and gloom that had fallen on everything. He could hear nothing but the beating of his own heart. He could think of nothing but the dreary void that was in his own breast.

The one bright and consoling factor amid all this drabness and depression was that Kurt and Lothar had returned alive and well. That was the one satisfaction that still remained to him, the one thing that reconciled him to all else, the one blessing for which he had to be thankful. Together they made plans for the future; they would have a short spell of rest and recreation, and then they would start work again; make a beginning with a new career.

But his eyes, instead of growing better, became worse. He said no word about it, but he realized it quite clearly. His mental depression too seldom left him. For a while it would go, and he would be himself again for a brief hour, then suddenly, deadly melancholy would seize him. In vain he fought against it and tried by sheer will power to rise superior to it; it was stronger than he.

They visited Anneliese at Margaretensee, and there were walks in the twilight along the bank of the lake, but Volkenborn found no delight in them. To his troubled mind the willows looked like reproachful vaguely defined human shapes that stretched their arms out to him; they cast shadows at his feet that threatened to enmesh them and to hold them fast. He could almost feel the meshes drawing together, striving to entangle him. Everything round him was dark and menacing, and he was afraid.

Anneliese's brother came home — came without either shoulder straps or side arm, but nobody noticed that. There was a family party to celebrate his return, and Volkenborn tried his best to rise to the occasion, but failed lamentably. Anneliese played the piano, and Volkenborn tried to listen, but he took no pleasure in her music. She seemed to him to be playing badly, but the fault really lay with him. It was he who had lost all capacity to enjoy. In deepest dejection, he sat listening, holding tight to his chair with both hands, as though he would keep himself there by main force. Anneliese gave him a smile, but his eyes wandered away, unable to sustain her glance.

The Volkenborns stayed the night, but Hans could not sleep. He could hear Anneliese's footsteps in the room next his own. Through the thin partition he could hear her making her preparations for the night. Then she opened the window and switched the light out, and he could hear her walking from the window. He knew she was feeling as disturbed as he was, and would also sleep but little that night. She too would be thinking how the afternoon had passed, of his strangeness, his silence, his inexplicable manner.

Volkenborn got up, put his dressing gown on and leaned out of the window. From there, he could see the lake and watch the full moon playing on the poplars. The night was so clear that he could see right across to the other bank. As he stood and watched the moonlight, his thoughts flew back to that miserable walk they had taken together in the twilight.

"No, Anneliese! my path in life is not yours. I cannot tell you why it is so, but I know that it is not from the depths of my being. My way is not your way. If I could only feel differently! If I could only find the bright and kindly path that I have lost. The way that lies before me is so dark, so menacing, so full of shadows. Why have I to tread this path?"

He felt unable to leave the window, and this one sentence echoed and reëchoed through his brain like some question to which there is no answer. No other thought would come to him, as from the lake and the trees rose the same question: "Why have I of all others to tread this path?"

As he drank in the sounds of the night, which brought only echoes of his own troubled soul, he fancied he could hear in the distance, far away, but drawing nearer, a strange, new voice — a voice which was both strange and yet familiar. Was it his dead comrade Werner? Was it Lieutenant von Kless? Was it Margrit? He could not tell. He could hear the voice, but it was so dim and vague that he could not distinguish it.

"You ask why," whispered the Voice. "Ask no more, Hans Volkenborn! Ask no more! Complain no more, but live! Tread the path for our sakes!

Suffer, that we may not have suffered in vain! Live, that we may live! We died that others might live. We hand on the torch of life to you. It is not for you to doubt, but it is for you to struggle and to conquer; from your sufferings, from your bleeding wounds let knowledge, faith, love of your fellow man and hope spring, until they blossom and bring forth fruit; the fruit of a greater, more beautiful, and nobler future! Live, Hans Volkenborn, live and struggle!"

His eyes seemed on fire. White specks floated before them, until he seemed to see nothing but one great, confused, white light. The banks of the lake faded into one blur, and the moonbeams seemed to be dancing strangely among the leaves of the trees. Then, as his tortured eyes sought to pierce through this confusion and obscurity, the pain became more intense, and from the blinding white glare shot up the dreaded, beautiful violet sphere; like a blinding violet star it hung suspended before him, while beyond it lay the night, cool, peaceful and at rest.

THE END

Afterword

CASEY CLABOUGH

The young soldiers passed by the graves of their comrades and, many of them, without knowing it, were drawing nearer to their own.

Zero Hour, 192

Georg Grabenhorst (1899–1997) was born in Hannover and spent most of his life in the Lower Saxony region of Germany. Having served as a *Fahnenjunker* during World War I, he studied at the Universities of Marburg and Kiel, earning a doctorate in philosophy from the latter institution. He published volumes of fiction and nonfiction but remains a minor literary figure both in his home country and abroad.

Grabenhorst's *Zero Hour* was published in Germany as *Fahnenjunker Volkenborn* by the Leipzig publisher Koehler and Umelang in 1928, prior to its publication a year later in the United States by Little, Brown. Among many English-speaking readers of Great War literature, an inaccurate belief persists that there has been a poverty of German material in English. This misconception is traceable to the circumstance that many of the German titles brought out in English during the first two decades after the war—including *Zero Hour*—quickly went out of print. Among the best of these translated books, most of which are now hard to find, are these works of fiction and nonfiction: Paul Alverdes's *Changed Men*, Rudolph Binding's *A Fatalist at War*, Walter Bloem's *The Advance from Mons*, Ernst Glaeser's *Class of 1902*, Ernst Jünger's *Storm of Steel* and *Copse 125: A Chronicle from the Trench Warfare of 1918*, Rudolf Kreutz's *Captain Zillner: A Human Document*, Ludwig Renn's *War*, Franz Schauwecker's *The Fiery Way*, Johannes Steel's *Escape to the Present*, Fritz von Unruh's *The Way of Sacrifice*, Georg von der Vring's *Private*

Suhren: The Story of a German Rifleman, Stephen Westman's *Surgeon with the Kaiser's Army,* Philip Witkopp's *German Students' War Letters,* and Arnold Zweig's *The Case of Sergeant Grischa.* This list is far from inclusive, but it illustrates the range of German literary works that made the transition into English in the years following the Great War. The majority of them also are books of formidable quality, the publishers and translators of the 1920s having chosen carefully those titles they believed most likely to succeed among readerships in England and the United States. The problem—also the problem in any publishing era—is that other books covering the same general topics received greater publicity, were chosen for book clubs, and were deemed by influential reviewers to be more accessible and/or of greater merit. Grabenhorst's novel is a strong one; but its competition included war books by Ernest Hemingway, John Dos Passos, Robert Graves, Siegfried Sassoon, and–on the German side–Erich Maria Remarque, as well as several of the authors noted above. Indeed, Louis Kronenberger's 17 November 1929 *New York Times* review of *Zero Hour* scolded the book for saying "very little that has not been said before."

Grabenhorst makes memorable the experiences of his protagonist, Hans Volkenborn, through the quality of his descriptions and the underlying conflicts and juxtapositions they create. At one point, Grabenhorst contrasts the sun, water, and sensual joy of the novel's opening ocean scene with the despair of the front's filthy, corrupted environment: "Hans Volkenborn, crouched behind earthworks thrown up at the edge of a shell crater, was breaking off lumps of dry soil from the edges and letting them fall into a pool of dirty, yellow water. . . . Bending over, he could see his own gray image reflected in the muddy water. He began taking shots at it with the clods, amused to see how his face became distorted by the splashes. Then he stopped. A filthy rat crept over the edge and stood looking at him, its ugly head stretched out, listening" (*ZH,* 16). Here Grabenhorst achieves an alteration in milieu and conveys what that transition means for Volkenborn. In a matter of pages, Grabenhorst convincingly traces Volkenborn's shift from careless, golden youth to bored and troubled soldier. Surrounded by ugliness and destruction,

Volkenborn despises both his surroundings and the grimy image of himself.

Like many war poets on both sides of the lines, Volkenborn cannot function as a capable soldier. His agonies are his own, yet he becomes a representative figure. His name when translated into English ("born of the people") provides positive connotations about him. As a German everyman of the Great War, even his most personal experiences are the stories of thousands of similar young men, German and non-German. Even at its most uneventful and mundane, *Zero Hour* offers interesting and occasionally profound commentary on military life. For instance, chapter 2, "The Lieutenant," constitutes a social history of the noncombat aspects of the German military during the Great War.

For Grabenhorst, ideals, beliefs, and all other considerations finally are irrelevant in war. In the end, one is left only with the fellowship of those who fight alongside him: "The same fate broods over all, yet each feels himself alone. Each struggles to maintain his individuality and yet is conscious of the ties of comradeship; for comradeship is, by now, the one splendid and ennobling thing that holds them all together. It is a thing they all accept without asking themselves on what it is based. Is it another word for duty, regiment, country? There are many names for it, for those who have imagination enough to find them" (*ZH*, 95).

Beyond capturing the nuances of the Great War from a German perspective, Grabenhorst is concerned with the timeless archetypes of war. The element of chance appears with enough regularity as to seem almost unrealistic: a machine gun's previous position blown to bits only seconds after it takes up a new one, Volkenborn's being recalled shortly after having been designated for leave, the seemingly random deployment of companies to areas of certain death or comparative safety, the sudden death of a friend standing at one's side. Some soldiers view this as luck or providence, others as the senseless, inevitable movement of events. Volkenborn's comrade Pongs holds the latter view, rhetorically inquiring, "Are we to be grateful to God for such meaningless chance?" (*ZH*, 220). Similar musings develop into philosophical statements concerning the general nature of warfare. When he discusses at great length the impressions and outlook of the representative young German soldier, Grabenhorst might be describing those of any youthful combatant during any conflict, past or future:

> It is an essential part of the soldier's calling to be able to deal with any situation and make himself at home everywhere. To none is this easier than to a healthy young man who is not given to reflecting too profoundly. But to such a one this life has definite dangers. All this normal, regular and homely in him is suppressed, and, on the other hand, adventurous and nomadic instincts are developed. To the soldier in the field, every day brings some new situation, and nothing seems lasting. The morrow brings constant changes. For this reason he accepts all the day has to offer him of good or bad, and worries but little about the future. To be ready for everything is his most essential quality. But necessary as these qualities are on active service, they are calculated to unfit him for civilian life. However adaptive he may prove himself, will he ever again be able to settle down to an organized and peaceful existence. Such a transition may be easier for the older men, but for the youngster who has passed the most impressionable years of his life in active service it will prove in many cases impossible. (ZH, 140)

Grabenhorst's combat sequences most often are rendered in darkly imaginative and highly visceral translated prose that effectively captures the agonies of mind and body beyond the conflict at hand. As Volkenborn lies beneath heavy debris in a trench, Grabenhorst captures his impotent agony: "He tries to stand up, to force this mass of earth aside that is holding him down, but his arms are pinned and he cannot move them. He is in such pain that he tries to cry out, but he is being strangled and cannot utter a sound. His chin is being forced down against his chest, a weight lies across his forehead, and a red-hot iron is searing his temples. The heat and pressure are so intense that his eyes feel as if they were melting, running away in red-hot drops of liquid. They seem to him to be red, red as fire, and sparks flash from them" (ZH, 237).

Volkenborn does not retreat from war's awful truths, nor is he transformed into a monster by them. Instead, he achieves a tenuous and partially despairing balance between idealization and duty, hope and necessary evil. His is not the familiar military narrative of suffering made over into disillusionment and pacifism. Nor is it a romantic tale of hawkish, problematic chivalry. One of Volkenborn's strengths is that despite his great suffering he often manages to view his involvement in war and the struggle itself in dispassionate terms. As his doomed comrade Pongs points out, "War is nothing more than a Stock Exchange speculation" (ZH, 212).